BOZWICK ABEL

PLAINS OF COLORADAS

— PARIAHS OF WAR —
• VOLUME 2 •

Plains of Coloradas (Pariahs of War Series Book Two)
Copyright © 2020 by Bozwick Abel, Monticello Publishing

www.facebook.com/bozwick.abel

All characters and events in this book, other than those clearly in the public domain, are fictitious and any resemblance to real persons, living or dead, is purely coincidental.

All rights reserved. No part of this publication may be reproduced, distributed, or transmitted in any form or by any means, including photocopying, recording, or other electronic or mechanical methods, without the prior written permission of the publisher, except in the case of brief quotations embodied in critical reviews and certain other noncommercial uses permitted by copyright law.

For permission requests, write to:
bozwickabel@hotmail.com

Ordering Information:

Quantity sales. Special discounts are available on quantity purchases by corporations, associations, and others. Orders by US trade bookstores and wholesalers. For details, contact the publisher at the address above.

Editing by The Pro Book Editor
Interior and Cover Design by IAPS.rocks

ISBN: 978-0-578-74573-2

1. Main category—Historical Fiction
2. Other category—Action & Adventure, Drama

First Edition

TABLE OF CONTENTS

PROLOGUE *1*

CHAPTER 1
A Day with the Devil *5*

CHAPTER 2
Trouble at the Jailhouse *19*

CHAPTER 3
The River and Reward *33*

CHAPTER 4
No Gold and No New Beginning *43*

CHAPTER 5
The Beast That Lies Ahead *53*

CHAPTER 6
The Prospectors on Cactus Hill *63*

CHAPTER 7
Here Comes the Rain *73*

CHAPTER 8
An Unmarked Grave *83*

CHAPTER 9
The Taos Three 89

CHAPTER 10
The Crescent Moon 99

CHAPTER 11
Newspaper and Coffee 105

CHAPTER 12
Stories of Socorro 111

CHAPTER 13
Major of Mora 119

CHAPTER 14
Adversaries in Ambush 125

CHAPTER 15
A Shot of Fox Smooth 135

CHAPTER 16
All Went Quiet 145

CHAPTER 17
The Little Lady 155

CHAPTER 18
Unforeseen Happenstance 163

CHAPTER 19
Who the Hell is Quinn? 173

CHAPTER 20
The Familiarly Strange Man 179

CHAPTER 21
> *A Bullet in the Head* 195

CHAPTER 22
> *Get the Horses Ready* 203

CHAPTER 23
> *Two-Headed Snake* 211

CHAPTER 24
> *The Woman and the Warriors* 219

CHAPTER 25
> *The Toothless Coyote* 227

CHAPTER 26
> *An Unwelcome Visit* 237

CHAPTER 27
> *A Sheep among Wolves* 245

CHAPTER 28
> *There Will Be No Peace* 263

CHAPTER 29
> *General Intermission* 279

CHAPTER 30
> *Sol de Coloradas* 289

ABOUT THE AUTHOR 293

ACKNOWLEDGEMENTS 295

This book is dedicated to Native Americans whose spirit and countless acts of bravery still resonate across the open plains like the thundering hooves of the American buffalo.

Mexican Republic

- San Juan
- Taos
- Mora
- Santa Fe N.M.
- Santa Rosa
- Socorro
- Magdalena
- Chiricahua Apache
- Western Apache
- Mescalero Apache
- Silver City
- Tucson
- Lordsburg
- Deming
- El Paso
- Domingo
- Santa Rita Mountains

Rio Grande River
Santa Fe Trail
St. Louis MO.
Mtn. Route
Cimarron Route
El Camino Real
Gila River

PROLOGUE

THE EARLY AFTERNOON SUN BEAT down on the Taos constable as he rode across the open plain. The sweat from his brim rolled down his forehead. He squinted, trying to keep it from running into his eyes.

His heart pounded, sounding like the horse's hooves beating against the hard ground as he further distanced himself from the Apache warriors. He raised his shoulder as high as he could to wipe the sweat from his face. Meanwhile, he continued twisting and pulling the rope that secured his hands to the saddle horn, trying to break them free.

Observing the wide-open land around him, Mitchell felt like a lone sheep among wolves in the open plain without his pistol, Mitchell knew that's exactly what he was.

As the landscape rolled slightly down hill in front of him, three riders moved in the direction he headed. Unable to see the men through droplets of sweat hanging from his eyebrows, he brought his horse to a stop. He closed his eyelids tightly and blinked repeatedly, but the sweat pooling there and its burning sensation made it difficult to keep his eyes open.

Just down the hill, the three horses were less than fifty yards away. They came to an abrupt stop, and the riders turned toward him.

After examining the riders, Mitchell caught a glimpse of a familiar face.

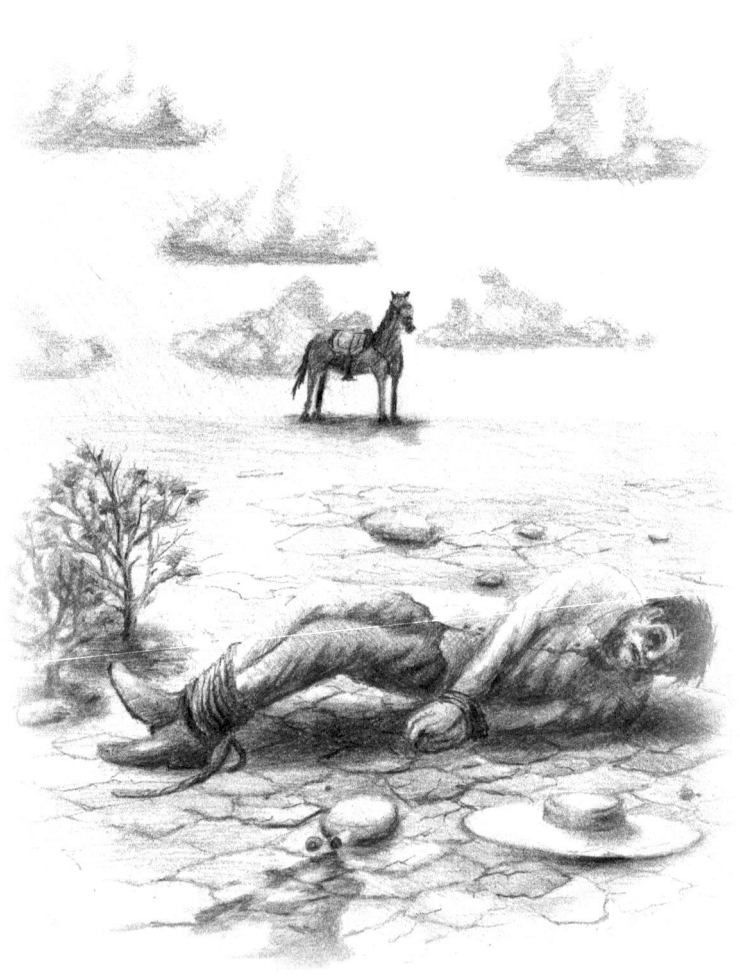

CHAPTER 1

A DAY WITH THE DEVIL

THE SOUND OF GUNSHOTS AWOKE the Mexican outlaw from his forced siesta. His eyes squinted from the bright rays of the sun and the throbbing pain of the blows he'd taken to the head. He shuffled around on the dirt-covered hilltop, looking for the men who had beaten him and stolen his mount. There was nobody in sight except a lone horse about fifty feet away, but he heard men yelling down the hillside in the direction of the Santa Fe Trail and figured they were less than a hundred yards away. He frantically wrestled with the ropes that held his hands and feet, and after violently kicking several times, the rope around his ankle broke free.

The sound of footsteps advanced up the hill toward him. He fell back to the ground on his side and laid motionless, soon hearing a man climb on his horse followed by the steady plodding of horse hooves drawing near.

"Juan, you awake?" asked the man.

Juan did not react to the man's calls.

"Juan, can you hear me?" asked the man again.

Juan remained motionless.

A moment later, the sound of hooves was heard again, slowly disappearing down the hill as the man rode away.

Juan opened his eyes, keeping his face hidden against the dirt, and looked side to side for the man while being careful not to move. He then popped up, resting his weight on his elbow as he continued to look around.

"Bastards," Juan whispered.

Sitting up, the outlaw worked at loosening the rope around his wrists. After several minutes with no luck, he reached over for a canteen sitting next to him, only to find it empty. He tossed the canteen aside, then hopped to his feet, and quickly moved south, opposite the way the man had ridden off. The area was low hills, rocks, and dirt with little vegetation. The dry, brittle ground and small rocks crunched beneath his feet as he looked back several times to make sure he wasn't spotted.

A group of shrubs stood about two hundred yards ahead, and Juan picked up the pace to get there as quickly as possible. The hot sun beat down on him as he lumbered toward the vegetation, fidgeting with the rope around his wrists and ducking low. Upon reaching the shrubs, he took cover and peeked over to check behind him. Still staring off into the distance, he chewed at the rope until his teeth hurt.

"Damn it," he grumbled to himself, grimacing in pain.

After catching his breath, Juan stood and continued south. Fifteen minutes later, he came across a cluster of pine trees. He stopped at one and rubbed the rope against a branch until the strands began to fray. As he tugged his hands apart against the binding, the last of the fibers snapped, and the rope dropped to the ground.

Thank God, he thought.

He looked around for a few minutes before continuing south. After nearly a half hour of running from tree to tree to take cover and rest, followed by two hours of walking, he felt confident that he had distanced himself far enough from the outlaws.

He desperately looked for a creek to get a drink of water. His head pounded from the earlier blows of the man's pistol. Juan's anger grew with each step, thinking about his compadres who had turned on him along the Santa Fe Trail. He was convinced they would have killed him if he hadn't skedaddled before they returned.

After another half hour of walking, he found a trail frequently used by rancheros in the area. He followed the trail across the arid landscape for an hour as he slowed. His headache and dehydration intensified with each passing minute. With no signs of water and several hours from sunset, he took shelter in a shaded area at the base of a pine tree.

Lying on his back, he closed his eyes. Juan rested in the cool shade for almost a half hour until he drifted to sleep. A short time later, he heard the wheels of a wagon approaching from the north.

He sat up and carefully observed the approaching two-horse buckboard wagon and the man steering it. Juan studied the man until he felt safe to emerge from the cover of the trees. Walking down a short hill, he stood by the trail and waved at the driver.

The driver slowed his horses, coming to a stop about fifteen feet from Juan.

"Hola," said Juan as he continued walking toward the man.

"Hola, amigo," replied the man. "You can stop there," he quickly added, reaching down and picking up a rifle.

Juan stopped and raised his hands. "I am no harm to you, señor. I am in desperate need of water."

"What happened to you?" asked the man. He regarded Juan with his squinted eyes, the rifle resting on his lap.

"I was jumped by outlaws. They pistol-whipped me and stole my horse," said Juan, lowering his hands.

"Where?" asked the man.

"A few hours of hard riding from here along the Santa Fe Trail," explained Juan, pointing north.

The man glared at Juan and gave no response.

"I don't have any weapons, señor. I am exhausted," added Juan, sensing the man's apprehension.

The man rubbed his chin and stared at Juan for a several more moments. Then he nodded. "Ok, amigo, climb on up."

"Gracias," said Juan as he walked to the other side of the wagon. He stepped on the rung and pulled himself up, finding a seat next to the man.

The driver smacked the reins, and the horses stepped forward, pulling the straps and horse collar tight.

The man next to Juan was slightly overweight. With mostly gray hair, a red, long-sleeve shirt, gray wool trousers and suspenders, Juan guessed him to be in his midsixties. The man reached by his side, pulling out a canteen and handing it to Juan.

Juan nodded his thanks and quickly took the canteen.

He loosened the cap, then raised the canteen to his mouth. After several large gulps, he handed it back.

"Keep it, son," said the man. "I have another right here." He reached down and lifted a canteen, placing it on his lap.

Juan immediately raised his canteen to his mouth again, taking a few more large drinks. "Gracias, amigo. Damn glad you rode by." After tightening the lid to his canteen and wiping his mouth, Juan looked at the driver and extended his hand. "Name's Juan."

The driver accepted Juan's hand and replied, "Devi."

Juan nodded and opened his canteen again for yet another drink. After closing the canteen, Juan glanced over at Devi. "Where ya heading?" he asked.

"Socorro."

Juan nodded and shifted toward the back of the wagon, seeing a few wooden boxes and two sacks of flour. Juan then watched the trail ahead.

"How about you?" asked Devi.

Juan shook his head, looking at the landscape. "I don't rightly know," he replied. "Lordsburg, or maybe Silver City…I have a few people I know there."

Devi nodded. "Well, I can get you to Magdalena in the morning, but you will be on your own from there."

"I do appreciate that, señor. I surely would have been a goner had you not come along." Juan lifted his hat and wiped his brow. "Think we'll be gettin' to Socorro before sundown?"

"We should. We'll stop along the rio and water the horses and have a quick bite." Devi glanced at Juan. "Give you a chance to clean up a bit."

Juan nodded and then smiled. "Sounds good to me."

Devi looked back at the trail ahead. "Who were the men that took your horse?"

Juan leaned back and shook his head. "Some guys I was riding with. We rode up from Lordsburg heading to Taos, and I guess they had it planned to rob me at some point."

Devi nodded while keeping his focus on the road ahead. "You know their names?"

Juan nodded in return. "Yeah. One guy was named Eddie, and another was Red. Then there was this burnt bastard named Quinn."

Devi looked over at Juan. "I know of that man. You're lucky to be alive."

"Oh, I think they were gonna kill me, but there were some Indians on the trail they were planning to attack, so they paid little interest in finishing the job after they beat me unconscious." Juan lifted one of his feet onto the front board of the wagon, using it as a footrest. "Eddie came back for his horse and called my name a few times, but I acted like I was still unconscious. I ran out of there once I got the ropes loose, then hid in some brush while they were on the other side of the hill." Juan placed his hat back on his head. "I watched for them from the brush for a bit, but they didn't come back looking for me."

Devi nodded, and the two men continued on toward Socorro for the next couple hours mostly in silence, only talking briefly about the recent war with America.

Once the men reached the river, they climbed down from the wagon. Devi led the horses to the water, and Juan rushed to the river's edge, splashing water on his face and neck.

Juan smiled as the cool water dripped from his hair and ran down his shirt. After spending ten minutes cooling down and getting cleaned up, he found a seat on a rock near the rear of the wagon, where Devi sat.

Devi reached into a small sack and tossed Juan a good-sized piece of jerky.

"Gracias," said Juan as he quickly bit into it.

The men made quick work of the jerky, and just moments after swallowing the last piece, Devi jumped down from the wagon.

After taking note of the sun's position, Devi said, "We better get moving if we wanna reach Socorro before sundown."

Devi climbed into his seat.

Juan followed, standing alongside the wagon and looking up at Devi. "Want me to drive for a while?"

"No, I'm fine," replied Devi.

Juan promptly walked to his side of the wagon and climbed up.

"Yah!" yelled Devi as he smacked the reins.

The men continued for a little over two more hours before reaching Socorro. The town was not much to see, with just a few people on the streets and nothing more than a general store, blacksmith, and barber shop. The buildings were all equally run down as the dirt and dust blew across the mostly empty streets.

Devi navigated his wagon until reaching a small reddish-brown adobe home on the edge of town. The home was in rough condition, with crumbling mortar and cracks covering the exterior walls. He pulled the wagon around back to a small barn, bringing the hoses to a stop.

The sun had completely set, and darkness settled across the land.

Devi and Juan climbed down from the wagon, unhooked the horses from the breast collars, and walked them into the barn.

Devi threw down some hay for the animals, filled the trough with water, and opened the side door to let the horses free walk in the paddock. "Good enough. Let's get some sleep."

He walked out the door, and Juan followed closely behind.

As they walked toward the house, Devi stopped at the porch. "I'll grab you a couple blankets and a lantern, and you can sleep in the back of the wagon."

"Much obliged," said Juan as he stopped to wait on the porch steps.

Devi reached the door of the home, pulling it open with force—as the door was stuck—before disappearing inside. After a few minutes, the door opened again and Devi returned with blankets and a lantern.

"Here you go, son," Devi said, handing the items to Juan. "I'll see you in the morning, and we'll head over to Magdalena."

Juan grinned at the gray-haired man while holding the lantern and blankets. "I really appreciate all your help, amigo."

Devi nodded and turned away as he walked back toward the house. "There's more jerky in a sack in the wagon if you get hungry," said Devi, walking in the house and closing the door behind him.

Juan was happy to hear there was jerky in the wagon. He was more than hungry and knew he would have a hard time sleeping on an empty stomach. He walked briskly to the wagon and tossed the blankets in the back, setting the lantern inside it. Then he went to the front of the wagon and grabbed his canteen. Climbing over boxes inside the wagon, he picked up the light and looked for the jerky. After a short search, he located the sack and helped himself to the three pieces inside.

Juan moved the boxes and sacks of flour to one side of the wagon, lying on his back on the other side. After a few moments, he grabbed a sack of flour, using it as a headrest. It was a nice night, and the temperature was perfect for sleeping outside. He gazed at the stars but soon found himself thinking about Eddie, Quinn, and Red.

He was angry his so-called friends betrayed him, but he was happy to finally be away from the dangerous men. Quinn killed without hesitation. Juan figured those men were going nowhere but to the end of a hangman's rope. He smiled just thinking about it, pulling the blanket over himself and closing his eyes.

The next morning, Juan was awakened by Devi hitting a stick on the side of the wagon. "Get up, son."

Juan raised his head quickly and looked over wagon's edge.

Devi held up a small plate of beans and bread. "Here, eat up, and we'll get moving."

Juan rubbed his eyes, then took the plate from Devi's hand. "Obliged," he said.

Devi walked toward the barn. "I'll get the horses hooked up."

Juan stared down at the plate, then lifted the fork, and began eating. He heard the barn door open and glanced at Devi to see how he was doing. The man walked out with one of the horses, placing a collar around the animal's neck. Juan climbed onto the wagon's seat and took the reins to hold the horse.

After a few minutes, Devi walked back into the barn and came out with the other horse. Realizing how quickly Devi was getting the horses hooked up, Juan started eating more rapidly.

Devi stood beside the wagon and looked up at Juan. "All set?" he asked.

Juan scooped the last of the beans into his mouth and

placed the fork on the plate to hand it over. "Gracias," he said as the man walked toward the house.

"There's water in that barrel. Be sure to fill your canteen," said Devi, pointing toward the porch as he disappeared into the home.

Juan filled his canteen, and after just a few moments, Devi reappeared with his hat in his hand. "All right, let's get moving."

After climbing up and finding his seat, he cracked the reins. The two men rode down the short trail to the main fairway and were on their way. Magdalena was a couple hours ride from Socorro, but at the pace they were going, it was sure to be much less.

Juan thought Devi seemed to be in quite a rush to get him to Magdalena, but he didn't take it personally. He just figured the old man was busy, and Juan greatly appreciated the man going out of his way to take him a little closer to his destination. The sun rose fast, and it was sure to be another hot day. Juan was already dreading the long trek to Silver City. He thought maybe he could get lucky and find a wagon heading that way to ride along.

Juan looked over at Devi, who focused on the road ahead. "I sure appreciate all you done for me. I truly do," said Juan as he reached for his canteen.

"That's no problem, son. I hope things work out for you."

Juan nodded. "Yeah, me too… I'll tell you what. After I get through this rough patch and get back on my feet, I'll drop you off some money for all your help."

Devi glanced at Juan. "Don't worry about that. You come through here again, just stop by and say hello." He looked at the road ahead.

Juan leaned back and pulled his brim down, blocking the sun, to get as much rest as possible over the next hour. About forty minutes later, Juan lifted his hat and saw the little town of Magdalena in the distance. This town surprisingly appeared to be even smaller than Socorro.

As they pulled in the town, they did not see a single person. Juan glanced around in all directions, then at the general store with a Closed sign on the front door.

Damn, thought Juan. "Anyone live here?" he asked.

Devi brought the horses to a stop. "Not many. Even less now since American soldiers started coming through."

Juan picked up his canteen and stepped down from the wagon. He looked in all directions, seeing nothing more than dust and tumbleweeds blowing in the distance. He then walked toward Devi, still sitting in the seat and holding the reins.

Devi reached in his pouch and pulled out a little sack of jerky and bread, tossing it to Juan. "Here you go, son. This should hold you until you reach the next town."

Juan smiled, then reached up to shake the man's hand. "Gracias, Devi. I will see you again, friend."

Devi smiled back, accepting his hand, then nodded. After releasing Juan's hand, he cracked the reins, and the horses lunged forward.

Juan turned to watch his new friend turn the wagon and slowly ride off in the distance. Juan then turned west to the long road ahead. He opened the sack and pulled out a piece of bread. He placed the piece in his mouth and held it with his teeth, then closed the sack, and put it in his pocket. Taking a bite of the bread, he started walking.

As the first hour passed and not a single person was seen in either direction, Juan started to feel like he was the only man on earth. Even animals were seldom seen. As another hour passed, he was convinced he had died on that ridge along the Santa Fe Trail. This was surely hell, and Devi was the devil.

CHAPTER 2

TROUBLE AT THE JAILHOUSE

Just outside Santa Fe at the newly constructed Fort Marcy, General Johnson sat at his desk, writing in his journal. A knock sounded at the door.

"It's open," said the general without looking up.

The door opened, and Corporal Rhoades entered the room, stopping to salute. Still focused on his journal, Johnson made a few more marks on his page before glancing up.

"Yes?" said the general.

"I have Private Maydew with me, sir. You requested to see him."

Laying his pen down, the general said, "Send him in, Corporal, and you can leave us."

The soldier saluted again and walked away.

A moment later, Private Maydew entered the room. He stopped by the entrance and saluted.

Johnson saluted the soldier and pointed at a chair on the

other side of his desk. "Private Maydew, please come have a seat."

"Yes, sir," replied Maydew, seating himself.

"How's our prisoner?" asked Johnson.

"Fine, sir," he replied.

"Sheriff Ricks still there?"

"Yes, sir. Although I believe his deputy is coming soon to relieve him for the night."

Johnson nodded and reached for a cigar. He gestured toward them, offering one to Maydew.

"No, thank you, sir."

Johnson lit the cigar with an eye cracked on Maydew. "Well, I imagine you're curious about why I summoned you?"

"Yes, sir," replied Maydew. "I guessed it was because of the prisoner's condition when we arrived here from Taos?"

The general fixed his eyes on Maydew, taking in a long draw from his cigar before releasing the smoke across the desk, then nodded. "Well, that was disappointing. However, that's not why you are here." He reached for a letter lying on his desk and then leaned back in his chair. "This letter is dated April 8, 1847," said the general, taking another hit from his cigar. He then began reading, "General Johnson, Fort Marcy, Santa Fe Nuevo Territory, please be advised after careful consideration and formal nomination by Daniel S. Dickinson, Private William Maydew has been selected to attend the United States Military Academy in West Point, New York. It's the immediate request of the United States Army that Private William Maydew report to General H. S. Stanton, Fort Jefferson, St. Louis, Missouri, where further travel arrangements have been made, sincerely William L. Marcy, United States War Department."

The general lowered the letter before glancing up at Maydew. The young man sat across from him with a large grin on his face.

"Congratulations, son," said the general, leaning forward and reaching across the desk to shake the soldier's hand.

"Thank you, sir," replied a beaming Maydew.

The general folded the letter and then handed it to Maydew. While the soldier reread the letter, Johnson leaned back in his chair, peering at the private while giving him a few moments to absorb the news. Maydew made a quick read of the letter with the grin still on his face, then he folded and placed it in his pocket.

"I will send two soldiers who will accompany you to St. Louis." The general took a long hit of his cigar, then stood from his desk. "Get your belongings together, and you will head out at first light tomorrow morning."

Maydew stood from his chair and saluted the general. "Yes, sir," he replied enthusiastically.

"Make us proud, Private," said the general.

"I will, sir," replied Maydew, saluting. Maydew was about to turn, and then he glanced down at the cigars on the desk.

Noticing where the private stared, General Johnson said, "Help yourself."

Maydew smiled and took a cigar from the box, "Thank you, sir," he said, saluting the general.

"You are dismissed, Private. Close that behind you," said Johnson.

Maydew placed the cigar in his mouth and walked out, closing the door behind him.

The general sat back down at his desk, took another hit of

his cigar, and then reached across his desk for a recent battle report.

A few hours later, General Johnson left the room, locking the door behind him. Walking down the hall and into his quarters, he removed his hat, coat, and shoes. He sat at a small desk to write a letter to his wife, Clara. After a few minutes of writing, there was a knock on the door.

Puzzled and a bit annoyed, the general glared at the door. "What is it?" asked the general with narrowed eyes.

"It's Corporal Rhoades, sir. I am sorry to bother you, but there's been trouble at the jailhouse, sir."

"What trouble?" asked the general as he stood from the chair.

"Corporal Stevens…he's dead, sir," replied Rhoades.

Johnson dropped the pen from his hand and reached for his boots. "Be right out." He shook his head.

After putting his boots on, the general grabbed his coat and hat. He opened the door and walked briskly past Rhoades. The corporal quickly saluted his general and followed closely behind him.

"What happened, Corporal?" asked Johnson, moving hastily down the corridor.

"The Mexican prisoner, sir. He tried to escape."

"Where is the prisoner now?" asked the general.

The two men continued walking until they reached a door leading outside, where several other soldiers started to gather.

"Dead, sir," replied Rhoades.

Johnson shook his head and started putting on his coat. "Get my horse, Corporal."

"Yes, sir," replied Rhoades, quickly exiting the door.

Johnson turned to the soldiers, who saluted the general.

"Return to your barracks, soldiers. I will brief you all in the morning," said Johnson.

"Yes, sir," said the men as they quickly scurried off.

The general opened the door and walked outside. Moments later, Rhoades appeared, leading the general's horse.

Johnson climbed up and adjusted his position in the seat. "Get a horse, Corporal, and follow me to town."

"Yes, sir." Rhoades rushed away.

Moments later, a soldier on patrol rode into the yard, and Johnson called for him.

"Soldier, follow me to town," said Johnson.

"Yes, sir," said the soldier.

They left the yard and headed to Santa Fe, soon joined by Corporal Rhoades and the three men, continuing toward Santa Fe at a quick pace.

"What do you know about Stevens, Corporal?" asked Johnson, still reeling from the news Rhoades had given.

"Only he was shot by the Mexican prisoner, sir. One of Ricks's men informed us about a half hour ago."

"How did the prisoner get a weapon?" asked a confused Johnson while glancing over at the corporal.

"Don't know, sir," replied Rhoades, shaking his head.

"What about the Indian prisoner?" asked Johnson.

"They said he escaped but is hurt pretty bad," answered the corporal.

Johnson shook his head, and his blood boiled. He could not understand how the prisoner could have possibly escaped. Johnson had given clear orders to stay away from the prisoner. He had even left one of his own soldiers at the jailhouse to help guard the Mexican prisoner until he could be identified as Lieutenant General Wells's killer.

As the general's anger rose, so did the speed of his horse. He anxiously wanted details. As the general turned through town, it wasn't long until he found groups of people gathered. The bodies of several men were lined along the street, close to where the brazen escape had escalated to an all-out shootout and ended with a vicious fistfight. After stopping his horse in front of the bodies and seeing the Mexican prisoner among the dead, the general glanced around for Corporal Stevens, who was not among them.

"Where is Sheriff Ricks?" asked the general.

"At the jailhouse," replied a man standing nearby.

The general nodded and turned his horse, riding away. Upon arriving at the jailhouse moments later, Johnson noticed several men out front, including Sheriff Ricks.

"Sheriff!" Johnson called. He jumped down from his horse and tossed the reins to Corporal Rhoades, still on his horse and alongside the general.

Sheriff Ricks turned toward the general and removed his hat, looking down as Johnson walked quickly toward him. Sheriff Ricks was clearly distraught, with red face and watering eyes. He looked around, not making eye contact with Johnson.

"I am sorry, Johnson," said the sheriff, shaking his head.

Johnson quickly nodded, creasing his brows. "What the hell happened? And where is Stevens?"

Ricks shook his head. "He's inside. Doc Roberts is in there, but Stevens…he's gone, sir."

Johnson rushed up the steps and into the jailhouse, Ricks quickly on his heels. Upon entering, he glanced around the jailhouse and rushed toward the men who'd gathered by the gate of the cell, which stood across the long room. Reaching the men, he looked down and saw a body covered with a blanket.

The men watched as the general knelt and lifted the blanket, revealing his soldier with a large hole in his head. The general pulled the blanket back over his dead comrade, looking at the large amount of blood on the floor around him and inside the cell. He glanced at the blood splattered on the wall. Johnson stood, shaking his head, and turned toward Ricks, who stood nearby.

"What the hell, Sheriff?" said Johnson with clenched fists as the blood raced to his face.

"I am truly sorry, Johnson. I don't understand how this happened," said Ricks. He shook his head raised his hands.

"Tell me what you know," Johnson said. He squinted his eyes and crossed his arms.

"Well, I was here just a few hours ago when Deputy Collins showed up, and I headed to my store. Wasn't more than an hour later, I heard gunshots and came running outside." The sheriff paused. His eyes watered, and he flailed his arms about, then he pulled his hat off, and punched inside it. "Saw the Mexican and Indian getting on a horse after killing a few innocent people, including Joe the barber." Ricks wiped a tear running down his cheek. "They were about to escape when I pulled my pistol and shot the Mexican, and I'm pretty sure I hit the Indian too." Ricks shook his head and put his hat back on while biting is lip.

Johnson peered at Ricks. "What happened then?" he asked.

"Well, the Mexican died on the ground right in front of me, and the Indian charged us on his horse, then rode out of town. I quickly sent six men after that Apache son of a bitch. Haven't heard back from them yet." Ricks looked toward the floor at the soldier's body and shook his head. "I am truly sorry, General."

Johnson closed his eyes and drew a deep breath, then exhaled forcibly. He then looked back at Ricks. "Where's your deputy?" he asked.

Doc Roberts quickly spoke up. "He's at my office down the street. Had to pull a bullet out of his leg and bandage him up."

"I need to talk to him," said Johnson.

"He's in bad shape and needs his rest, sir," replied the doctor, facing Johnson.

"Take me to him," Johnson replied through his teeth.

Roberts grabbed his black leather bag, which rested on the desk beside him. "All right," he said, pacing toward the door.

Johnson and Ricks followed the doctor. Once outside, the general looked at Corporal Rhoades.

"Get Stevens to the fort right away, and I'll be there shortly. Tie my horse off at that post," said Johnson, pointing to a nearby hitch post.

"Yes, sir," Rhoades replied. He got down from his mount, then walked the horses to the post, and tied them off.

The patrol guard also got down, tying off his horse to help Rhoades with Stevens's body.

Johnson, Sheriff Ricks, and the doctor walked briskly down the street, past many people still gathered in town. Once reaching the doctor's office door, the men quickly entered. In a room just past a desk and chairs was another small room, and Collins lay on a bed with his leg lifted and bandaged.

When Johnson entered the room, he turned up the lantern

sitting on a small table. Alongside Collins's bed sat a woman, who stared at the three men.

"Hello, ma'am," said Johnson.

"Hello," she replied, wiping her eyes.

Sheriff Ricks walked toward the woman and put his hand on her shoulder. "How you holding up, Margie?"

The woman smiled, placing her hand over the sheriff's. "I'm fine."

"Would you mind giving us a few minutes?" asked Ricks.

"Of course." The woman stood from the chair and smiled at the men. She leaned over and kissed the deputy's cheek, then quickly left the room.

Collins glanced around at the three men now gathered over him.

"How you feelin' son?" asked Ricks.

"Like hell, but I'm alive," he quickly responded.

Ricks smiled, then pointed over at the general. "This is General Johnson, and he has a few questions for you."

Johnson nodded to Collins. He removed his hat and extended his hands out at his side, then shook his head. "What the hell happened in there?"

Collins looked over at the sheriff, then back toward Johnson. "The prisoners got into a fight, and the Mexican appeared to be knocked out by the gate." Collins grimaced in pain as he tried to sit up a little in the bed. "Your man Stevens approached the gate to investigate after ordering the Indian to stand back."

Collins reached for water by the bedside and took a quick drink, then he looked at the men gathered around him. "We thought the Mexican was possibly dead," he explained, then placed the cup back on the table. "Stevens knelt down and reached in to feel for a pulse, and that Mexican feller jumped up quick as lightning and grabbed Stevens's arm."

Collins shook his head and shifted in the bed a little more, still trying to get comfortable. "That Mexican bastard slammed Stevens so hard into the metal bars and 'bout knocked him out, then put him in a choke hold. Before I could react, the Mexican had Stevens's pistol and was holding it to his head." Collins looked over at Ricks. "Then that Indian bastard came over and helped hold Stevens while searching for the key to the gate!" Collins shook his head. "Was a goddamn set up from the beginning." His eyes closed, and he clinched his jaw.

Johnson glanced up at the ceiling, remembering his direct instructions to Stevens to stay away from the prisoner. He then looked back down at the deputy. "Go on," he said.

"Well…I told him to drop the weapon several times, but without any hesitation, the Mexican pulled the trigger, and Stevens fell to the floor. Then he began firing at me," explained Collins.

"What did you do then?" asked Johnson.

"Well, I turned around quick as hell and ran for the door to go find the sheriff," replied Collins, motioning toward his leg. "That's when the Mexican shot me."

Johnson bowed his head, staring toward the floor in deep thought. Moments later, he raised his arm and wiped his brow with the sleeve of his coat before putting his hat on.

He then looked at Collins. "Thanks, Deputy." He pointed to the man's bandages. "Rest that leg." He looked at Ricks and the doctor. "Gentlemen." He nodded and turned toward the door.

"Rest up, son," said Ricks, patting Collins on his good leg and quickly following the general.

Johnson walked past the woman in the room sitting at the desk. "Ma'am," said the general, tipping his hat while walking briskly toward the front door.

He heard Ricks closing in behind him.

"Wait up, General!" said Ricks, breathing heavily.

Johnson stopped a moment, then continued walking once Ricks caught up to him.

"What should we do with that dead Mexican feller?" asked Ricks.

"You killed him, you bury him," replied Johnson, continuing to walk at a quick pace.

Ricks looked away from Johnson, shaking his head. Then he turned back. "We can't bury that murdering bastard in our cemetery. The people around here won't go for that!" said Ricks about out of breath, struggling to keep up. He reached forward, tapping the general on the arm. "Hold it now, Johnson," said Ricks, taking deep breaths with his hands on his hips.

The general stopped and turned around to face the sheriff.

After catching his breath moments later, Ricks stood back up straight. "I can't bury that bastard in town," explained Ricks.

"Then take him out of town and bury him. Just be sure to mark his grave," replied Johnson.

"Fine," said Ricks. "What was that bastard's name?"

"Domingo," replied Johnson.

"Yeah that's right—Domingo," said Ricks. He bit his lip and shook his head. "What a dreadful man," he added. He looked over at Johnson, still shaking his head.

After another moment, the general exhaled forcefully, turned, and continued walking toward the jailhouse. Ricks exhaled loudly as well. Then Johnson heard the sheriff's footsteps and heavy breathing closing in behind him again. Johnson rolled his eyes and clenched his jaw, having had more than enough Sheriff Ricks for one night.

"What are you gonna do, Johnson?" asked Ricks, having caught up to the general and walking alongside him.

Johnson looked at Ricks. "What do you mean?" His brow creased.

"Well, aren't you gonna send men out after that savage?" asked Ricks.

"You already sent men after him. Besides, you said you shot 'im. He won't get too far," said Johnson, now looking forward.

"Yeah, well, I think…um…well that's true," said Ricks, scratching his cheek and nodding. "But we need to make sure he's dead!" Ricks pointed his index finger in front of him and opened his eyes widely.

"Those prospectors still at your ranch?" asked Johnson.

Ricks regarded Johnson with a creased brow. "Yeah, what of it?"

Johnson peered at Ricks through the corner of his eye. "Send them after Red Sleeves. They captured him the first time." He smirked as he reached his horse and untied it from the hitching post. He then lifted himself into the saddle and glared down at Ricks standing alongside the horse with his hand on the horse's muzzle. "Domingo killed Corporal Stevens, and Domingo is dead." The general looked around at the many people still in the streets, then stared down at Ricks. "If you want Red Sleeves, grab some men and go after him."

Ricks rubbed his beard and shook his head in what appeared to be deep thought.

Johnson hastily turned his horse away, and Ricks moved his hand from the horse's muzzle.

"It's late. Good night, Sheriff," said Johnson, spurring his horse. He quickly rode away, disappearing down the dark street.

CHAPTER 3
THE RIVER AND REWARD

Red Sleeves rode hard through the darkness, maneuvering through a valley of many trees and steep hills before stopping along the Santa Fe River. He led his horse to water so the exhausted animal could drink. At six miles away, Red Sleeves felt safe enough to tend to the several wounds he had received during his brazen escape from the Santa Fe jail.

The bones in his knuckles were exposed, and a deep cut sliced across his palm when he had grabbed a knife by the blade from his attacker.

He ran cool water over his hands before splashing some on his face. His entire body ached. Red Sleeves pushed on his ribs and grunted from the intense pain that followed. A rib was at least cracked, if not broken. He examined the gunshot wound to his leg, but luckily, the bullet had only grazed him.

As he waded in the waist-deep river, Red Sleeves raised his hands high above him and celebrated his freedom. A few moments later, he lowered his arms and listened for any approaching horses. Feeling confident that no one followed him, he walked back to his horse and searched the saddlebag for any food or useful items.

He discovered leather gloves, a bandana, and a small bag of crackers. After scarfing down the crackers, he rolled the bandana and tightened it around his hand. Walking his horse into a heavily wooded area away from the river, he tied it off to a tree and found a small piece of soft ground to sleep.

After finding a comfortable position, he thought about his tribe and family. It had been well over a week since he left them, and he was sure they were moving south toward the Gila River, as he instructed before he and Black Knife, who the prospectors knew as Half Breed, had left Lordsburg.

Red Sleeves knew most of the land in the Nuevo territory like the back of his hand. Although it was dark, he knew where he was. He planned to set out a couple hours before daylight, gaining a head start on any soldiers or posse searching for him.

His pistol laid across his lap, and he continued to listen for the sounds of horses or men. No sounds other than an occasional critter scampering across the dry brittle ground greeted him.

Red Sleeves thought of his friend, Domingo, who had saved his life in the final moments of his escape. Red Sleeves relived the escape in his mind, wondering what he could have done differently to save the brave Mexican man. It seemed they'd fought half the town, and it was pure luck that either of them survived. It just happened to be him who made it out alive.

With only two bullets left in the pistol he had acquired, Red Sleeves knew he could not fight any soldiers or posse looking for him. He needed to make his way south and prepare the tribe for the impending fight.

Inching closer to sleep, he made plans to return to the very town he'd escaped when the morning came. He was certainly not about to leave his horse Whom'tu behind.

After a long night, Sheriff Ricks rode north to his ranch located on the outskirts of Santa Fe. The sheriff was slumping in his saddle with his eyes barely cracked open and a frown fixed on his face. Still heavily thinking about his barber friend and killing that Mexican, Domingo, and equally disappointed the posse he'd sent out after Red Sleeves had returned less than a couple hours later, empty handed.

Riding along the dark trail, Ricks wondered if Red Sleeves still remained in the area. The thought made him perk up and glance warily around, then quickly spur his horse to rush them along. As Ricks reached the fence line of his ranch, he eyed the three prospectors on his porch, smoking cigars and drinking.

Ricks stopped his horse next to a stump. Swinging his leg over, he stepped onto it before walking his horse to the fence and tying it off.

Joe, Henry, and Bill said a quick hello once the sheriff reached the porch, offering him a seat and a drink of whiskey.

The sheriff grabbed the bottle and took a large swig before he sat in the chair with a blank stare.

Noticing the sheriff's odd behavior, the men looked at each other.

"What happened to you, Sheriff?" Said Joe, glancing at Bill and Henry seated a few feet away, then back at Ricks.

Without responding, the sheriff took another large swig

before pulling a cigar from his front pocket. He sat the whiskey on the table, taking the candle next to his drink to light his cigar.

After several moments passed without a response, Bill rubbed his neck. "You doing all right, Sheriff?"

The sheriff placed the candle on the table and leaned back in his chair. "Oh yeah, just fine boys," he answered Bill in a sarcastic tone. He took a long drag of the cigar and then released the smoke slowly from his mouth. "However, I have some bad news for y'all." Ricks cocked his head to the side.

Joe leaned forward. "What do you mean?"

"Well, you know that Apache son of a bitch you brought in?"

"Yeah, What about 'im?" replied Joe.

"He escaped." Ricks raised his hands and shook his head.

Joe's eyes opened wide. He stood and turned toward Bill and Henry.

Henry put his hand to his head and leaned back in the chair. Bill looked toward Ricks, who took another swig of whiskey.

"What do you mean escaped? How?" asked Bill, staring intently at Ricks.

Ricks looked over at Bill and shook his head. "I don't know. But the bastard killed a few folks and rode east out of town."

The prospectors looked at each other, stunned by the news. After a few short moments, Joe fixed his gaze on Ricks.

"What about the reward from Silver City?" asked Joe hastily.

"What about it?" replied Ricks, crossing his legs in front of him.

"We still get it right? I mean, it's not our fault he escaped. We did our job bringing him in," said Joe.

"Yeah, that's right," said Henry, adjusting the bandage around his shoulder. "We should get our reward."

Ricks looked around at the men. "Reward for what exactly? Red Sleeves is gone."

"Goddamnit, Sheriff, this is bullshit!" said Joe in an angry tone.

Ricks closed his eyes, and his face turned red. Opening his eyes, he leaned toward Joe. "I don't give a shit about your reward," said Ricks, staring angrily at Joe. "You dumbasses didn't even know you had Red Sleeves until I told ya!" Ricks shouted as Joe quickly returned to his seat. "Now I have men dead in that town, including a good friend of mine and a deputy who might lose a leg!" He banged his fist against the arm of the chair. "I don't give a fuck about your reward!"

Ricks's wife opened the front door, noticing her husband on the porch. "What's all the shouting about?" she asked with an angry glare.

"Oh, I am sorry honey, It's nothin'. I'll be heading inside shortly," replied Ricks with a half-hearted smile.

She peered at the men gathered on the porch, then back toward her husband. "Ok, well, just quiet down and watch your mouth."

Ricks smiled again as she walked into the house, shutting the door behind her.

The sheriff turned his attention back to the prospectors. He lowered his tone. "Look, y'all are still alive, so just be happy with that."

Henry shook his head then rubbed his chin. "No, Sheriff,

we delivered Red Sleeves to you, and we should get the reward from you or from Silver City Mining Company."

Bill nodded in agreement.

Henry continued. "I think if you explain—"

"Goddamnit, you asshole!" Ricks hollered, cutting Henry off. "I am not discussing the fucking reward!" His eyes bulged as he stared at Henry.

Henry turned away, fixing his gaze to the floor. A moment later, the front door opened again.

"Goddamnit!" shouted Ricks. He raised his hand in disgust and looked across the yard.

Ricks's wife appeared again. "Come inside now!" she said, her hand on her hip.

Ricks turned toward the door and glared at his wife, this time without the smile. "I will come inside when I damn well please," he said slowly.

She stared at her husband without blinking, her jaw clenched. Silence ruled as the two glared at one another.

The three prospectors turned away to escape the awkward silence, talking among themselves.

The angry woman slowly turned inside and slammed the front door so hard the vibration was felt throughout the entire porch.

Ricks reached for the bottle of whiskey and took a drink. He placed the cigar back into his mouth and stared at the three men, who discussed what they should do in the morning. Ricks understood the men being upset about the reward, but there were much larger things to be upset about, like the loss of life that had just occurred. Even though Ricks was annoyed with the men and mostly wanted them to leave, Ricks had offered the men to stay at his ranch a few days. Even though the circumstances had changed, he planned on honoring that agreement.

"You boys don't have to run off in the morning," said Ricks, interrupting the men's discussion as they turned toward him. Ricks pulled the cigar from his mouth. "Y'all can stay here a couple more days." He motioned toward the barn. "You can take those two horses you got from the Indians to Mick at the stable house in the morning. He'll probably give you good money for them." He took another drink from the bottle and placed it back on the table.

"Thanks, Sheriff," said Joe as he reached for the bottle.

"If you do decide to stay, y'all can help me with some fencing. I'll pay you for it," added Ricks.

"We appreciate that, Sheriff," said Joe with a quick nod. "We're not sure what we're going to do yet."

Ricks nodded and stood. He stretched his arms above his head and closed his eyes while yawning deeply. He looked at his front door, dreading the thought of facing his wife. He figured, once he told her what happened, she would cool down pretty quick, but Ricks was exhausted and didn't feel much like talking at all. He hoped she had gone to bed, and he could wait until the morning to talk about it.

"Well, boys, maybe I'll see you in the morning, If not, good luck to ya." Ricks reached to shake Joe's hand, and the other man rose to his feet. Ricks looked at Henry and Bill and gave a quick nod before opening the front door to head inside.

As he shut the door behind him, he glanced toward the living room, where the silhouette of his wife sat in the darkened room. She stood from the sofa and swiftly approached her husband. The oil light shone across the room, reflecting her lowered brows, fiery eyes, and the flyswatter in her hand.

Ricks held his hands in front of him. "Wait, honey, hear me out!" while backing into the kitchen. His words seemed to have no effect on her as she continued closing in.

She raised the flyswatter high above her head, swinging it down on her husband repeatedly as he covered his head and face. "Don't you ever talk to me like that!" she shouted still delivering the blows to his head.

"Stop it now and listen!" shouted Ricks while making a quick escape around her. He rushed toward their room, his wife on his heels. He attempted to shut the bedroom door, but she pushed it open to continue the onslaught. As the smacks of the flyswatter pierced throughout the house, so did the yelps of the sheriff.

CHAPTER 4

NO GOLD AND NO NEW BEGINNING

Before the morning sun rose, Red Sleeves awoke. He listened to the sounds around him for signs of danger before taking his horse back to the river. After checking his wounds again and ensuring the horse drank his fill, he climbed onto the mount and headed for Santa Fe.

Darkness covered the land as Red Sleeves silently rode the same path he came. Looking down every so often, he checked his horse's tracks and remained alert to any movement or sounds. After a mile, Red Sleeves found a trail leading toward town. He followed it, making good time. Before long, he was within a mile of Santa Fe.

He rode off the trail, using the trees and brush as cover. Once the town came into view, he jumped off his horse and tied his mount to a tree. The sun was just starting to peek above the eastern sky when he knelt in the brush and surveyed the area.

Red Sleeves swiftly moved toward town on foot to get a

better view. He stopped for a few moments, ducking to the ground. He stood up, dropping quickly back to the brush when he noticed a wagon riding his way. It had two horses tied to the rear, and another man on horseback rode alongside it.

The trail was around fifty yards ahead of Red Sleeves, and since dawn had not fully broken, he figured the men would pass without noticing him or his horse, currently tied up over the hill eighty yards behind him.

Slipping behind the brush, Red Sleeves positioned himself to get a good look at the men as they passed. After a few more minutes, the wagon rolled by, and he had a clear view of the men inside and the man riding his horse beside it. It was none other than the three prospectors who had beat him and killed his companion along the Santa Fe Trail just days ago.

Red Sleeves fixed his eyes on the horses tied to the rear of the wagon, smiling when he saw Whom'tu. After the men passed and Red Sleeves could move safely, he made his way to his horse, climbed up, and rode parallel to the men and wagon while hidden from view in the thick brush.

After the men stayed to the left at a fork in the trail, he knew where they headed. He kicked the horse repeatedly, picking up speed as he rode a ways ahead of the slow-moving wagon. Surveying the trail, he looked for a good spot to ambush the men.

It wasn't long until he found the place. The trail passed through a tight rocky opening before widening. Surrounded by a ridge on each side, it hit another tight rocky opening a few hundred feet ahead.

Red Sleeves tied his horse off a distance away and walked toward the trail. It came into view about fifteen feet below him. Standing on the rock cliff, he looked in the distance as the wagon came into sight. He dropped down and readied his pistol. Only having two bullets, he wasn't sure how he would use them, but he knew the man on the horse—possibly Joe—would be his first target. The wagon could not escape nearly as quickly, and it would reduce the chances of the men getting away.

Joe grabbed some jerky from his pocket. Taking a bite, he glanced at the two men in the wagon as they continued east, away from Santa Fe. They turned toward Taos at the fork, planning to survey the land there. Although they'd missed out on their reward and the secret spot of promised gold, the men had all their money and a couple new horses. The sun reached above the tree line, bringing in another hot day.

"Joe, you have more of that?" asked Bill.

Joe reached into his pocket and steered his mount closer to the wagon, tossing Bill and Henry a chunk of jerky. "Well, boys, we have a long hot ride ahead of us, but we should reach Taos tomorrow morning, I would say." Joe glanced at the wide-open land. "We'll make camp along the river and cook us a fine meal," he said with a grin.

"All we got is beans and a little mutton back there," Henry replied. He pointed his left thumb behind him and held the reins with his other hand.

Joe nodded and smiled. "Well, that still sounds mighty fine, Henry." He looked around and raised his chin. He was happy to put Santa Fe behind him and start prospecting again. After a few minutes passed, he finished his jerky and spoke to the men. "Felt li'l bad for that sheriff," Joe shook his head. "But what a dumb son of a bitch, huh?"

Henry laughed. "Yeah, no kidding! How you let a half dead Indian escape out of an iron cell?"

Bill chuckled as well. "Yeah, that bastard cost us twenty-five hundred bucks!"

Joe grinned. "How 'bout that wife? Oh my lord." He rolled his eyes.

Henry put his head down and laughed, stomping his foot on the floor of the wagon. "Boy, she sure beat the hell out of that poor dumb bastard!"

Bill jumped in with a hoot. "Oh hell, yeah! All you could hear was smack! Ouch! Smack! Ouch!" Bill made a hand gesture of swinging a stick every time he said smack.

The three men laughed loudly. They passed an opening through a ridge line, which had been hit with dynamite a few years before for easier traveling.

Joe shook his head, continuing to chuckle. "I bet she would've came after all of us, if she didn't wear herself—"

Bang!

A shot rang out. Joe reached for his shoulder, nearly falling from his horse. A second shot hit Joe's horse in the leg. The animal reared up, spilling Joe to the ground, and crashed down on Joe's leg. Pain raced up his spine.

Joe shouted in agony, and Henry drew the wagon to a stop. Bill jumped down from the wagon while reaching for his holster to grab his pistol. Henry also left the wagon and took cover under it, careful not to put much stress on his injured collar bone.

"Joe!" Henry shouted. "You ok? Where did he get you?"

Joe flailed, grabbing at his leg.

Bill scanned the ridge for the shooter.

Henry crawled away from the wagon—his bandage restricting his movement—to get Joe.

Bill stopped him, shouting, "Stay put, goddamnit! They're trying to draw us out." He scanned the ridge while Henry retreated under the wagon.

Joe breathed heavily and yelped in pain.

"Joe, can you make it over here to the wagon?" Henry asked.

Joe made a slow crawl toward the other man, dragging his leg behind him.

Henry glanced at Bill. "You think it's that Apache bastard out there?"

Still unable to see signs of anybody, Bill said, "I don't know. I guess it could be or maybe a few of his friends?"

Joe had dragged himself within a few feet from the wagon, and Henry reached out with his good arm to drag him under. Bill remained focused on one end of the ridge, not noticing the fast-approaching horse from the other end until he heard the sound of hooves beating forcefully against the ground.

Bill jumped to his feet and took aim at the approaching rider.

Bang! Bang! Bang!

Three shots rang out. They hit the charging man's horse each time as the rider ducked below the animal's neck.

Bill steadied his pistol to fire again.

The stumbling horse drew ever closer.

Bill underestimated the speed and distance of the charging animal. Before he could pull the trigger, they collided, throwing Bill, horse, and rider in all directions. The pistol flew from Bill's hand. He landed hard on his back, and his legs were thrown above him, rolling him head to toe several times.

The horse collapsed to the ground with such force that the saddle broke free and skidded across the ground. Dust and dirt flew in the air and blocked any visibility of the rider. The horse kicked its legs, snorting and moaning in pain.

In shock, Henry and Joe peered from underneath the wagon as their eyes darted back and forth, waiting for the dust to clear. Through the dust, they saw Bill sit up. He was covered in dirt, and blood ran from his head and down his face. He scrambled around on all fours, looking for his pistol.

Joe and Henry watched as two feet wrapped in animal hide moved toward Bill at a slow pace.

"Bill, look out. He's coming!" yelled Henry, reaching for Joe's holster for his pistol.

Joe recognized Red Sleeves, the man they had captured just days before.

The Indian approached Bill, who was on his knees with his hands held above his head. Red Sleeves stopped when he reached Bill, staring at him for a moment. Putting the pistol to Bill's head, he pulled the trigger. Blood and brains spilled onto the ground.

"Holy shit!" Henry shifted toward the other side of the wagon, away from the Indian. "What the fuck now, Joe!" he asked.

Joe held his shoulder and lay on the ground. "Shoot him, Henry," he said with what strength he could muster.

Henry's heart pounded. He gave a frantic jerk of his head, and then he fired a couple blind shots from under the wagon. A loud thump sounded above them from inside the wagon. The sudden noise spooked Henry, and he fired a few more rounds into the wood planks above him. The gun clicked, its chambers empty. He opened the pistol to dump the spent cartridges and reached for ammo from Joe's gun belt.

As he reached, he locked eyes with Red Sleeves. The Indian knelt beside the wagon and stared straight at him.

Henry froze.

Red Sleeves kept unblinking eyes locked on him.

Henry raised his hand and let go of the pistol, his eyes wide. "Please," he said with hands and jaw trembling.

Henry, Joe, and Bill had traveled with this very Indian just a week ago, hoping to find wealth and establish their budding company.

Henry quickly realized there was no gold, no reward, and no new beginning.

This was the end of the road, and Joe knew it more than anyone. He did his best to play dead in his last-ditch effort to survive. Joe stopped his heavy breathing and lay motionless beside Henry. He kept an eye cracked on Henry, watching his comrade shake in fear and beg for his life.

Red Sleeves noticed the poor acting job by Joe, seeing his hands trembling with fear as a bead of sweat ran down Joe's cheek. The Apache chief glanced at Henry as the corner of Red Sleeves's mouth quirked in a smile.

Henry took notice of the Indian's small grin and smiled back in response.

Bang!

Red Sleeves fired the pistol.

Henry's head flew backward, and he collapsed to the ground.

Red Sleeves noticed Joe's whole body shudder at the sound of the gunshot as the smoke from the barrel spewed out from under the wagon. Red Sleeves stared at the man's leg. Twisted in unnatural ways, Red Sleeves knew it was broken. The Indian hovered over Joe for a few moments and grabbed the pistol lying beside Henry's lifeless body. He then unhooked Joe's gun belt, pulling it away to watch it skid across the ground. Retreating from under the wagon, he rose to his feet and searched Joe's dead horse. Once done, he climbed onto the wagon and searched it as well.

Joe heard Red Sleeves walking around the wagon before jumping onto it and going through their gear for several minutes. He saw Red Sleeves feet close to the Apache's horse and heard Apache words being spoken. Red Sleeves feet disappeared, and the horse's legs were all Joe could see as Red Sleeves rode into the distance.

Joe wiggled forward for a better view, catching a glimpse of the Apache riding through the rocky ridge and leading Half Breed's horse behind him. As the sound of horses faded in the distance followed by an eerie silence, Joe quickly looked over at Henry, then squirmed from under the wagon. He pulled himself closer to Bill and shook his head at the sight of his longtime friend's injuries.

"Goddamn savage," he muttered to himself.

Joe pulled himself onto the wagon's seat, grimacing at the effort. Using his hand, he lifted his broken leg inside and cracked the reins. Turning, he directed the wagon back the way they'd come, bucking the cart as its rear wheel rode over Henry's lifeless body.

Cracking the reins several times, Joe continued looking behind him, praying Red Sleeves didn't return.

CHAPTER 5

THE BEAST THAT LIES AHEAD

JUAN FOUGHT SEVERE DEHYDRATION AND hunger during his trek to Silver City. With each footstep, he became weaker. The hot sun beat down on him, forcing him to find shade anywhere he could as he walked along the road.

After Devi left him the day before in Magdalena, Juan hadn't seen a single person since. He had at least another full day of walking before he would reach his destination, and he wasn't sure if he would make it. Several pine trees stood ahead, slightly off the trail. As he neared, he left the path and climbed a gently sloping hill. Upon reaching his destination, he sat, tugging his hat off and wiping his brow. Leaning against one of the trees, he closed his eyes and relaxed. Minutes passed before he heard a strange noise in the woods behind him.

Juan opened his eyes and turned to peer around the tree. When he heard nothing, he shifted his back against the pine and got comfortable.

The noise started again moments later.

Convinced something lurked in the woods, he distinguished scraping noises and breaking sticks with an occasional snort. Taking a deep breath to calm his pounding heart, Juan stood and crept toward the unusual sound. After convincing himself he was surely in hell over the last day, he could only imagine what beast lay ahead of him.

He turned and twisted though the trees and brush, often stopping and listening to determine where the unknown sounds came from. He continued cautiously until he realized whatever made the noise was just ahead of him. After walking another fifteen feet, he knelt behind a tree. Heart pounding, he peeked around it.

A clump of low brush blocked his view as he attempted to scan the area. Ready to proceed forward, he noticed a large leather strap trailing down a tree nearly twenty feet in front of him. The strap moved side to side, and he heard sticks break with each pull. Puzzled, Juan continued toward the twisting strap, attempting to discern the source of the sound.

"What the hell?" he mumbled, standing upright to get a better look.

Juan found a horse tied to a tree, and it was in bad shape. It lay on its side, the strap pulling its head off the ground toward the tree. The horse appeared to have been tied there for some time. Blood trickled along the bridle where the animal had been pulling on the strap. Juan looked around before approaching the horse.

"Easy, boy." Juan held his hands in front of him.

The horse twisted about and snorted with an occasional whinny.

Juan unhooked the strap, releasing the frightened animal

from the tree, and held fast to the strap. The horse tried unsuccessfully to stand, and Juan did his best to calm the animal.

The frantic horse continued trying to stand, losing its balance and falling back to the ground over and over.

Juan put his weight on the animal to keep it from standing. "Easy now, boy. Stay here a sec," he said.

The horse eventually calmed down enough for Juan to release his hold. He noticed several canteens along the saddle and reached for one. Cracking it open, he took several large drinks. Looking at the horse, he could tell it was severely dehydrated, so he did his best to pour some water into the animal's mouth.

The horse took down a few good drinks of water before Juan returned the canteen to his own mouth. Pouring some water on the horse's head and neck, he rubbed it around to cool the animal.

"There, boy. Doesn't that feel good?" Juan asked, pouring some on his own head.

The canteen was empty within minutes, and he reached for another. Juan dug a three-inch-deep hole with a stick in front of the horse's muzzle and filled it with water. The horse put its snout in the hole and slurped the water up. Juan took several more drinks before taking inventory of the horse's saddlebags.

He found bullets, money, a knife, dried meat, a tinderbox, a small pot, beans, a bandana, a bedroll, and several canteens of water. Juan wondered why the horse was abandoned in the middle of nowhere, surmising that the owner of the horse had gone out to hunt and had been injured or killed.

Whatever the case, Juan could not believe his good fortune, but then, the smile he wore dissipated. His eyes darted, and he fidgeted, wondering if this was a test within hell, much like the eating of the apple in the Old Testament. Juan shook his head to dismiss the thought before looking around to see if a snake would appear. He chuckled.

The horse seemed calm, and Juan decided to see if it could stand with help.

"Ok, ole boy," Juan said, standing over the horse. He reached down, pulling on the cheek piece of the bridle to help the animal stand.

The horse tried to lift itself up, its front legs in front of him. The horse's rear leg muscles shook, barely strong enough to lift the animal. With a few more pulls from Juan, the horse finally stood.

"There you go, boy!" Juan said with a grin, rubbing the horse's neck and muzzle.

He slowly walked the horse to a little patch of weeds and grass, allowing it to graze. A tree stood near the area where the horse ate, and Juan smiled at his new friend. "Ok, I have to tie you up again. I promise I won't leave you."

The horse continued eating as Juan tied the strap around the tree. Although in weak condition, he was sure the horse would be fine. He returned to the saddlebags, pulling a rifle out of the sling.

"Wow!" he exclaimed, a huge grin lighting his face. "A Winchester repeater!"

He noted that the rifle was fully loaded before returning it to the sling and grabbing a few pieces of mutton and a chunk of bread. Although a little hard, the bread didn't appear to contain any mold.

Juan guessed the horse had been there for at least three days, perhaps even a week. He picked up the canteen he'd opened earlier and finished it off. Two full canteens remained.

He walked to the front side of the horse with the small pot and filled it with water. The horse pushed its snout inside and drank.

He poured the rest of the canteen in the pot. "There you go, boy."

After rubbing the horse's neck for a few minutes, Juan stood and put the canteen around the saddle horn before looking the horse over for injuries. When he didn't see any, he said, "I think I am going to call you Lucky." He raised his hand to his chin. "I guess were both pretty lucky I found you."

After another hour had passed and Juan and Lucky both had several more drinks of water, he led the horse back to the road leading to Silver City.

He knew he could not ride the weak animal, so Juan led the horse along the dusty road while looking for a creek to refill the canteens and get Lucky another good drink. As they continued south, he noticed several horses and wagons moving in his direction.

Juan continued walking, watching as dust rose into the sky from a distance. Juan soon realized many horses and wagons lumbered in his direction. Juan stared hard, realizing it was the US Army.

Unsure of the situation, he decided to take cover and hide behind some trees and brush around one hundred yards off the road to let the soldiers pass. He pulled Lucky along, rushing away from the dusty road and out of sight. After reaching his hiding spot, he stood alongside Lucky and gazed at the soldiers as they approached.

The line of horses and wagons began passing by, and Juan couldn't believe the size of the army. Juan guessed there was over thirty wagons, several hundred horses, and a couple thousand men. He watched until he noticed two soldiers on horses looking in his direction. He pulled Lucky further into the group of trees another thirty feet, tying him off before returning to his original position.

Upon his return, he peeked around a tree to look at the soldiers. Now, he saw three men on horses looking his way, and one of them had field glasses.

"Oh shit!" Juan whispered, ducking further in the brush.

A few moments later, he lifted his head and looked at the soldiers, only to see five men riding his way at a quick pace.

"Cripes," grumbled Juan. He leaped to his feet and ran to Lucky.

Lucky staggered as he attempted to pull himself onto the horse, struggling to stay upright. Juan tried to get the horse to run, but he was still too weak. Juan jumped down to lead Lucky the opposite way of the soldiers.

Moments later, the sounds of sticks cracking under hooves could be heard as the approaching soldiers closed in on him.

Juan stopped.

Seconds later, they appeared in front of him through the trees, their pistols drawn.

Juan raised his hands quickly. "Whoa! Whoa! What's the problem?"

The soldiers stared at him with jaws clenched and lowered brows.

One soldier pointed toward Juan and said to another soldier, "Get his rifle."

The soldier rode toward Juan, pulling the rifle from the sling before retreating a few yards away. It was obvious they were angry, and Juan's eyes darted back and forth still uncertain of the soldiers' motives.

"What's your name?" asked one of the soldiers in Spanish.

"Juan Moraga."

"Where are you coming from?" asked the soldier.

"Magdalena." Juan's eyes shifted from one soldier to the next.

"Why are you hiding from us?"

"I wasn't hiding from you. I wasn't sure who was coming or if it was safe," Juan replied.

The soldier turned to his comrades and spoke in English. Juan knew a little English and could make out some of what they said, but little made any sense to him.

After a brief discussion among the soldiers, one turned to Juan and rested his hands on the saddle horn. "You're coming with us. Don't try and run, or we'll shoot you."

Juan drew his chin back toward his neck somewhat surprised. "What?" He raised his hands and turned his palms up. "Why do I have to go with you?"

The soldier fixed his eyes on Juan, his face turning red. "Because I fucking said so!"

Juan's brow creased and eyes squinted.

"Now get on your horse and hand me the rein!" the man instructed, pointing at the animal.

Juan shook his head. "The horse is too weak. We had a long journey from Magdalena."

The soldier swung his horse around and held his hand out for Lucky's rein. Juan handed it to him.

"Get on the back of his horse," said the soldier, pointing to another sitting on his horse nearby.

Juan walked toward him, and the soldier pulled him up, where he found a seat on the rump.

The soldiers rushed back toward their waiting caravan as

Juan struggled to stay on the back of the horse. After reaching several more soldiers on horseback alongside the line of wagons, the man Juan rode with pushed him off the rear of the horse, and he fell to the ground.

"What do we got, Sergeant?" asked one of the men.

"Not sure, Major. But this could be our man, sir."

The major walked toward Juan and stared at him intently. Juan wasn't sure what was happening, but he figured this was certainly the man in charge.

The major turned toward the other soldier who still rode on horseback. "Sergeant Warden, go get Jenkins."

"Yes, sir," replied the sergeant, riding swiftly down the line of wagons.

"What's your name, boy?" asked the major.

"Juan Moraga," he said, rising to his feet.

The major pulled a cigar from his pocket while looking down the line of wagons. "My name is Major Bolan, United States Army." He then glanced back at Juan. "Why are you running from us?"

Juan quickly shook his head. "I wasn't running. I didn't know who was coming, so I just got out of the way."

Major Bolan stared at Juan, nodding before looking down the line at two approaching soldiers. As they reached Juan and the major, one rider glared at Juan for several moments and moved his head side to side.

"That him?" asked the major.

The soldier slowly shook his head. "I can't say for certain, sir. He looks about the same age and certainly resembles him, but I can't say with any confidence, sir."

The major nodded his head a few times. "All right, men, let's get these wagons moving! We aren't stopping till we reach

Santa Rosa." He then addressed a nearby soldier. "Sergeant Warden, shackle him on his horse and tie it to a wagon."

As the major turned his horse away, the soldier replied, "Sir, he said his horse is weak and can't carry him."

The major stopped his horse. "Well, then shackle him and throw him in a wagon."

"Yes, sir," replied the sergeant. The man moved toward Juan after pulling irons from his saddlebag.

"What is going on?" asked Juan, slowly backing away.

"You look an awful lot like a man we been searching for. Until we know for sure, you're coming with us." Sergeant Warden grabbed Juan's wrist, forcing it into the shackle.

Panicked, Juan plead his case. "I didn't do anything, What man? How do I look like him?" asked Juan.

Sergeant Warden smiled before leading Juan toward a wagon. "You're a Mexican, and that's close enough!"

The sergeant reached one of the nearest wagons and instructed Juan to climb inside. Another soldier entered and sat across from him to keep guard. Moments later, the sergeant tied off Lucky to the rear, climbed on his horse, and rode away.

Juan stared at Lucky, his new friend, and asked the soldier if the horse could have some water.

The soldier shook his head. "We'll stop again in a few hours."

Seconds later, the wagon began moving at a very quick pace, rapidly covering the same ground Juan spent the day before desperately walking.

CHAPTER 6

THE PROSPECTORS ON CACTUS HILL

Sheriff Ricks fed his pigs and walked into the barn to get his horse, placing the saddle on its back. After a long day and sleepless night, he was none too excited about heading into town, but there were plenty things for him to get done.

What bothered him the most was having to bury the Mexican outlaw who killed his friend and shot his deputy in the leg. Ricks knew the townsfolk wondered what he was going to do about the Apache who'd escaped. Ricks had already made up his mind to offer a reward on the savage, and hopefully, some bounty hunters would do the work of catching him.

Ricks led his horse out of the barn and climbed onto the saddle. Just as he was about to spur the horse, he saw a wagon approach at a quick pace. Ricks gazed at it momentarily before realizing it was the prospector's wagon.

Ricks gave a little kick to his horse and rode ahead. When

the wagon came closer, he noticed Joe hunched over in the seat. Ricks spurred his horse faster.

Blood covered Joe's shirt, and the man grimaced, holding his shoulder. "Sheriff, it's Red Sleeves!"

Ricks looked down the road but didn't see anything "Where?"

Joe pointed over his shoulder, squinting his eyes while hunching over. "Back there. He got Bill and Henry."

Ricks glanced down the road again, eyes wide and jaw hanging open. He looked back and forth a few more times before noticing the extent of the other man's injuries. "We need to get you to the doc. Move over!"

Ricks tied his horse to the wagon, noticing his wife at the door. "Stay inside and lock the doors!" he shouted, watching as she disappeared inside.

Ricks climbed into the wagon, grabbing the reins. "Yah!" He cracked the reins, and the two men rode to town.

Joe's leg was clearly broken, Ricks thought, as Joe's shin and foot flopped around in front of him. "What the hell happened, Joe?" he asked.

They bounced down the bumpy trail, throwing an injured Joe around the seat.

"Slow down!" yelled Joe, pulling himself back into the seat.

"Sorry, Joe, but we need to get you there and real quick like!" urged Ricks.

Joe braced a steadying right hand to the bottom of the seat. "We were heading to Taos, and that Apache bastard ambushed us."

Ricks eyed Joe before turning back to the road. "Well, what happened to Bill and Henry?"

"Dead," replied Joe, lowering his head. "Shot them both in the head."

"Goddamn that Apache bastard," said the sheriff through his teeth.

Ricks spat out the side of the wagon. He turned his attention to Joe, who seemed more lethargic than before.

"Hang on, Joe. We're almost there." Ricks put a hand on Joe's shoulder to stabilize him.

As the sheriff rode into town, several people gawked at the wagon. After noticing their sheriff, they called for him.

"Not now!" shouted Ricks.

He waved his hand at them as he rode past, heading toward Doc Roberts's office. Once Ricks stopped the wagon, he jumped down and rushed across the porch, swinging the door open.

Doc Roberts lifted his head while pulling off his spectacles and setting the paper on the desk. "Hello, Sheriff."

"I need you to come outside right now. I got a hurt man out here!"

Doc scrambled to his feet. The two men rushed outside, and Doc jumped into the wagon to examine Joe. "Help me get him inside."

Doc stood next to Joe and pulled him to the side of the seat. Ricks, still slightly out of breath, was a heavy man. He walked toward the wagon and stood nearby, watching.

Noticing Cliff and William Taylor walk by, Ricks said, "Hey, fellers, help the doc carry him inside."

"What happened to him?" asked William as they came closer.

"That damn Apache son a bitch got him," explained Ricks.

William and Cliff each grabbed one of Joe's arms and

shoulders. The doc grabbed Joe's feet, carefully handling the man's broken leg. Joe yelped in pain as they walked up the steps, Ricks following closely behind.

They carried him into the room that Deputy Collins still occupied, healing from his leg injury. The deputy gaped at the four men as they walked into the room.

Doc Roberts released Joe's feet while William and Cliff continued holding him. He then opened a closet and pulled out a cot, setting it near Collins's bed.

"Lay him down here," said the doc.

William and Cliff brought Joe closer to the cot, laying him down gently.

The sheriff stood by the door, giving them room to work. He looked toward the deputy, shaking his head. "Red Sleeves got him."

The deputy rose onto his elbows, his eyes wide. "No shit."

William and Cliff turned shocked expressions toward the sheriff.

"The same Indian who escaped last night?" asked Cliff.

The sheriff nodded and turned toward the brothers. "You boys interested and going after him? I need to get a posse together to get that savage before he kills someone else."

William and Cliff turned toward one another with raised eyebrows.

"Umm, Sheriff, I don't know. That might be better for the law or bounty hunters," explained William.

Cliff nodded his agreement.

The sheriff cocked his head to the side and closed his mouth.

William raised his hands. "Sheriff, we ain't the law. We just—"

"You're looking at the only law around here!" Ricks face turned red, and his eyes bulged.

Cliff and William stood still as the sheriff pulled off has hat and wiped his brow.

Ricks looked down at the floor, shaking his head before turning his eyes back to the brothers. He knew assembling a posse to go after such a dangerous savage would be difficult. Ricks thought of Mitchell, a constable in Taos who had several of his own men and a real hatred for Indians.

"All right, you cowardly bastards," said Ricks, putting on his hat. "Do me favor then. Head over to Taos and tell Mitchell what's happened here."

William shook his head.

Cliff cleared his throat and took a breath. "That Apache is still out there, Sheriff." He raised his hands. "It's Red Sleeves, for Christ's sake," he added, creasing his brow.

Ricks clenched his fist and shook his head. "You pussy asshole cocksuckers, he's gone, goddamn it!" He pounded his fist against the wall, knocking a picture from it.

The doc glared at the sheriff.

"Sorry, Doc." Ricks pushed the broken picture with his foot toward the wall.

The doc turned back to Joe, cutting his shirt to look at the bullet wound in his shoulder.

Ricks took a breath and turned his attention back to William and Cliff. "Look, he probably just came back for his horse." He gritted his teeth as he turned to Joe. "I told you assholes to sell that fucking thing!" shouted Ricks.

Cliff held out his hands beside him and leaned back before dropping his arms again. "All right, Sheriff. We'll go get Mitchell in the morning."

Ricks shook his head and pointed toward the door. "No, right now, boys! Take that wagon out front and go by my store. Take what you need for the trip and move out!"

Cliff shuffled his feet, looking down at the floor as William bit down on his lip, gazing at their sheriff before William gave a heavy sigh. "Goddamnit, all right." He threw his hands to his sides.

The sheriff nodded to the brothers. "Thanks, boys, I'll let your women and family know where you're headed."

Cliff rolled his eyes and left the room, walking past the sheriff as he did so. William started to walk out, but he stopped and accepted the sheriff's hand. He then nodded and walked slowly toward the open front door.

Ricks turned his focus to Doc Roberts. "How's it looking?"

The doc had cleaned the wound and covered it with a bandage, and Joe seemed to be somewhat comfortable.

"Well, the good news is the bullet passed through his shoulder without major bone damage. But it will take time to heal." The doc slid his chair close to Joe's feet and began cutting his pant leg. "For the leg, I am not sure yet."

Deputy Collins glanced back and forth from Joe to Ricks before fixing his eyes on the sheriff. "Why in the hell would that bastard come back right after escaping? You really think it was for the horse?"

Ricks shrugged his shoulders. "I don't know. I just said that to make them dumb bastards feel better about heading over to Taos."

Collins smiled and lay back, shaking his head. "Some crazy times we're living in."

"Sure the hell is," Ricks whispered, watching the doc a

moment longer before turning to leave. "See you later. I'll be back in a few hours to check on ya."

The sheriff walked out the door, disappointed to find several people waiting to talk to him. He raised his hands waiving them at the crowd. "Move back. Move back," he said, taking off his hat to address them. "Listen, folks, we had a hell of a couple days, so let's not make this any harder than it needs to be." The sheriff then placed his hat back on his head, looking toward a few men close by. "I need you three to go bury that Mexican bastard somewhere in the outskirts of town."

The men glanced at each other and shrugged their shoulders as Ricks turned toward the crowd.

One of the men raised his hands. "Bury him where, Sheriff?"

Ricks rolled his eyes and turned back. "Shit, Pete, I don't give a damn. Just get rid of him." The sheriff regarded those gathered around him. "Now, listen, that man laying inside and his partners were attacked by Indians this morning, So I don't want no one leaving town alone, you hear?" said the sheriff.

Many in the crowd nodded.

"I sent two men to get Mitchell in Taos, and I am sure he will come help us track that savage down." Ricks pointed in the direction of Fort Marcy, just outside of town. "I'm going over there later today to talk to General Johnson and see what help he can offer securing the town until those savages who did this are killed or captured!"

He raised his finger in front of his face, his eyebrows drawing close together in a glare. "I promise you we will get the Apache bastard. Now, when Mitchell arrives, I am going to need some volunteers to go looking for Red Sleeves." Lowering his finger, he pointed at several nearby men. "In the meantime, you men head out on the Cactus Hill trail and get those two dead miners."

Ricks removed his hat and placed it in front of his chest. "Now we got graves to dig for our friends we lost yesterday. So let's get them buried and avenge this senseless loss of life." He put his hat back on and looked over at the hitching post. He didn't see his horse. "Goddamnit, those dumb assholes took my horse with them."

Dropping his shoulders, he threw his hands down beside him and started walking toward the jailhouse. The crowd following behind him, asking several questions.

"Nothing else to say. folks, Read it in the paper tomorrow!" shouted Ricks. He waved his hand up and continued down the street, shaking his head over his now-missing horse.

CHAPTER 7
HERE COMES THE RAIN

RED SLEEVES RODE ALONG THE Rio Grande River before reaching the Santa Fe Trail an hour later. With Whom'tu and the supplies he took from the prospectors, he was set for a long ride and not worried about any posse that might be after him. He proudly rode along the trail, rubbing Whom'tu's neck several times and talking to his old friend.

Not only was he happy to be alive and have his freedom, but he was overjoyed to have his trusty steed back. For many hours, he rode east along the Santa Fe Trail, leading Half Breed's horse behind him. He passed several wagons and rancheros along the way.

The strangers stared at the tall Indian, and a few even seemed to recognize him, but no one dared to challenge the lone Apache.

After a time, Red Sleeves steered Whom'tu and Half Breed's horse to the bank of a river for a drink. He climbed down from his horse to scout the area. He examined the terrain and led Whom'tu along roughly fifty yards until he came upon the body of his friend, Wuyan Black Knife, whom the miners called Half Breed.

Red Sleeves removed Black Knife's necklace from the badly decomposed body. He cut two branches from a nearby tree, using the knife he took from the prospectors. Assembling a travois, he laid Black Knife onto it. He dragged the man's body behind him and found a nice resting place higher on the ridge.

He used a large stick to dig a shallow grave, then laid his friend inside, covering him with dirt and branches. After a few moments of prayers, Red Sleeves stuck the stick in the ground beside the grave and wrapped Black Knife's necklace around it.

"Sleep well," said Red Sleeves to his friend.

He mourned a bit longer, then turned to Whom'tu, who stood a few yards away. Red Sleeves grinned and walked over to unhook the travois. Rubbing the horse's side, he hopped on and rode to the Santa Fe Trail, continuing east.

He eventually reached a bend in the trail. Scanning the area, he fixed his eyes along the ground and ridge for several minutes before noticing a small piece of rope hanging from a nearby limb. He rode to the hanging rope and looked at it for several moments before continuing to ride. After another ten minutes, he turned Whom'tu south and stopped. He stared in the distance before turning his face to the sun.

"Let's go home, Whom'tu," he said, kicking his feet a few quick times.

The horse took off, driving its hooves into the brittle ground and bringing a smile to Red Sleeves's face. He was eager to see his wife, his children, and his tribe again. He smiled even more at the thought of how surprised they would be to see their chief alive and well.

Just after 5:00 PM, General Johnson finished reading a letter he had received from General West, currently stationed in California. The general was moving southeast across the southern region of Alta California, and he would enter the New Mexico territory within a month. Johnson, never caring for the man or his treatment of the Indians, was none too excited about the impending arrival.

The American forces had begun to congregate, planning their march south, deeper into Mexico. It wouldn't be long before Johnson received orders to move south along the Camino Real, which would lead him directly to Mexico City.

A knock sounded at the door as Johnson reviewed an inventory log.

"Come in," he said.

Corporal Rhoades walked inside and gave a quick salute. "General, sir, Wells's brigade is just arriving."

Johnson nodded. "Thank you, Corporal. Have the men set up their tents and get the cooks going. Have them brief me in the morning." Johnson looked over the log again. "I am sure they are hungry and exhausted."

"Yes, sir." Rhoades saluted before spinning on his heels to walk toward the door.

After reviewing the fort's inventory, Johnson pulled out a folder that housed his plans to build a prisoner of war camp at Fort Marcy. Even though it would be a couple more days before the rest of the brigade arrived, the arrival of much-needed manpower would help complete the work at a faster pace.

Major Bolan had taken a portion of Wells's brigade to Mora to quell a recent uprising that started months earlier in Taos. It was Johnson's plan to promote Major Bolan to brigadier general when he arrived in Santa Fe now that Lieutenant Wells was dead. After looking over the plans and materials still needed, another knock interrupted him.

Johnson laid the folder on the desk. He reached for a cigar and lit it, staring at the door. At the next knock, the general took his time to respond. "What is it?"

"Corporal Rhoades, sir, I have Sergeant Warden requesting to see you."

Johnson took a long puff of his cigar and leaned back in his chair. "Come in," he replied, crossing his arms.

Corporal Rhoades opened the door, and in walked Sergeant Warden. The sergeant saluted the general, and Johnson saluted him in return.

"Welcome back, Sergeant," said Johnson.

"Thank you, sir. I apologize for the intrusion, but I have some news about Wells."

Johnson nodded and reached for the ashtray. "You can brief me in the morning, Sergeant. I'll need a full battle report and exactly the number of prisoners we have as well."

"Will do, sir," replied Warden.

After a moment, Johnson glanced up. "That's all, Sergeant."

"Yes, sir, General. I just want you to know we got him, sir," said Sergeant Warden, smiling. "We captured him alive, sir."

Johnson cocked his head sideways, leaning back in his chair to stare at the sergeant. He tapped his fingers on the armrests.

Sergeant Warden narrowed his eyes and tilted his head at the general's lack of reaction to the news.

After an awkward silence, Johnson leaned forward, putting his elbow on the desk and resting his chin in his hand. He then released his chin and rubbed his forehead. "Caught who, Sergeant?"

The sergeant tilted his head to the other side. "Well…the Mexican, sir. The man who killed Lieutenant Wells."

Johnson shook his head. "I was afraid you were going to say that." He sat back in his chair and heaved a sigh, staring at Warden. Waving his hand, the general motioned him to come closer. "Come have a seat, Sergeant, and tell me who you have and where you caught him."

Warden crossed the room and found his seat. "Sir, we were heading toward Santa Rosa when we came across a lone Mexican on an exhausted horse that was well supplied with food and water. The man saw us coming and went into the trees to hide. We sent several men after him and then had Jenkins identify him."

Johnson rubbed his face. "Did Jenkins identify him as the killer?"

Sergeant Warden nodded. "He said it looked a lot like the man he'd seen in Wells's tent. The Mexican was really acting strangely, sir."

Johnson nodded and placed his cigar on the ashtray. "Well, sergeant, we already caught the man who was believed to have killed Wells, and he was killed trying to escape."

Sergeant Warden leaned back in his chair and stared at the floor, scratching his beard. He looked back up at Johnson. "Well, sir…I don't know what to say sir."

Johnson nodded and stared at his desk, deep in thought.

"Yeah. Me either." After a few moments, the general asked, "Where is the man you captured?"

"Outside, sir, still shackled in a supply wagon and under guard."

Johnson stood and picked up his cigar. "Take me to him, Sergeant. Let's get to the bottom of this."

Warden stood from his chair and saluted. "Yes, sir."

Sergeant Warden led the way through wagons and troops, some still arriving. Many soldiers paused in unloading their wagons to salute their general as he walked through their ranks. The clouds above signaled an impending storm, and the men hurried to pitch their tents.

Warden walked to a supply wagon with a horse tied to the rear, where two soldiers stood guard. Johnson stopped in front of the soldiers as they saluted him. Johnson saluted back and peered inside the wagon.

The prisoner's face was cut and swollen, and blood stained his shirt. The shackled man sat on a wooden box, looking back at the general.

"You speak English?" asked Johnson.

The Mexican shook his head.

Johnson then asked the man in Spanish, "What's your name?"

"Juan Moraga," replied the prisoner.

"Do you know why you are being held?"

Juan raised his shoulders and slowly shook his head.

"We had a man attacked by a Mexican shortly before they came across you, and it's my understanding you ran and hid in the trees to avoid detection," said the general.

Juan shook his head again. "I wasn't running. I just figured I would get out of the way."

Johnson looked at the man for a few moments in silence before he gave a slight nod. "Ok, sir, I need you to tell me exactly where you been, where you were coming from, and where you were heading, the days before you encountered my brigade."

Juan shuffled toward the back of the wagon, closer to the general. He raised his hands, and the claps around his wrists pulled tight to a chain attached to his ankles. "It was a lot that happened the days before," explained Juan.

The general looked up as a few raindrops hit his brim. Then he turned his head quickly back at Juan. "Tell me quickly and don't lie to me. Your freedom depends on it."

Juan bit down on his lip, then looked at the general. Leaning forward, he began telling his story. "I was riding with a few men I met up with in Lordsburg. One of the men I encountered a few times asked if I wanted to ride along to Taos to look for bounty work." Juan rubbed his eyes and continued. "On the way, we came across a small group of Indians on the Santa Fe Trail."

Johnsons ears perked up, and his eyebrows drew close.

Juan continued. "A couple men I was riding with wanted to kill them and take their horses and scalps, but I told them let's keep moving. One man pulled me from my horse and pistol-whipped me until I was unconscious." Juan pointed to the marks on his face and head best he could before the chain drew tight.

Johnson began connecting the dots between this man's story and the dead Indians Stevens and Maydew had come across while bringing Domingo to Santa Fe. Johnson nodded. "Go on," he said, glancing at the sky as the rain picked up.

"I woke up to the sound of gunshots. My wrists and feet were tied, and a rag was crammed in my mouth. I broke free, then quickly got out of there." Juan shrugged his shoulders. "My horse was gone, so I began running as fast as I could, just in case they came back for me," he added. "Met a man along the road who gave me a ride to Magdalena, and from there, I journeyed on foot toward Silver City."

Johnson nodded, then looked at the horse tied at the rear of the wagon, and pointed. "If you didn't have a horse…then whose horse is this?"

Juan looked at the animal and grinned. "Strangest thing, I found this horse tied to a tree while resting in the shade."

Johnson bit down on his lip and cocked his head. "What do you mean *found*?"

Juan glanced at Lucky, then fixed his eyes on Johnson. "Just exactly that," replied Juan. "It was tied to a tree and appeared to be there for a few days, maybe more. It was a lucky break for me and the horse. The saddle had several canteens of water and some food, which pretty much saved my life."

Johnson nodded and rubbed his beard, thinking about what the Mexican had told him. "These men that attacked you along the Santa Fe Trail, what were their names?"

Juan shifted his weight for a more comfortable position. "Red, Eddie, and this mean bastard Quinn."

Johnson nodded to the prisoner and turned toward Sergeant Warden standing nearby. "Ok, Sergeant, tell Jenkins to come to my office in the morning. I want him to get a look at the Mexican who tried to escape and see if he is the man who attacked Wells."

The sergeant saluted the general. "Yes, sir."

Johnson walked back the way they came.

In the distance, he heard the prisoner shout. "Am I free to go?"

The sergeant looked at the prisoner and shook his head, then at the soldiers standing guard. He said, "I want two soldiers guarding this man at all times. Understand?"

The soldiers turned toward Warden. "Yes, sir," they replied, saluting the sergeant.

The rain poured down, and the sergeant rushed to the nearest tent the soldiers had just pitched.

CHAPTER 8
AN UNMARKED GRAVE

THE NEXT MORNING AT THE jailhouse, Ricks sat at his desk, drinking coffee. He read the news about the brazen escape of Red Sleeves and Domingo. All the blood in the jail had been cleaned up, and things were slowly returning to normal.

The sheriff shook his head several times, clearly irritated. The story seemed to glorify the ruthless Apache and his courageous return for his horse the day after.

"Dumb assholes," Ricks muttered to himself.

He closed the paper and tossed it on his desk. Ricks looked forward to Mitchell's arrival, which would finally put an end to Red Sleeves once and for all. The sheriff had already posted wanted signs with a twenty-five-hundred-dollar reward for Red Sleeves, dead or alive. Unfortunately, there were not many in Santa Fe interested going after the dangerous Apache.

Ricks expected Mitchell to bring several of his own men who didn't know any better. He picked up his cup of coffee and leaned back in his chair. He had just touched his cup of coffee to his lips when the front door opened.

The sheriff stared at the door as light rushed into the room. General Johnson entered, and a soldier accompanied him.

Ricks smiled. "Howdy, General, this is a nice surprise! I was planning on heading over later to see you." He took a quick drink before placing the coffee cup back on his desk.

"Hello, Sheriff," said Johnson. The general walked to his desk, the soldier close on his heels.

Ricks motioned to the chairs on the opposite side of the desk. "Have a seat, General."

Johnson looked toward the chairs. "Thanks Sheriff, but we don't have a lot of time."

Ricks leaned back. "Ok, General, what can I do for ya?"

Johnson removed his hat and wiped his brow before pointing his thumb at the soldier. "This is Private Jenkins. He witnessed the attack on Lieutenant Wells."

Ricks nodded to Jenkins.

"Where is Domingo's body?" asked Johnson.

Ricks froze for a moment, then replied, "We buried him. Just like you asked General."

"I need you to take us to him and bring a couple shovels."

Ricks scratched his beard. "What's going on, General?"

Johnson put his hat on his head. "Well, it seems we might have had the wrong Mexican, and I need Jenkins to identify his body to make sure we got it right."

Ricks shifted in his chair before grabbing his hat. Standing up, he looked at Johnson, his brow creased. "Well, General, I had a couple men bury him. So we need to go find one of them to takes us to 'im."

Johnson first shook his head. Then he nodded with a

slight eye roll. "Ok, Sheriff, let's get going, and we can discuss what you needed to see me about on the way."

The three men moved as one toward the door.

Ricks and Johnson waited as Pete surveyed the ground, looking in several directions. He walked about ten feet before turning to walk back, kicking at the ground. He shook his head. "I think he's more over yonder way," the man explained, pointing in the distance.

He led his horse away from the three men on horseback, watching him wander about. The group followed along until Pete stopped.

"Oh yeah, right through here somewhere," he explained, pointing toward the nearby ground.

Johnson turned toward Jenkins, who sat astride his own horse next to the general. "Hop down and help him look."

"Yes, sir," replied Jenkins. He climbed down from his mount and searched.

General Johnson examined the hills and the road in the distance, looking for any people riding by, such as the Apache, Red Sleeves.

Pete searched the ground for disturbed dirt. "Wow, that rain really came down last night…covered up our tracks pretty good."

Johnson crossed his hands over the saddle horn and clenched his jaw. As more time passed, Sheriff Ricks squirmed in his saddle and continued shifting his eyes to the general. Johnson noticed the sheriff's glares but stoically kept his eyes ahead. After a few more minutes with no luck finding the grave, Johnson's lips tightened. "Sheriff?" Johnson said, his voice clipped.

Ricks moved his mount closer to the general and adjusted his hat. "Yes, General?"

"Do you remember me telling you to mark the grave after you buried the Mexican?"

Ricks removed his hat and scratched his head. "Um… yeah, I sure do, General."

Pete was now shaking his head and looking across the ground, listening to their conversation. "You never told us to mark it, Sheriff," said Pete.

Ricks eyes bulged, and his face turned red as he glared at Pete. "You goddamn lie!"

Pete stalked back to his horse and climbed up. "He's buried through here somewhere. You find him. I'm done with this!"

"I told those fools to mark it. I swear, General. I did!" the sheriff said to Johnson.

The general's expression was blank as he regarded Ricks. Moments later, he turned his head to Jenkins, who had continued looking for any signs of Domingo's grave. "C'mon, Jenkins, lets head back."

"Yes, sir." Jenkins climbed atop his horse.

Johnson turned his mount, bringing it to a stop next to Ricks and leaning toward him. "As far as the Apache goes, he's your problem."

Ricks stared at the general momentarily, then clenched his jaw as his eyes found Pete. Johnson spurred his horse, and Jenkins followed alongside him, trotting back to Fort Marcy. Johnson heard Pete and Ricks arguing behind him. He spurred his horse again and quickly distanced himself from the two fools.

As Johnson and Jenkins rode silently toward the fort, the general used the time to think about things. Although it would have been nice to have Jenkins identify Domingo as the killer, Johnson was confident the story Juan had told him was true, and Domingo was indeed the man who had killed Wells.

Johnson shook his head as he thought of Sheriff Ricks's incompetence. *What a bungler*, he thought.

Once they reached the camp, Johnson steered his horse toward the wagon housing the prisoner. Johnson stopped his mount and gazed at the soldiers before glancing at the prisoner, who lay on his side.

The soldiers saluted their general.

"Good morning, sir," said one of the soldiers.

Johnson nodded and pointed to the prisoner. "Undo his shackles."

Juan lifted his head when he heard the men talking close by.

Johnson looked at Juan, and the prisoner regarded him with eyebrows lifted. "You are free to go," explained the general.

A smile formed across Juan's face. "Gracias."

The soldiers reached for the keys, unhooking the shackles from Juan's feet and hands. Juan rubbed his wrists after the shackles were removed and climbed from the wagon. He then looked up at Johnson and nodded, then turned toward Lucky.

"Escort him out of camp," said Johnson to Jenkins.

"Yes, sir."

Just as Johnson turned his horse, Juan stopped him. "Excuse me." Juan pointed to the sling on his horse. "My rifle?"

Johnson looked from Juan to Jenkins. "Do we have his rifle?"

Jenkins shook his head. "I am not sure, General."

Johnson turned to the soldiers who had been keeping guard. "What about you?"

"I believe Sergeant Warden has it, sir," one soldier answered.

Johnson turned back to Jenkins. "Ok, ride to the sergeant's tent and get his rifle."

Jenkins nodded to the general. "Yes, sir."

Johnson regarded Juan once more, then addressed Jenkins. "Give it to him once he's out of our camp and make sure it's unloaded."

Johnson spurred his horse and rode quickly toward the entrance of the fort.

CHAPTER 9

THE TAOS THREE

William and Cliff Taylor rode into Taos after a nearly sleepless night. Heavy rain had fallen on them while they camped. They navigated through town, riding past several carriages and pedestrians along the street. Mud from the horse's hooves flung onto the kickboard as the wagon slid side to side.

With the sheriff's horse still tied to the rear of the wagon, they parked along the street in front of the jailhouse and climbed down. After tying the horses to the hitching post, they walked up the steps and went inside.

A man sat at a table and loaded his pistol as they entered. "How can I help you, fellers?" the man asked.

William removed his hat. "Are you Ben Mitchell?"

The man sat his pistol on the table and glanced at the two men, raising an eyebrow. "Sure am, although I don't recognize you, boys."

"My name is William." He pointed his thumb toward the

man beside him. "This is my brother, Cliff. We rode here from Santa Fe. Sheriff Ricks sent us to find you."

Mitchell leaned back in his chair and crossed his arms. "Well, you found me."

William neared the table, and Cliff followed closely behind him. Cliff stared at the bottle of whiskey on the table.

"Help yourself," Mitchell offered, nodding toward the far wall. "There's glasses over there on the counter."

"Thank you kindly," said Cliff, walking toward the counter.

William remained in front of the table opposite Mitchell, and he glanced at Cliff. "Grab me a glass too." He turned his eyes to Mitchell, who was just raising his glass up for a drink. "Sheriff Ricks sent us here to ask for your help dealing with some Indians around Santa Fe."

Mitchell opened the chamber put a lead round into his Colt Walker revolver.

The young man continued. "We had some people attacked the other morning. Two were killed, and one is in really bad shape."

"We believe it's the same Apache who escaped the jailhouse the day before," added Cliff, stepping toward the table.

Mitchell's brows drew close as he spun the cylinder, setting the pistol back on the table in front of him. "What Apache?"

William opened his mouth to answer, but Cliff returned just then with the glasses and found a seat at the table. He reached for the bottle and filled the glasses. William pulled out a chair and sat down as well.

After pouring the whiskey, Cliff looked at Mitchell. "Red Sleeves, sir, him and this Mexican feller escaped the day before."

Mitchell rubbed the back of his neck. "The Mexican escaped?"

William took a drink from his glass before nodding. "Well, the Apache did. He killed a few people in the process, and then he came back the very next day and killed two more!"

Mitchell looked back and forth a few times at the brothers and waited for one of them to continue, but they were busy enjoying the whiskey. He then focused on William, speaking slowly. "Yes, I get it, but what about the Mexican? Where is he?"

William raised his glass of whiskey. "He's dead. They got him, but Red Sleeves got away."

"I'm sure you will be reading it in the paper soon enough," said Cliff, raising his glass.

Mitchell lowered his head. Then he rubbed his hand across his face.

Cliff looked at William, shrugging his shoulder at Mitchell's reaction.

Mitchell raised his head. "Red Sleeves could be a hundred miles away by now, boys," said Mitchell, spinning his empty whiskey glass on the table with his fingers.

William nodded. "Yeah, I suppose, but since he attacked more people after escaping, Sheriff Ricks would rather be sure."

Mitchell tilted his head, then picked up the bottle, and filled his shot glass again. "General Johnson and his men still there?"

Cliff nodded. "Yes, I believe so."

Mitchell took a quick drink before setting his glass on the table. "What about you, boys? You gonna ride out after Red Sleeves?"

Cliff and William both shook their heads.

"We'd rather not, sir," William said.

Mitchell smiled and nodded. "All right, I will get some men together and head over there as soon as I can."

Cliff and William both grinned.

"We appreciate it, sir, and so does the sheriff," said a smiling William.

"What kind of reward Ricks have on Red Sleeves?" asked Mitchell.

William shrugged his shoulders. "He mentioned twenty-five hundred."

"I am pretty sure Silver City Mining Company has a reward for him too," added Cliff.

Mitchell stood from his chair and slammed the last bit of whiskey in his glass. "Sounds good. Where you staying tonight?"

The brothers looked at each other for a second, then back to Mitchell. "Well, sir, if it's the same to you, we're gonna head back," said William.

Mitchell nodded to them and grabbed his hat from the table, placing it on his head before starting for the door. "Ok, let Ricks know, once I get some men together, we'll head out. We should be there fairly soon."

Cliff and William slammed the rest of the whiskey in their glasses and followed Mitchell. Once outside, the men shook hands. Mitchell walked down the street as Cliff and William began untying their horses from the post.

"That was easy enough," said Cliff, pleased with the results.

"Sure was, now let's get home," replied William.

The two men climbed on their mounts and rode southwest, out of Taos.

Mitchell meandered down the street and said hello to a few people before walking into the saloon. He searched for Pete or Frank.

Not seeing them inside, he stepped toward the bar and nodded to the bartender. "Hey, Bob, you seen Frank or Pete?"

"Not today." Bob picked up a glass, wiped it with a rag, and placed it in front of Mitchell. He then poured a small glass of whiskey and sat the bottle next to the glass.

"Thanky," said Mitchell, lifting his glass before turning to the patrons inside.

Eight people sat at the tables, and Mitchell knew most of them. They nodded and raised their hands in greeting. Mitchell didn't recognize the three men sitting at the back of the room. He picked up his hat from the bar and walked toward them.

As he approached, the men turned toward Mitchell, and their conversation halted. Mitchell saw two Mexicans and a white guy, and one of the Mexicans had what appeared to be burn scars on his hands and face. Getting a better look at the men, Mitchell figured they were either outlaws or bounty hunters.

As Mitchell stood alongside their table, the three men stared at Mitchell silently.

"Good afternoon, gentlemen," said Mitchell.

"Good afternoon," the white man replied.

The other two men nodded.

"I know just about everyone around here, but can't say I met you fellers before," said Mitchell.

The man with the burns on his face looked down at his glass and replied, "Just passing through."

Mitchell nodded and pointed to the chair. "May I?"

"Sure," the man replied.

"My name is Mitchell, the town constable." He reached his hand toward the man with the burns.

"Pablo," replied the man, accepting Mitchell's hand. "That's Ramon, and that's Ed," he explained, tilting his head toward the men at the table.

Mitchell nodded to the men and found his seat. "You boys from around here?"

"No," Pablo replied, looking at Mitchell before lowering his eyes to his drink.

Mitchell curled his lip. "Well, then what brings you to Taos?"

Pablo shrugged his shoulders. "Get a drink, sell a couple horses."

Mitchell smirked. "So where you heading?"

"Not sure yet," Pablo replied.

Mitchell could tell these guys were not going to be much for conversation. He shook his head and gave a slight smile before tossing his hat on the table. "Well, let me just get to the point then. I am looking for a few men to help track down some Indian savages who just attacked civilians in Santa Fe."

Pablo, Ed, and Ramon looked at each other and then back to their drinks.

Mitchell took note of the men's ears perking up when he mentioned savages and Santa Fe. "You boys come across them?" he asked, looking around the table.

Pablo leaned back in his chair and raised his glass to his mouth. Placing it on the table, he said, "Yeah, we came across some savages along the Santa Fe Trail. It looked to us they were set up for an ambush."

"What happened?" asked Mitchell.

"We made it through ok." Pablo smiled and looked back at his comrades, who also began to grin.

"Ok, well, are you up for it?" asked Mitchell.

Pablo's smile broke, and with his expression blank, he asked, "What's it pay?"

"I hear twenty-five hundred, possibly more. I'll split it with you if you boys are interested?"

Pablo lowered his eyebrows and drew in his chin. "Split it, hell. There's three of us and one of you. Two thousand for us, and five for you," said Pablo, still staring at Mitchell.

Mitchell chuckled. "You didn't think I'd be going alone, did you?"

Pablo sat quietly with his eyes fixed on Mitchell, biting his lip.

"No, sir, I have two other men coming with us. We will need all the help we can get," Mitchell added.

Pablo looked at his comrades.

Ed nodded, and Ramon shrugged his shoulders.

"All right, lawman, you got a deal," said Pablo, raising his glass to Mitchell.

Mitchell raised his own glass, and they both took a drink. Setting his glass down, Mitchell grabbed his hat and stood. "All right then, see you boys in the morning at the jailhouse. Be there at sunrise." He waited for a reply before walking away.

Ramon looked at his comrades with a creased brow. "Goddamnit," he muttered before slamming his empty glass down.

Mitchell looked at Ramon, then back at Pablo. "We good?"

Pablo grinned. "Yeah, we're good."

Mitchell turned and headed toward the exit. Just as he reached the batwing doors, Pete and Frank came inside.

"Hey, Mitchell, whatcha up to?" said Pete, with raised brows and a smile.

"Hello, fellers," replied Mitchell, nodding to both men. He set his hat on his head and placed a hand on Pete's shoulder. "Why don't you boys follow me to the jailhouse and have a drink there? I have something I wanna talk to you about."

Frank and Pete glanced at each other and back toward Mitchell.

"All right," said Pete. "Let's go."

The three men exited the saloon and walked back toward the jailhouse. Mitchell told them what had happened, starting with the escape of the prisoners in Santa Fe and the death of the Mexican, Domingo.

CHAPTER 10

THE CRESCENT MOON

After leaving Fort Marcy, Juan and his horse, Lucky, rode along the dusty street into Santa Fe. The townsfolks seemed anxious as he passed through, many not responding to Juan's friendly gestures. Juan stopped at a general store and loaded up on food and water before heading back south toward Silver City.

After Bob, the store clerk, helped him gather the supplies he needed, Juan looked at the row of whiskey bottles behind the counter. "Have a bottle of Fox Smooth over there?" he asked, pointing toward the liquor.

Bob glanced over his shoulder, then looked at back at Juan. "Fox Smooth? What's that?"

Juan smiled. "Oh, never mind. Just give me a bottle of whatever whiskey you have."

After leaving the store with his supplies, Juan climbed atop Lucky. He put his hat on his head and a cigar in his mouth, then patted Lucky on the side of his neck. "C'mon boy," he said, giving a little kick to the horse's side.

Juan kept a slow pace with Lucky, who was still a little too weak for any hard riding. He figured it would take him several days to reach his destination, being careful not to overstress the recuperating horse. After thinking about it for a few moments, he decided he would stop and see his new friend, Devi, along the way.

He wanted to share a drink and a cigar with the man who had helped him just a few days before. He also wanted to give Devi a little money for his trouble, as he'd said he would. Half the day was already gone, but Juan planned to ride into the night for a few hours before setting up camp to make up for his late start.

Juan felt like he traveled the whole territory three times over in the last week, and he didn't look forward to the long trail ahead. However, he couldn't help but smile at his luck in finding the fully stocked horse and the new shiny rifle. Finally away from the dangerous outlaws he had been traveling with, the feeling of a new life was just ahead, somewhere in the wide-open plains in front of him.

He looked forward to reaching Socorro, and the thought of it brought a smile to his face. He gave another little kick to Lucky, speeding up just bit more. As the hours and the tumbleweeds rolled by and he passed a few wagons here and there, darkness fell across the plains. Juan kept riding, having a difficult time seeing the trail in front of him. He knew he would have to stop and make camp before long.

Little Feather peered through the trees. The land was covered in darkness, the only light coming from the crescent moon above. The tribe had reached their destination earlier that day, with hours spent putting together their wickiups in preparation for a long stay. Several hours before sunrise, he'd noticed a lone rider in the distance.

Positioned on a small cliff overhang, Little Feather had a good vantage point. The tribe slept on the green prairie, surrounded by several groups of pine trees. A small fire burned, shedding little light on the camp. Little Feather raised his rifle, keeping a keen eye on the ever-approaching rider. Seeing only one man, Little Feather didn't alert the others, confident in the advantage of surprise on his side.

Just out of reach, the rider abruptly stopped. Little Feather lowered the rifle and watched every movement the man made. He raised his rifle again, looking down the sight squarely fixed on the man's chest, and put his finger to the trigger.

Surprisingly, the man raised his hand in a friendly fashion. Little Feather lowered the rifle and stood. After staring at the rider for a few moments, a smile came across his face when he realized who the man was. He scrambled from the high platform, sliding down the rocky slope, and ran straight toward the man.

As Little Feather got close, he noticed the smile on the face of Red Sleeves. Little Feather stopped in front of his chief, then he grinned ear to ear and embraced him. The two men began laughing as the joy of seeing each other overtook them.

"Chief, we feared you were dead!" said Little Feather.

Red Sleeves smiled. "I almost was, Little Feather."

"Your teeth are gone," said Little Feather with a chuckle, reaching his fingers toward Red Sleeves's mouth.

The chief leaned away from Little Feather, still grinning. "I lost one tooth for every white man I killed."

Little Feather laughed and embraced Red Sleeves once more, beaming over the safe return of his chief. After a few moments of celebrating the arrival of Red Sleeves, Little Feather looked to the ground, and his smile slowly disappeared.

"What is it, Little Feather?" asked Red Sleeves.

"The others were killed along the Santa Fe Trail. We found them and buried them a few moons ago."

Red Sleeves nodded and didn't seem surprised by the news. "Do you know who killed them?"

"No," replied Little Feather, hanging his head.

"We will find out, Little Feather. But for now I am just happy to be home," said Red Sleeves, placing his hand on Little Feathers shoulder. Red Sleeves handed his reins to Little Feather. "Whom'tu is thirsty, and I am exhausted." The chief walked toward the wickiups lined a short distance away.

"Want me to wake the elders?" Little Feather asked.

Red Sleeves stopped and faced him. "No, I would like to spend time with my woman. I will see them in the morning."

Little Feather grinned then nodded to his chief as Red Sleeves disappeared into the darkened camp. He led Whom'tu and Black Knife's horse to a nearby creek. Then he scurried up the rocky formation, a rifle in his hand and a smile on his face.

Red Sleeves entered his wickiup and lifted the animal hide flap to peer inside. His two children slept on the left side of the wickiup. He looked on the other side to see a buffalo skin wrapped over his wife, White Bird, who was also asleep. He slipped inside, being careful not to wake his children, and sat next to White Bird.

He could barely make out her face in the dark, but he gazed at her and smiled for several moments before he undressed. He lifted a side of the buffalo skin, placing himself along his wife and feeling her warm body against his.

She opened her eyes and lifted her head to face him. Although first startled, the little light inside the room captured her glowing smile and her teeth in the darkness. Red Sleeves smiled back, and she pulled him tightly to her.

He kissed her, rubbing his hand up and down her thighs, occasionally making a quick stop between her legs to feel her warm entrance with his fingers. Moments later, White Bird ran her fingers over his hand as he rubbed her breast.

Feeling the injuries on his hands, she lifted her head. "You are injured. Let me get some water and yarrow plant," she said softly.

Red Sleeves drew himself closer to her and smiled. "In the morning," he whispered.

He continued touching her body. Shortly after, he found himself submerged in complete happiness, a surreal feeling that he had not felt in many weeks. As he lifted her leg and put himself inside her, the feeling of happiness turned into heaven.

CHAPTER II
NEWSPAPER AND COFFEE

THE MORNING FELT COOL BUT pleasant. Sheriff Ricks had just left Doc Roberts after checking on Joe, still recovering from his injuries. Doc had cleared Deputy Collins the day before, and he rested at home under his wife's care.

It relieved the sheriff to learn that his deputy wouldn't lose his leg after all. He walked along the street and stopped at his store, getting a hot cup of coffee and newspaper before he strolled into the jailhouse. Walking straight to his desk, he set the coffee and newspaper down. He removed his hat and wiped his brow with a bandana. After he tossed his hat and bandana on the desk, he reached for his spectacles and found his seat. He kicked off his boots, grabbed the paper and his coffee, then leaned back in his chair. Placing his feet on the desk, the sheriff lowered his spectacles over his eyes and adjusted his weight in the chair.

The room fell quiet as he read an article about recent American victories against the Mexican Republic. While reading, he sipped his coffee and relaxed. As the sheriff lifted the cup to his lips for another sip, the front door swung open and slammed against the wall. It struck a nearby coatrack that fell over with a bang.

Ricks jerked his head toward the door. Coffee spilled across his lap when he leaned forward, bringing the chair's front legs to the ground with a jerk. He pulled his feet from the desk and squirmed around for his pistol, keeping his eyes fixed on the front door.

The sheriff squinted as the sun's bright rays glared through the entrance. He pulled off his reading spectacles and tossed them to the table. A silhouette of a man with a tall hat came into view. Ricks held his hand over his eyes, still unable to make out who it was. The man took a step forward, and he noticed a black vest. Ricks face heated as the man gave a low-pitched rumbling laugh.

"Goddamnit, Mitchell! You about gave me a fucking heart attack!" shouted Ricks.

Mitchell continued to laugh as he stooped down to fix the overturned coatrack. "Damn, Sheriff, you sure are jumpy these days." He grinned and walked toward the desk.

Five more men entered behind him.

Ricks grabbed his bandana and cleaned the coffee from his lap and the table. He shook the newspaper off the side of his desk, and droplets of coffee fell to the floor.

"You asshole," the sheriff said, standing to retrieve a rag from the counter. "I just got that fuckin' coffee!" He returned to the table, shaking his head and glaring at Mitchell. "That's a good way to catch a bullet."

"Sorry, old friend. I was just foolin'," said Mitchell. He reached across the table to shake the sheriff's hand.

Ricks huffed and looked at the floor momentarily before he turned to Mitchell and accepted his hand. "Well, you're an asshole. But I am damn glad to see you," he said.

Mitchell nodded, finding a seat in front of the sheriff's desk. The five men stood behind him. He pulled a pipe from his pocket and lit it, watching Ricks clean the desk and gather himself.

After Ricks sat, Mitchell pulled the pipe from his mouth. "Heard you had some trouble with some of the natives?" he asked.

Ricks raised his cup to his mouth, emptying what little remained inside. "Yeah, you heard right." He shook his head. "The fucking Apache Red Sleeves and that dirty Mexican bastard went on a damn killing spree." Ricks's face heated as anger coursed through him.

Mitchell took his hat off and tossed it on the table. "What happened to the Mexican feller?"

"I shot him," replied Ricks. "Damn bastard killed one of Johnson's men and shot my deputy, then was attacking folks in town."

Mitchell gave a slight nod while keeping his gaze on Ricks. "Strange. He seemed like an all right fellow back in Taos."

Ricks glared back at Mitchell before reaching toward his boots. "Well, he wasn't!"

Mitchell mouth quirked in a small smile, and he tilted his head toward the men behind him. He motioned to each of them with his thumb. "That's Pete and Frank." He turned his head the other way toward the men on his right. "That's Ed, Pablo, and Ramon." Then he faced the sheriff.

Ricks looked at each man and nodded while putting on his boots. "Hello, gentlemen."

The men nodded to the sheriff.

Mitchell took another hit from the pipe, waiting for Ricks to reemerge from under the table as the sheriff still tried to wiggle a boot on.

Ricks finally sat back in his chair and looked at Mitchell. "The three asshole miners that brought Red Sleeves here were attacked the next day by the savage after he escaped."

Mitchell shook his head. "Was it revenge you think?"

Ricks nodded. "Yeah, maybe, or he wanted his damn horse." He shrugged his shoulders. "I told those ninnies to sell that fucking thing."

Mitchell removed the pipe from his mouth and raised an eyebrow. "Sounds like a risky thing to do for a horse?"

Ricks put his hat on. "Well, I don't know, but he killed two of them, and the other is just down the street with a bullet hole in the shoulder and broken leg."

Mitchell leaned back in his chair, raising his hands beside him. "Red Sleeves is most likely a long way from here by now. He would know a posse or soldiers would be coming for him."

Ricks shook his head. "Johnson ain't gonna do a damn thing!" The sheriff pointed toward the front door. "And the people out there ain't nothing but a bunch of lily-livered meaters."

Mitchell smiled at the sheriff and remained quiet.

Sherriff Ricks gazed back at Mitchell and lifted his hands, palm side up. "I don't have anybody willing to join you fellers."

"Well, I think we have enough to bring in Red Sleeves." Tapping his steamer in the ashtray, Mitchell dumped the ashes and packed it full of tobacco. He struck a match, taking several quick puffs as the smoke hovered about the desk. "So what's the reward for bringing in Red Sleeves?"

"Twenty-five hundred, and Silver City is offering twenty-five hundred as well," replied Ricks, standing abruptly from his chair.

Mitchell followed his lead and stood as well.

Ricks reached his hand across the desk. "I appreciate you, Mitchell, and best of luck out there."

Mitchell nodded and accepted his hand. "We'll circle the town to make sure he isn't hiding nearby, but I am pretty sure he headed south by now."

Ricks shrugged his shoulders. "Yeah, fine, whatever you think Mitchell." He reached down and grabbed his cup from the desk, walking toward the door. "I hate to cut it short, but I have to go get some coffee." He nodded to the five men behind Mitchell as he walked past. "Good day, fellers."

Ricks heard the men talking and following behind him as they left the jailhouse. He walked toward the general store, but Mitchell called to him.

"Ricks!"

The sheriff stopped and turned.

"After we circle the town, we are gonna need five hundred of that reward money if you plan on us chasing after Red Sleeves?"

Ricks sighed, then nodded. "Fine. Come back and see me in a day or two, and I'll have it." As Ricks began to turn away, he stopped himself midturn and faced Mitchell again. "And be sure to knock next time, goddamnit!" And then he turned and continued down the street.

CHAPTER 12
STORIES OF SOCORRO

After two days of traveling and a few miles from Socorro, the road had become dustier. Parched pine trees and sparse vegetation hung on for dear life, awaiting the next good rain.

Juan lifted his canteen, taking a couple large drinks before placing the canteen over the saddle horn. After a nice, cool morning and finding that his horse seemed to be fully recovered, his mood had turned more positive. He whistled the song "Roll On, Silver Moon," singing out loud the words of the few parts he knew.

As he entered the town, he quit his yodeling and kept his song to a low whistle. Many folks looked at him as he passed, most with a smile, and Juan tipped his hat to them. He followed the same road he had traveled just days ago with Devi and saw his new friend's familiar adobe home.

He rode to the side of the house, stopping out back by a tree, and climbed down. Juan tied Lucky off to the tree and then raised his hands above his head, stretching his back and yawning deeply. He rubbed Lucky's neck and looked for Devi, but he didn't see him outside. Spotting Devi's wagon and horses, he thought his friend must be in the house.

Juan walked toward the porch and went up the steps to knock. He heard footsteps inside and stepped back, waiting for the door to open. Moments later, the door cracked, and Devi peaked out before fully opening the door.

"What happened? You get lost?" asked Devi.

Juan chuckled and then pulled off his hat. "No, sir, I told you I would be back."

Devi grinned and stepped outside. Juan noticed his friend's dirty clothes as the other man walked toward a chair on the porch.

Devi pointed at another nearby chair. "Grab a seat, son."

Juan nodded and sat. Pulling a cigar from his pocket, he handed it to Devi. The old man leaned forward, accepting the cigar. Juan reached in his pocket again and grabbed one for himself. He struck a match and leaned toward Devi, who drew in several puffs under its flame.

Juan lit his cigar and shook his hand, allowing the flame to disappear. Juan looked over Devi again, taking note of the dirt-covered trousers and shirt. "What you been up to, Devi?"

The old man leaned back in his chair and shook his head. "Wife died last night. I buried her out yonder," he explained, pointing in the distance to an open field behind the barn.

Juan's brows furrowed, and he dropped his shoulders. He looked at the floor, then back at Devi. "Sorry, friend. I don't know what to say."

Devi looked away, closing his eyes momentarily. "No apology necessary. She's been sick for some time."

Juan nodded. "I'll be right back."

He stood from the chair and went to his saddlebag. Grabbing out a bottle of whiskey and a few coins from his money pouch, he walked back to the porch. He handed Devi the bottle, and the older man quickly accepted, pulling the cork top and taking a couple large swigs. Devi handed the bottle back to Juan, who sat down.

Lifting the bottle to his mouth, Juan took a drink and replaced the cork. He set the bottle on a table nearby. "I want to thank you again for the ride, food and water the other day. If it wasn't for you, I'd been a goner." Juan placed the coins on the table and looked at Devi. "For your trouble, friend."

Devi nodded. "Thank you kindly," he said, placing a finger to the coins and examining them.

Juan reached for the bottle again and took another drink, then passed it over.

Devi took a swig and held it in his hand, resting the bottle on his leg. "You see anymore of Quinn?" he asked.

Juan shook his head. "No. Luckily, I haven't." He chuckled and leaned back in his chair. "Man, I had some couple of days, let me tell ya. After you left me in Magdalena, it got really strange."

Devi drew his chin toward his neck. "Like how?" He leaned forward and placed the bottle on the table.

Juan shook his head. "I was about dead when I came up on that horse." He pointed toward Lucky. "Then these American soldiers arrested me, saying I killed one of their men." Juan shrugged his shoulders. "Then they took me clean up to Santa Fe, only to release me the next morning." Juan rubbed his neck. "Let me tell you: I am exhausted of riding."

Devi's lips parted slightly. "Well, you may be tired, but

you're really lucky to be alive, especially after riding with that murderer Quinn."

Juan nodded and looked at Devi for a few moments, drawing a large drag of the cigar. After releasing the smoke from his mouth, he reached for the bottle. "How do you know Quinn?" he asked, sensing the old man knew more than he did of the outlaw.

Devi pulled his cigar from his mouth. "Oh hell, I knew that li'l bastard now for many years. I was friends with his father, Ricardo."

Juan took a drink from the bottle, then leaned back in his chair with raised eyebrows.

"Well, not his real father. His adopted father," added Devi.

Juan stared at Devi and scratched his chin. "Where was this at?" he asked.

Devi put the cigar in his mouth and pulled off a shoe, lifting it upside down and allowing small stones to fall from it. "Right here in Socorro. Ricardo lived just right up the street." Devi put his shoe back on. "Quinn started running around with this other troublemaker named Ramon, and it went to hell from there."

Juan looked toward the barn before looking back at the man. "Yeah, now, Ramon I do know a little. Met him a few times before, and he convinced me to ride with them." Juan shook his head. "Wasn't too long before I realized that was a mistake," he added.

"You know the story of Quinn as a boy?" asked Devi.

"Sure don't," replied Juan.

Devi pointed to the bottle still resting on Juan's lap, and Juan handed it over.

The old man took a swig and then set it back on the table.

"Quinn's family had a little home near the Gila just southeast of Lordsburg, and they were attacked by Apache Indians," said Devi, taking a quick hit from his cigar. "Killed everyone but him and his grandma, then burnt the house down. That's where he got those burns all over him."

Juan sat back in his chair with a creased brow.

"Ricardo and a friend of his was riding back from Tucson and saw smoke billowing in the sky," Devi added.

After a few moments passed in silence, Juan asked, "What happened then?"

Devi tilted his head to the side. "Well, they followed the source of the fire and found Quinn and his grandma severely burned, lying on the ground." The older man rubbed his beard. "Then they buried his family not far from the house and brought the boy and old woman back here to Socorro." He paused, taking another hit of the cigar. "The old woman died before they arrived, So Ricardo raised Quinn as one of his own."

Juan shook his head. "Wow, that's some story, Devi." As he took a hit of his cigar, he digested what Devi told him.

"It wasn't too long before Ricardo realized his mistake. Damn boy became wild and started robbing about everyone in town." Devi shook his head. "Ricardo tried to set the boy right, but Quinn and that other scoundrel Ramon nearly beat Ricardo to death."

"Yeah, I could see that happening," Juan said.

Devi shrugged. "Eventually, they rode off together, not to be seen for many years, but stories still come in from time to time."

Juan's brow creased. "What stories?"

Devi reached for the bottle. "Well, the Indians seem

to think Quinn is some evil spirit or something." He took a quick drink of whiskey and smacked his lips. "Just high-tale-type stuff. They gave him different names, like 'the Boy,' 'the Raven.' I suppose they don't know the whole story," he added.

Juan nodded. "I remember Red calling him Raven a couple times, but I didn't bother asking why. I just figured it was on account of his raven-feather necklace."

Devi nodded. "Well, it was probably best you didn't. Rumor has it he'll kill you if you do."

Juan shook his head, gazing at the barn before his eyes trailed up to the sky. "Yeah. I tell you this world ain't nothin but a bunch of niggards and bounders." He leaned way back in his chair and stretched his arms and back, followed by a yawn.

Devi nodded. "I think about everyone at some point could be considered as such, but he is certainly a cut above the rest."

Both men grinned and chuckled.

Devi took one more swig from the bottle and placed it on the table, then stood from his chair. "I am going to get cleaned up. I have a stew cooking inside."

Juan nodded at him and reached for the bottle. "Sounds good."

Devi pointed to the barn. "Go ahead and get your horse squared away and bring your gear inside," said Devi. "You're more than welcome to stay a few days if you like."

Juan placed a hand on the man's shoulder. "That's mighty kind of you. I appreciate that."

Devi nodded and opened the door to go inside. He stopped and looked back at Juan. "Grab some wood when you get a chance. We'll sit around the fireplace later and continue our stories," said Devi.

"Will do," replied Juan.

Devi stopped for a second like he had something else to say. Then he went inside and closed the door behind him.

Juan stood from his chair, placing his cigar in his mouth and the bottle on the table. He walked to Lucky and led the horse to the barn.

Later that night, the two men sat around the fireplace and shared stories. Juan asked Devi if he had any children or family nearby. Devi was reluctant to share much information about that. He only stared into the fire, but he eventually stated that he had children in deep Mexico, adding that he hadn't seen any of them in a long time.

A few days turned into many weeks as the two men became friends, and they much enjoyed each other's company. Juan helped Devi around the home with many needed repairs, and Devi introduced Juan to several people in town.

Overall, the people were friendly, although they were not happy about being under American control. Most still considered themselves to be part of the Mexican Republic and were loyal to it.

When the time came for Juan to leave for Silver City, he loaded his horse with plenty of food and water. The men shook hands, and Juan assured Devi they would see each other someday soon.

CHAPTER 13

MAJOR OF MORA

Just before noon on a hot sunny day, Major Bolan and his one hundred cavalry—consisting of four wagons and six cannons—came to a halt less than half a mile from Mora.

The major pulled out his field glasses, surveying the town and its surrounding terrain for several moments. He pointed to his left and instructed the soldiers to place the cannons on a ridge a hundred yards away.

The men and wagons moved, following their commander's orders.

The major continued to look through his field glasses at the large white church in the center of town. Many horses and men moved about, seeming to prepare for a fight.

A single rider headed toward him, holding a white piece of cloth in his hand. He waved it above his head.

"Captain Taylor," said Bolan, removing the field glasses from his eyes.

"Yes, sir," replied the soldier.

"Follow me and let's see what this is about," said Bolan.

Taylor saluted his commander, and they rode down the hill about fifty yards.

The approaching rider stopped twenty feet from the major and captain.

"What's your name, sir?" asked Bolan in Spanish.

"Miguel Garcia," replied the man.

Bolan placed his hands on the saddle horn and stared at the man.

Taylor pulled his pistol from the holster and rested it across his lap.

"How many men are down there?" asked Bolan. "And what are their intentions?"

The Mexican man turned and pointed toward town. "Maybe two hundred señor." He looked back at the major. "They are ready to fight, but they are also willing to talk."

The major looked from Taylor to Miguel. "Well, that's what we're doing here, amigo. So talk," he said sternly.

The Mexican shrugged. "They are willing to lay down their arms if they can go free," said Miguel.

The major shook his head. "Many will go free, but none that were involved in attacking Taos," replied Bolan.

Miguel looked around and scratched his beard. "Well, that's a good chunk of them down there, along with a lot of innocent people who will die if a fight does come."

The major nodded. "Tell the rebels to lay down their arms around that tree up yonder, then walk to that fence, and get down on their knees with their hands behind their heads." Bolan pointed to a pine tree and a fence line in the distance.

Miguel looked where the major pointed. "Then they go free," he said.

Bolan grinned. "No. Then they become prisoners and taken to Santa Fe." The major lifted his hat and wiped his brow. "It's better than dying."

The man looked at the major and Taylor briefly, then shook his head. "I don't think—"

"Tell them they have a half hour to comply, or we open fire." the major said, cutting him off. He turned his horse, and Taylor followed him back toward their brigade.

Once they reached their original position on the ridge, the major looked at his watch and checked the time before placing it back in his pocket. He reached for his field glasses, watching as a group of men crowded around Miguel, who filled them in on the major's demands.

"Captain Taylor," Bolan said, "Have the artillery take aim right at the church in the center of town and wait for my signal."

Taylor saluted his commander and rode quickly toward the line of cannons on the ridge.

Major Bolan looked through his field glasses again, watching as several women and children moved toward the fence. Groups of men walked toward the tree, their rifles in hand, placing them on the ground before walking toward the fence to join the women and children.

One of the men was Miguel, and for a moment, the major thought no battle would come. However, no more than fifty men stood in the group along the fence, and it appeared that not many more were coming. Far short of the two hundred Miguel had said were in town, the major surmised.

The major looked to his left as Taylor rode toward him.

Glancing at his watch, the major saw that the people in town still had fifteen more minutes left to surrender.

When Taylor neared, he saluted and brought his horse to a stop a few feet away. "All set, sir."

Bolan looked through his glasses at the town, and it appeared no others were surrendering. The major turned toward Taylor. "All right, Captain, looks like that's about all. They only have about thirty horses down there, so they won't be able to escape—at least not many of them."

Taylor saluted the major and rode away to ready the cavalry.

The major looked at his pocket watch again and shook his head. "Oh, hell with it," he said, placing his watch back in his pocket. He raised his hand above his head, looking at his artillery, and brought it down quickly.

Boom! The cannons fired almost simultaneously.

The ground rumbled, and smoke filled the sky. The sight of the large cannonballs was quickly lost in the sky, and silence fell across the land. Moments later, a large explosion—followed by five more—shook the town, throwing horses, men, dirt, and pieces of buildings in all directions.

A large portion of the church collapsed, and fire from a barn nearby rose into the sky. The men, women, and children along the fence fell flat to the ground, covering their ears and heads as fire and smoke rose high above the town.

Major Bolan signaled for his artillery to reload. Moments later, he raised his hand and brought it down quickly. "Fire!" he shouted.

Boom! Another round of cannon fire shot from the ridge and barreled toward town.

The second round of cannon fire all but collapsed the

church. Mexican rebels rushed out from under it, several going a few feet before collapsing to the ground. Fire engulfed the barn, igniting several roofs.

"Reload," shouted the major.

His men scrambled to meet his demand.

Captain Taylor rode up beside the major. "The cavalry is ready, sir," he said, looking at the center of town engulfed in flames.

The major looked at the captain. "Very well." He turned to his artillery and signaled them again. "Fire!"

Bolan and Taylor watched together as cannonballs ripped through the town and sent the remaining men fleeing in all directions.

The major pulled the field glasses from his eyes and turned toward the captain. "Send in the cavalry, Taylor. Take anyone who surrenders alive and kill the rest."

Taylor saluted the major and rode away. Moments later, a stream of close to eighty cavalry rose on the ridge and rode toward Mora. The major watched through his binoculars as fifteen rebels on horseback fled from the far side of town, only to quickly be cut down by Taylor and the cavalry. Within fifteen minutes, the remaining rebel forces were either dead or had surrendered.

Major Bolan and ten of his cavalry rode toward the town. By the time they reached Mora, his soldiers had those who surrendered rounded up as the American cavalry circled them. Forty rebels remained in the circle, and soldiers bound the prisoners' hands. The major rode to the fence line and looked down at the frightened group. He then looked at the town as fire spread across it.

Glancing at the women and children, he caught a glimpse of Miguel staring at him.

The man's eyes protruded, and his brow creased. Miguel rose to his feet, wielding a pistol, and pointed it at Bolan. He pulled the trigger. Within a second, several cracks of gunfire behind the major struck the Mexican and sent him to the ground.

The woman drew their children close as screams filled the air.

Hearing the commotion, Taylor jumped on his horse and rode toward his commander.

Major Bolan turned his head toward the captain. Slowly leaning to one side, he fell from his horse, holding his stomach.

Within moments, Taylor jumped from his horse and slid across the ground to his commander's side. He lifted his head from the dirt and pulled him onto his lap.

Blood spewed from Bolan's mouth as he coughed, shooting blood in Taylor's face. Taylor rubbed the major's head, then turned to yell for a medic as the major gripped Taylor's wrist. As more soldiers arrived alongside them, the major's eyes rolled back in his head, his grip released, and his lifeless hand fell to the ground.

CHAPTER 14

ADVERSARIES IN AMBUSH

MITCHELL AND HIS MEN RODE south along the Camino Real near the town of Magdalena. They had circled Santa Fe two months earlier, and after zigzagging over many miles of rough terrain, they had seen no sign of Red Sleeves or any other Apache.

Although fatigued, they still had several hours of daylight left, and they would use every minute of it. Soon, they would leave the Camino Real, heading southeast toward the Apache stronghold along the Gila River. Knowing they could be easily outnumbered, they would have to be extremely cautious. Heavily armed with plenty of ammunition, the men were ready for a long fight if it came to that.

Mitchell hoped to catch the Apache chief by surprise. He knew the Chiricahua Apache warriors were in low numbers after several years of fighting against the Mexicans. He also knew Red Sleeves was injured and would most likely be with the tribe while the men were out hunting. If he could locate the tribe and attack in the late morning, it would be their best chance of capturing or killing the Apache chief.

Growing up in the same town, Mitchell had known Frank and Pete for a good chunk of his life. Ed, Pablo, and Ramon, on the other hand, were strangers to him. He had been riding with the men for many weeks, but he didn't really care for them. Something about their demeanor made Mitchell have a hard time trusting the rough-looking men.

Pablo especially seemed difficult to get along with. Mitchell asked Pablo about his necklace lined with raven feathers, and he had received an angry glare. That was two days ago, and the two men hadn't shared a single word since.

Most nights after a long day of riding, the men often set up separate camps, making it obvious to Mitchell that they cared for him as much as he did of them. However, they had to set all differences aside while they traveled through such a dangerous territory. They all agreed that they would need to work together to catch Red Sleeves.

After leaving the trail, they headed into some small cliffs and an extensive valley, keeping a keen eye out for any tracks or Apache on the ridges ahead. They rode for a couple more hours without a sign of the Apache before taking a break at the bank of the Gila River.

After climbing down from their horses, Mitchell stood a good twenty feet from the river, studying over his map with Pete and Frank and planning their next move. Around thirty feet away, Pablo sat with Ed and Ramon along the riverbank.

Pablo suddenly rose to his feet, pulling Ramon and Ed by the shoulder, and the three men led the horses away from the river. They moved beside Mitchell and hunkered down.

"Apache coming this way." Pablo pointed away from them.

"How many?" asked Mitchell.

"Looked like four or five."

Mitchell closed his map and put it in his pocket. "Ok, men, let's move our horses back out of sight and wait for them to pass. If we see Red Sleeves, we ambush them, but let's try to get him alive."

Pablo squinted his eyes at Mitchell. "What?"

Mitchell glared at Pablo, and his brow creased. "What didn't you understand?" he asked, taking a step toward the man.

Pablo shook his head. "First of all, we don't leave our horses. Second of all, we ambush them regardless if it's Red Sleeves or not."

Mitchell took off his hat and wiped his brow, then stepped even closer to Pablo, and spoke through clenched teeth. "We wait and see if its Red Sleeves, and if not, we let them pass. Now, move your horse back and hide in that brush." Mitchell pointed opposite the river.

Pablo turned away and looked at Ramon. He walked to his horse and climbed up. "I think I'll stay on my horse. You fellers do what you want." Pablo turned his horse away from the men and the river, slowly riding away.

Ramon and Eddie climbed on their mounts and followed behind.

Mitchell put his hat back on and shook his head, then looked at Pete and Frank. "C'mon, move back, and let's take cover in the brush."

The men moved their horses well out of sight and walked closer to the river's edge to ready their pistols, concealed in the brush.

Mitchell glanced back to look for Ramon, Pablo, and Ed,

but he didn't see them anywhere. "Those fucking morons. They are gonna blow our cover," he whispered to Frank and Pete, who were just feet away.

A few minutes later, Mitchell heard the heavy sound of horse's hooves beating against the ground and the cracking of brush and sticks. Mitchell quickly lifted his head turning to the source of the sound, which started behind him, and glanced toward the direction of the Apache. The sound of brush was silenced by the cracking of guns and shouting.

Mitchell stood, and Pete and Frank rose as well. Running toward the river, Mitchell looked in the direction of the gunfire. Several horses without riders crossed the river, and a couple of them stood on the bank. Mitchell motioned for Pete and Frank as they rushed to their horses. The three men jumped into the saddles and rode hard toward the fight along the bank of the Gila.

As they reached the part of the river where the skirmish had ensued, Mitchell saw a wounded older Apache man. A dead Apache woman floated in the river. Another woman lay dead along the riverbank. He glanced around, finally seeing Ed and Ramon, riding down the riverbank toward him.

Mitchell's face heated, and his eyes widened until he felt them bulging as he rode toward them. "What the fuck!" he shouted. "Where the fuck is Pablo?" Mitchell turned his horse continuously, water splashing under the animal's legs as he looked for the man.

"He rode after one of them who got away," replied Ed.

Ramon stayed tight lipped, giving an expressionless stare.

"Goddamn dumb son of a bitch!" Mitchell shouted.

Pete climbed down from his horse and looked at the old Indian, sitting still and showing no sign of escaping. Blood trickled down his face from a cut on the forehead. Pete moved to the woman along the bank and rolled her over. She appeared to be knocked unconscious. Pete knelt beside her and felt for a pulse.

From his mount, Mitchell looked at the old Indian and pointed toward him. "Frank, tie his hands together." He then looked back at Ed and Ramon. "I told you dumb fucks not to attack until we knew it was Red Sleeves!" he shouted at them, clenching his teeth. "Now, you have killed a woman and let one of them get away."

Ed and Ramon only stared at Mitchell with jaws clenched and unblinking eyes.

Mitchell pulled his pistol and pointed it at Ramon. "Whatcha you gonna do, boy?" He moved his mount closer to Ramon, his pistol only feet from the man's head.

Pete and Frank drew their pistols, pointing them at Ed before the man could move.

A tight-lipped Ramon stared back at Mitchell for several moments. He then smirked and looked at Ed, tilting his head. Turning toward Mitchell, Ramon focused straight forward and drew a deep breath before he forcefully exhaled. He clicked his tongue twice and gave a slight kick, and the horse moved forward.

Ed steered his mount toward Ramon, and the two men meandered across the river, up the bank, and vanished into the brush heading south.

Mitchell put his pistol away, and Frank and Pete did the same.

"Dumb bastards," said Mitchell, shaking his head.

Climbing from his horse, he walked to the Apache woman, still motionless in the river. He dragged her onto the shore.

He put his hand to her neck and felt for a pulse, then lowered his ear to her mouth. Shaking his head, he rose to his feet.

"She dead?" asked Pete.

Mitchell glanced at the old man still sitting on the bank, then over at Pete. "Yup," he replied.

Frank finished tying the old man's hands, and Pete examined the unconscious woman. Pete found a cut to her head, probably caused by a blow from the butt of a rifle. Her wrist was broken, from the way her hand lay awkwardly beside her. He moved the woman's hair from her face and lightly tapped her cheek a few times.

The woman's eyes opened and wandered in different directions in an apparent daze.

"She's coming to," said Pete.

Mitchell stood over them and looked down at the woman.

Her eyes locked on Pete, and she became frantic, attempting to get to her feet and escape the men. Mitchell and Pete quickly subdued her, and Frank rushed over with some rope to tie her hands.

"Careful of her wrist, Frank. It looks broken," said Pete.

After the woman's hands were secured, Mitchell surveyed the area, keeping watch for Pablo or his comrades.

Mitchell walked to the old gray-haired Apache man and knelt beside him. "What's your name?" asked Mitchell in Spanish.

The old Indian glanced at Mitchell, then looked straight ahead. "Gray Sky."

Pete and Frank walked the Apache woman closer to the old man and sat her beside him. The old man spoke to her in Apache, and she glanced from him to Mitchell and back.

She said a few more words to Gray Sky, holding her wrist and grimacing in pain.

Mitchell took note of their brief conversation. "What did you say to her?" he asked.

Gray Sky lifted his tied hands and placed his right index finger to his cheek, sliding it slowly down his face. "The scarred man…who brings great suffering," said Gray Sky.

Mitchell rose to his feet and glanced down at the two Apaches, shaking his head. "Great suffering, huh? I'd say I saved your life, old timer." He stepped away and walked to Pete.

"What's the plan, boss?" Pete asked.

Frank joined his comrades as Mitchell scratched his cheek, surveying the area.

"Well, it's going to be dark soon, but if we head out now, we should make it to Silver City before nightfall." Mitchell regarded the Apache prisoners. "I don't think we should make camp anywhere through here. If one in fact got away, they'll send fifty warriors to this very spot."

"That sounds good to me," said Frank.

Pete nodded, then looked at the two Apache prisoners. "What about them?" he asked.

Mitchell glanced at the Apache sitting on the bank. "Bring them. They might be useful to draw out Red Sleeves." Mitchell looked around and muttered to himself, "Or use as a bargaining chip if that war party comes looking for us." Mitchell pointed to the two Apache horses standing nearby. "Put them on their horses. Tie one to mine and one to Frank's horse."

He walked to his mount and climbed up, pulling his steamer from his vest pocket. He packed it full of tobacco and placed it in his mouth while watching Frank and Pete carry out his orders. He lit the pipe, drawing several large drags as the smoke rose above him. He then looked at the dead Apache woman on the riverbank.

Pete noticed the direction of Mitchell's stare and asked, "What about her?"

Mitchell removed the pipe from his mouth. He drew in a deep breath and gave a heaving sigh. "Just leave her. Their warriors will be coming through here soon enough."

Pete nodded and led the old man's horse toward Mitchell, handing him the lead rope. Mitchell spun the strap around the saddle horn a few times, then watched Pete hand Frank the lead of the Apache woman's horse before climbing onto his own mount. Mitchell gave his horse a quick kick, and the three men and their Apache prisoners rode away from the river. They navigated through some thick brush and trees, emerging into a narrow valley below heading straight toward Silver City.

CHAPTER 15

A SHOT OF FOX SMOOTH

A RATHER COOL NIGHT GREETED JUAN as he rode south along the Camino Real. He whistled loudly and rocked his head from side to side, looking for a nice place to camp. He had left Devi's home early that morning and was fifteen miles from Silver City.

Devi had supplied him plenty of jerky, biscuits, and fresh canteens of water for the trip, and the smooth trail made for easy riding. All in all, it was a pleasant trip so far.

After locating a nice spot to set up camp, he brought Lucky to a stop. He climbed down, leading the horse to the Gila River just thirty feet away to let the animal get a good drink. "How's this look, ole boy?" he asked, rubbing the horse's neck.

After a few minutes, he led Lucky to a nearby pine tree and tied the horse to it. Unbuckling the wide leather straps, Juan set the saddle on the ground about twenty feet away.

He walked around the area, searching for brush and small branches to start a fire.

A mostly full moon rose above him, lighting the ground, as he made several trips until he had plenty of wood. He grabbed the tinderbox from the saddlebag and tucked dry grass into the box, striking the flint a couple times before it ignited. He placed the box into the gathering of sticks and limbs, then tossed more dry grass around the box. Within moments, the fire started to gain strength. He reached for the box and placed it back in his saddlebag.

He laid out his bedroll and grabbed a cigar from his saddlebag along with a bottle of whiskey and a chunk of jerky. Seated on his bedroll, he placed the cigar and bottle down beside him, taking a large bite of jerky. The fire continued to grow as warmth surrounded his face and hands.

Chewing, he tilted his head back and watched the stars. He caught Lucky's eyes as they reflected in the fire and stared back at him.

Juan smiled. "Some night, huh, boy?"

Lucky snorted twice, and Juan's grin widened.

"Yeah, I know. I'm tired too," Juan replied as though he understood the horse's noises.

Finishing his jerky, Juan pulled the cork top on the whiskey bottle. He took a drink and replaced the cork before reaching for his cigar. He placed one end into a close flame from the fire until it began to smolder. Lifting the cigar to his mouth, he drew several mouthfuls of smoke.

Taking in the cool relaxing night, he whistled. After about ten minutes and several drinks of whiskey, he placed what remained of the cigar by the bottle, and it quickly suffocated under its own ash. After removing his hat, he set it on the ground nearby and leaned back, lying on his back.

A star shot across the sky, and Juan's heart warmed. He thought about his family in La Barca, hundreds of miles south. He had a rather large family in that area, including a brother, sister, and many cousins, aunts, uncles, nieces, and nephews.

His father had died in his sleep when he was a boy. His mother believed God had wanted him home, but Juan thought his heavy drinking gave him a heart attack.

Juan had first come to El Paso from La Barca four years ago to work as a ranch hand. He had bounced around the Nuevo territory working as a rancher, miner, and even as a bartender at a saloon in Las Cruces for a short time.

That was where he'd first met Red, a regular of the saloon. Red had been a patron there for several months before introducing Juan to Eddie and Quinn. They sold Juan on the idea of stealing and robbing until they gathered enough money to head south. There, they would live easy for the rest of their days.

After several months went by, and all the money they got with each score ended up quickly spent in the saloons, whorehouses, and a few lost card games, Juan grew tired of riding with the men. Then, after witnessing Quinn's dangerous and unpredictable behavior, it became too much for him to take. Juan might have been pistol-whipped, but he couldn't be happier about finally being away from those bastards.

He couldn't help but think he'd wasted much of his life having nothing more than his clothes on his back and a saddle to rest his ass in, although sometimes, he hadn't even had that much. In his early thirties, it was time to live a different way and build a life for himself. He wanted a good life with a good woman to share it.

Juan closed his eyes, listening to the sounds of the night as critters scampered and the crickets chirped. As the minutes went by, the sounds quieted, and all he could hear was his own deep breathing. Moments later, he fell asleep.

A little before noon the next morning, Juan was less than a half mile from Silver City, surrounded by foothills, cliffs, and unique rock formations. Ancient ruins of the Mogollon Mountain people, who'd lived high in the cliffs along the Gila River many centuries ago, were visible high in the rocky cliffs. Before the Spaniards began mining the area and forced the Apache elsewhere, the natives used the ruins as a campsite for many decades.

Predominantly a mining and trading town, Silver City housed tough men living an even tougher life. Juan continued forward until the series of mining camps came into view. The budding town contained a general store, jailhouse, doctor's office, blacksmith, saloon, and several merchants lining the street and selling goods from their wagons.

Juan observed the townsfolk as he rode through. Mostly men, they carried the obvious signs of being miners. Some walked with limps, had missing hands, or dirt covered their clothes and faces. Many neither tipped their hats nor nodded. Silver City mainly comprised of tough men who experienced either a constant pain in their hands or backs, with loneliness their constant companion.

Mining was not something Juan missed, along with the twelve-hour workdays and relentless push from the pit boss to keep digging. A friend, Dermot Shackley, had moved to Silver City a few years back, and Juan planned on looking him up while there. He continued past the merchant's wagons and blacksmith before stopping in front of the saloon.

After he tied Lucky off to a nearby hitching rail, Juan walked toward the swinging doors. He stepped on the porch and glanced to his left, noticing two Indians—an old man and younger woman—tied to a bench about fifteen feet away. The Indian woman glanced at Juan and made eye contact before turning her head. They appeared injured, and Juan thought they had perhaps been caught stealing.

He pushed through the saloon doors and walked toward the bar. Finding a stool, he took a brief inventory of the patrons. A couple men sat at the bar a few seats down, while several others talked, ate, and drank in groups.

"What can I get you?" asked the bartender.

Juan spun toward the bar. "I'll have a water and shot of whiskey," replied Juan. He took note of the patrons' food plates. "Is that stew they're having?"

The bartender nodded.

"I'll have some of that as well," said Juan.

The bartender sat a small glass on the counter and poured the whiskey while Juan took another look around the saloon. Catching a glimpse of two men watching him across the room, he shifted his eyes in another direction. Moments later, he looked back.

The men spoke to each other and continued to glance at him.

Juan drew his chin inward and curled his lip, then turned back toward the bar. *What the hell are they looking at?* he thought, reaching for his glass of whiskey.

Moments later, the bartender sat a glass of water and bowl of stew in front of him.

"Gracias," said Juan, taking a sip of the whiskey.

At a different and closer table than the two men he'd noticed, three men talked about the Apache in the area. Juan figured they had the Apache tied up out front. Juan tried to listen to the men without them noticing. From what he could hear, they had been in a shootout.

One man, who wore a black vest and tan hat, had a deep voice that carried across the room. It wasn't hard to make out his words. He mentioned the Apache, Red Sleeves, returning to Santa Fe. Then he mentioned Taos. Juan assumed they were bounty hunters.

Juan took a bite of his stew and looked over his shoulder where the two guys in the far corner continued to gawk at him. Juan looked toward the bar and shook his head. He tried to recall if he had met them in the past, but they didn't seem familiar to him.

He took a deep breath and sighed, muttering, "All right."

Slamming his glass of whiskey, he picked up the bowl of stew and his water. He stood and glanced at the two men, who conversed together. Juan approached their table. Once he was within ten feet of them, the men stopped talking and looked up. Juan halted just a few feet from the table.

"Hello, amigos." Juan made eye contact with each man. "Do I know you?"

The men shook their heads. "No, sorry, amigo," said one of the men. "You look familiar is all."

The men were dressed like ranch hands or line riders, wearing wool trousers, long-sleeve shirts, bandanas around their necks, and wide-brimmed hats. The men looked similar to each other, with similar mustaches and stubbly beards.

The men seemed friendly enough, so Juan looked at the seat in front of him before regarding them. "May I?" he asked.

"Sure, amigo," replied one man, moving his hat.

Juan placed his food on the table and nodded. He sat, smiling as he glanced at the men who stared at him. He extended his hand. "Juan Moraga."

"Luis Barreto," he replied, accepting Juan's hand. "This is my brother Jose."

The brother reached his hand out. "Hello, amigo," he said.

Juan nodded and reached for his spoon. "So who do I look like?"

Jose grinned. "Someone we haven't seen for quite a while," he replied.

"You look very similar to him, and we were taken back," added Luis.

Juan looked across the table and saw the men's whiskey glasses. "You boys hungry? This stew is quite tasty." He took another bite. "Good to finally have a warm meal. It's been nothing but jerky and stale biscuits for me lately," he added with a grin.

"Where'd you ride in from?" asked Jose.

Chewing his food, Juan shook his head. "You wouldn't believe it, amigo, but I been to Lordsburg, Santa Fe, Socorro, Magdalena, and back again in the last couple months."

The brothers looked at each other, their brows together.

"You running from someone?" asked Luis.

Juan chuckled. "No. Not running, but maybe *avoiding* is a better word." He looked back down in his bowl.

Jose turned his head to Luis and shrugged his shoulder.

Juan turned his gaze toward the brothers, chewing on the potato he'd just spooned into his mouth. "What about you, amigos?" he asked. "What y'all doing here?"

Jose reached for his glass of whiskey. "Selling some wool and getting some supplies."

Juan looked up from his bowl and set it on the table. "You have a ranch around here?" he asked.

Luis and Jose both nodded.

"Si," replied Luis. "'Bout twenty miles from here."

Juan looked around for a few moments before turning back to the brothers. "You looking for any help?"

Jose looked at Luis and then back toward Juan. "Ever done any ranching?" he asked.

Juan grinned. "Oh, yeah, Among many other things."

Jose and Luis nodded at one another and faced Juan.

"Ok…let's give it a try," said Luis. "We are only half owners, and other owner will have to agree as well, but I don't think that will be a problem."

Juan smiled. "Gracias, amigo. When we leavin'?"

Luis raised his palms. "Once the wool is sold, maybe two or three days." He shrugged his shoulders.

"That's fine with me," Juan agreed. "I am sick of riding and could use a couple days out of the saddle."

"Well, you can get a bed at any of the camps for a small fee. They have breakfast and dinner available you can help yourself to," said Jose. "They'll be trying to hire you, I'm sure."

Juan shook his head. "No way. I done my share of mining, enough for two lifetimes." He raised his glass for a drink of water. "Besides, have a friend in Silver City I'm sure will take me in."

Jose and Luis stood from the table.

"All right, let's meet back here in a couple days about this time, and we will head out, or just look for us and our wagon around town," said Jose. "I'm sure we will most likely bump into you."

Juan set his glass back on the table. "Sounds good. I'll be here. I think I might go camp in the cliffs tonight. Looks awful peaceful up there."

Luis plucked his hat from the table and placed his hand on Juan's shoulder, walking past. "Adios," he said, following his brother toward the swinging doors.

Juan nodded to the brothers. "Adios."

After a few moments of letting his food digest, Juan rose and strolled back to the bar to his original seat.

The bartender appeared in front of him again. "What can I do you for?"

Juan studied the bottles of liquor lined up behind the man. "How about a shot of Fox Smooth?"

The bartender's eyes grew close. Then he turned to study the row of bottles, tilting his head and scratching his beard.

CHAPTER 16
ALL WENT QUIET

PEDRO STOOD IN A WIDE-OPEN grassland, a mile and a half from the ranch. With his hands to his hips, he stood just feet from a sheep's carcass, stripped to the bones and surrounded by the animal's wool that swirled in the wind. With Luis and Jose in Silver City, he decided to ride out during the early afternoon to check on the flock.

Pulling off his hat, Pedro looked around and wiped his brow. "Damn lobos," he muttered to himself.

He shook his head, put his hat back on, and walked toward his horse—standing about forty feet away—when he noticed three riders coming over a hill in the distance. Pedro paused for a moment to see if he recognized them, blocking the sun by lifting his hat off his head. As the strangers drew closer, he stood alongside his horse and held the rein.

The men stopped about ten feet away, and Pedro studied the men. One man was mostly dressed in black with bad burns to his face and a raven-feather necklace. The other two wore similar styles of clothing, seeming equally as ugly and unfriendly.

The man with the feather necklace looked at Pedro, his face blank. He tilted his head back, peering at Pedro.

Pedro raised his left hand in a friendly manner. "Can I help you, amigo?"

The man nodded and edged his horse a little closer, holding out a piece of paper that looked like a map.

Pedro approached the rider and took the piece of paper from the man's hand, looking down at it. Rather than a map, it was a bunch of scribbles. It didn't make much sense to Pedro, and he drew in his chin, rotating the paper a few times.

He looked away from the paper and toward the man to hand it over when the butt of a pistol swung down at him. The weapon connected with the top of his head, and the force made Pedro stumble backward. His vision became blurry.

The man spurred his horse toward Pedro, sending him to the ground.

Pedro attempted to regain his stance, but the man's horse trampled him. He held his hands in front of him to protect his face and head from the barrage of hooves. This continued for several moments until a hoof caught Pedro on the side of his face. He heard some laughter, then all went quiet, followed by darkness.

Arabella stood in front of the counter, rolling dough, when Camille called her name.

"What is it?" Arabella asked.

"Laila took my necklace Papá gave me!"

Arabella stopped rolling, pausing momentarily as she

thought of the man she loved and missed before she continued working the dough. "Laila, give Camille the necklace."

After a few more moments lapsed, she heard yelling, followed by the girls' footsteps running from their bedroom into the kitchen. Arabella shook her head as she turned. Camille, with a guilty expression on her face and not making eye contact with her mother, placed her hands behind her back. Laila followed, in such a deep cry that no sound emerged from her mouth.

Arabella covered her ears, knowing what was about to come.

Laila drew in a deep breath and tilted her head back. Her high-pitched cry echoed throughout the house.

Her ears still covered, Arabella turned to Camille. "What did you do?"

Camille, hearing the anger in her mother's voice, covered her mouth as she began to cry and pointed at Laila.

Arabella waved the girls away. "Ok, that's it! To your room!" she said with authority.

The girls walked toward their room, covering their faces with their hands as their mother followed behind them.

"I can see you girls need a nap," Arabella said, pulling the door shut after the girls entered. "And don't come out until I tell you."

Arabella walked back into the kitchen and reached for the roller. Just as she pressed down on the roller, there was a knock at the door. She released the roller and peered out the window but did not see anyone on the porch. She took a few steps toward the door. She walked quietly when she noticed it was unlocked.

"Who is it?" asked Arabella, inching quietly toward the lock.

"We need water," replied a man on the other side.

Arabella reached the lock and tried to slide it, but she heard a small squeak of metal, and immediately, the door began to open. She threw her weight into the door, struggling to lock it, but the man pushed against it. Arabella wedged her feet against the table to keep the door from opening. The man's arm reached around the door through the six-inch opening, and Arabella clamped the man's hand between the wall and the door. The man grunted in pain as she found her footing and pressed even harder. With tremendous force from the other side, the door opened as she slid across the floor, taking the table with her.

Realizing she was not going to keep the man from entering, she retreated toward the living room. She was grabbed by the hair and dragged back into the kitchen. The man held her by the throat and pushed her against the wall, knocking over a nearby chair and choking her. Her eyes bulged, and tears ran down her face as she felt around for something to hit the man with.

Two other men entered the house, glancing at Arabella and looking around the kitchen.

The man choking her grabbed his pistol and put it to her cheek.

With the little air she had left in her lungs, Arabella whispered. "*Please.*"

She stopped fighting and stared directly into the man's eyes. He leaned against her and licked her mouth. Arabella turned her head, and the man released his grip from her neck.

Arabella drew a loud deep breath. Then she stumbled away, leaning against the counter and coughing.

The man moved beside her and pointed his gun at her head, squinting his eyes. "Are you gonna be calm now?"

Arabella nodded and rubbed her neck.

"Good," he replied.

He put his pistol in his holster and walked toward the table to toss his hat on it. Straightening the table, he lifted the fallen chair and faced it toward Arabella to sit. The other two men stood just feet away, and he looked at the men with him.

"Have a seat, Red," he said, pointing to a chair. "You too, Eddie."

Arabella shook, backing into the kitchen while keeping her eyes fixed on the men.

The man leaned back in his chair, crossed his legs out in front of him, and placed his thumbs in his belt. "Now, get us something to drink," he demanded.

Arabella wiped her face and rose to her feet, walking to the cupboard for three glasses.

"Huh-uh," said the man shaking his head. "Take that ugly prairie dress off first." He bit down on his lower lip.

Arabella looked at the man, a tear trailing down her face. "Please…my husband and ranch hands will be here soon."

The man grinned widely, "Nah. There ain't no one coming." He pulled off a boot, dumping dirt to the floor. After shaking it a few times, he put it back on and sighed, staring at Arabella. "Ok, I see you need some motivation." He pointed his pistol at her. "Now you lose that dress"—he pointed the pistol at her chest—"or die."

Arabella shook as her trembling hands undid the buttons

in front of her. She slipped her shoulders from the straps, and the dress tumbled to the floor.

The three men's eyes brightened and smiles lit their faces.

Arabella used one arm to cover her breasts and the other over her private area.

The man holding the pistol shook his head. "Oh, no. Don't cover up. You're beautiful." He pointed his gun away and set it on the table. He looked at the man next to him. "Isn't she pretty, Red?" he asked.

Red stared at Arabella with his mouth open as he took deep breaths. "Oh...she sure is, Quinn," he said without blinking.

The man turned to his other comrade. "What you think, Eddie?"

Eddie only nodded without saying a word.

Quinn looked back at Arabella. "Now, how about those drinks?"

Arabella filled the glasses with tea and walked them to the table.

Quinn reached to pull Arabella to his lap. He felt her breasts and ran his hand up and down her thigh. He then pushed her off him and spun her around, grabbing her backside.

"Look at this ass!" he said with a large grin.

He then stood from his chair and forced her back into the kitchen, pressing her against the counter. He put his finger inside her and forced her head down. He unbuttoned his pants, letting them drop to the floor.

"No…please no!" shouted Arabella, crying.

Quinn forcefully pushed himself inside her while holding her head to the counter. "Hold still damnit!" he shouted, smacking the back of her head.

The man pushed hard against her, and she put her hand between her abdomen and the hard counter. Minutes later, Quinn made a low groan and stopped. He pushed himself off her.

Arabella slowly fell to the floor. She curled into a ball and whimpered.

Quinn pulled his pants up and walked back to the table while buttoning them. He lifted the tea and took a big drink and smiled. "Man, that felt good."

He then looked over at Red, seeing his anticipation. "Well, go on, Red. Go try it out!"

Red quickly left his seat and unbuttoned his pants. He went to Arabella, still curled in a ball, and pulled her legs out as she kicked and yelped, begging for him to stop.

Red smacked her across the face. "Shut up and hold still!" he shouted, spreading her legs apart.

Within moments, he was inside her.

Arabella felt ready to pass out from shock and exhaustion. Tears filled her eyes, and she lay still. Minutes crawled and felt like hours.

Red climbed off her, pushing his weight up by placing his hand across her head and face.

Eddie then made his way to the kitchen. He pulled his pants down and climbed on her. Arabella made no attempt to stop the man, staring at the ceiling as tears streamed down her face. Eddie rocked back and forth on top of her, and she turned her head away from the man and closed her eyes. He pushed himself deep inside her and, after a series of small shudders, abruptly stopped.

He drew in a deep breath and then turned toward his comrades, grinning. "Whew!"

He then looked down at Arabella, grabbing her face to turn her toward him. He kissed her mouth forcefully as she pushed with all her might to get him off her. He spat on her and then rose to his feet. He kicked her foot as he walked slowly back toward the table.

Quinn drank down the rest of his tea as he stared through the bottom of the glass at Arabella, who curled back into a ball in the middle of the floor staring back at the man. After lowering his glass and slamming it hard on the table, he stood to his feet. "All right, boys, let's see what she has around here."

The men looked around the house, pulling open cupboards and drawers. Quinn and Red walked out of the kitchen toward the front room, and Arabella filled with rage. She jumped to her feet and went after the men, and Eddie grabbed her hair as she flailed her arms wildly.

Quinn, standing between the rooms, looked toward the girl's bedroom. "Well, what do we have here?" he said, disappearing from Arabella's sight.

In complete uncontrollable rage, she kicked and clawed Eddie as he did his best to subdue the woman.

Arabella screamed, "Bastards! I am gonna fucking kill you!"

Red reemerged from the living room and raced toward her, pulling his pistol and raising it above her head. "Shut the fuck up!" he shouted as the pistol rushed down, and all went quiet.

CHAPTER 17
THE LITTLE LADY

Mitchell, Frank, and Pete rose from their seats, putting on their hats to head for the swinging doors.

Mitchell walked out first and looked toward the empty bench. Twisted and frayed rope rested beside it. "Oh, fuck," he muttered.

"What is it?" Pete asked, hurrying alongside Mitchell to look at the bench. "No damn way!"

"Shit," said Frank, taking off his hat and hitting it against his thigh.

Mitchell knelt and picked up the ropes. "They were cut." He looked in all directions, his eyes focused on everyone and everything around him. He looked a short distance and noticed that the Apache horses were also missing. He stood while Pete and Frank joined him, searching for any unusual movements or whoever might have cut the ropes.

Frank put his hat back on then looked at Mitchell. "What do you wanna do, boss?" he asked.

Mitchell took a deep breath and exhaled, shaking his head. "I don't know about you, boys, but I had enough of this shit," he said, walking toward his horse.

Pete looked over at Mitchell. "You wanna go out looking for them?" he asked.

"They couldn't have gotten far," added Frank.

Mitchell pulled himself onto his horse. "No, I'm good. Let's go home, boys." He turned his horse and started down the street, heading toward the south side of town.

Frank and Pete climbed onto their horses and rode alongside Mitchell.

"Home is the other way," Pete said, scratching his cheek.

Mitchell pulled his steamer from his pocket. "Yeah, I suppose." He packed his pipe and glanced at Pete. "So are the Apache."

Frank nodded. "Good idea, boss. Let's take the long way around."

The men rode south for an hour, moving over rough terrain from steep hills to heavy vegetation. They reached a point high on the hill where they could see for some distance. The men stopped surveying the area, and within moments, Mitchell grabbed his field glasses and put them to his eyes. His mouth fell open.

"Well, well," said Mitchell in a low soft voice.

Frank asked, "What is it, boss?"

Pete reached for his own field glasses.

"Looks like our old friends are heading the same direction," explained Mitchell. "And they got their backs to us."

"They sure as hell do," said Pete, lowering the glasses from his eyes and turning toward Mitchell.

"Whatcha wanna do?" asked Pete.

Mitchell put the glasses back to his eyes. "Oh, I'd like to see who he has with him."

Pete looked through the glasses again. "Yeah, he does have someone riding with him."

Frank reached for Pete's glasses. "Let me have a look, Pete," said Frank. "You think that bastard took our Apache prisoners?"

Mitchell returned his field glasses to their case and placed them in his saddlebag. "It's a good chance," he replied. He looked in the distance, charting the landscape. "All right, boys, we're gonna ride straight up behind them, so keep it quiet as you can." He turned his horse. "And keep your pistols handy. Yah!" He spurred the horse forward.

The three men rode down the hill and into open plains at a quick speed. They were no more than a quarter mile behind Pablo and his gang. Mitchell's hat blew off his head. It flapped behind him, pulling the string tight to his neck. Frank already had his pistol drawn, and he kept one hand on the rein. Pete rode between the two men, spurring his horse repeatedly to keep up. Once the men got within a hundred yards, they came to a group of trees and took cover to give their horses a rest.

Pablo had turned his group northeast, which worked perfectly for Mitchell and his men.

"All right, we'll follow this tree line and pop out right in front of them over yonder." Mitchell pointed in the distance.

Pete and Frank nodded.

"Sounds good, boss," Pete said.

The three men set off at a much slower pace.

Minutes later, Mitchell got his first real look at the men and woman they had with them. He squinted at the rider on the back of Pablo's horse, and his lip curled. "Looks like a young girl he has with him."

Frank came to a stop alongside Mitchell. "What in the world is that bastard up to?" he muttered, shaking his head.

Pablo, Ramon, and Ed turned again, coming straight at Mitchell and his men.

The anger in Mitchell climbed at the sight of the burned bastard's face under his hat and his shit-eating grin. He waited a few more moments, then emerged from the woods fifty yards from Pablo, directly in his path. Spurring his horse, Mitchell raced toward Pablo and his comrades.

Pablo raised his hand to bring his group to a stop, then smiled. "Well, now…look who it is!" he said loudly.

Mitchell rode about twenty feet away from them before stopping. He sat in his saddle, his hands resting on his saddle horn as he stared at Pablo.

Pablo noticed Mitchell's demeanor and leaned back in his saddle, returning the same stare while placing his hands on the saddle horn to mock the man.

Ramon and Ed moved their eyes back and forth, watching Mitchell, Frank, and Pete for any sudden movement.

Pablo smirked. "What happened to you, boys?" he asked. "We came back to the river looking for ya, and y'all were gone?"

Mitchell remained quiet, staring at the man he had grown to hate.

"You fellers catch Red Sleeves yet?" asked Ramon, his sarcastic tone causing Ed to chuckle.

Pablo grinned, moving his hands to his sides. "Whatcha want, Mitchell?" His grin dissipated.

"What I want is to never see your ugly face again," said Mitchell through his teeth, his gaze steady on the man.

Pablo drew in his chin and raised an eyebrow. "Well… then get riding," he said.

Mitchell nodded. "Fair enough." He lifted his hat to his head. "But before we go, why don't you tell me where you got that girl from?"

Pablo's eyes widened, and he leaned to his side, looking behind him at the frightened girl on the back of his saddle. "Who? Her?" he asked. "Oh, I found her over yonder way." Pablo motioned behind him and turned his gaze to Mitchell.

The girl certainly seemed frightened, but she appeared not to be hurt. Mitchell noticed the young girl peeking at him around Pablo's shoulder, and her frightened eyes peered into Mitchell's.

"What's your name?" asked Mitchell in Spanish.

The girl's head popped up and stared at him without saying a word.

"Now, Mitchell, this is my niece, and I am taking her to her mother's…my sister's house."

Mitchell looked back at Pablo, then moved his horse a few steps forward. "I'll be taking the girl with me, Pablo," he stated. "Now let her down from your horse,"

Pablo smiled at Mitchell. Then he laughed as Ed and Ramon joined in. Moments later, Pablo stopped laughing.

His brow creased, and his eyes squinted. "You ain't takin'—"

Mitchell pulled his pistol with lightning speed. He pointed it at Pablo's head and pulled back the hammer before Pablo could react. Frank and Pete also drew their six-shooters, pointing them at Ramon and Ed.

"Let her go or die," Mitchell said in his low-pitched tone.

Pablo stayed frozen for a moment, glaring at Mitchell. He looked around at his men, disgust written across his face. "What you fuckers doing sleeping back there?" he asked.

Ramon turned away from Pablo, looking at the ground.

Pablo twisted in the saddle and pushed the girl down from his mount. The girl fell to the ground and stayed there, looking up at Mitchell.

Mitchell's gun remained pointed at Pablo with one hand, and he motioned to the girl with the other. "Come here, girl. It's ok now."

The girl climbed to her feet and walked slowly to Mitchell.

"Start riding, Pablo," Mitchell said.

Pablo glanced at Frank, then Pete, then to the sun. He squinted at the light before returning his gaze to Mitchell. "You know it's too bad, Mitchell." He adjusted his hat. "We would have made a good team." Pablo leaned forward in his saddle. "But least now, I don't have to share that reward money with you." Pablo then turned his horse and spurred it along as he rode slowly past Mitchell, who was only a few feet away, while continuing to glare at him.

Mitchell reached out and grabbed Pablo's rein, bringing the horse to a halt. "If I take this girl home and find her family dead"—he raised a brow before releasing the rein—"I'll come looking for you."

Pablo grinned at Mitchell. "C'mon, boys." He turned his horse away.

Mitchell watched the men ride away for a few minutes before looking down at the girl. He put his pistol in his holster and extended his hand toward her. She reached up, and he lifted her onto his horse, sitting her in front of him on the saddle.

The girl appeared to be ten or eleven years old. She was visually shaken, as her teeth nervously chattered like she was cold.

Mitchell placed his hand on her shoulder. "It's all right now. We got you."

He spurred his horse in the opposite direction of Pablo and his men. Looking at the tracks, he backtracked the outlaws' trail.

Frank and Eddie returned their pistols and rode beside Mitchell.

"Let's follow their tracks. It will take us back where they came from." Mitchell leaned forward, and with a small smile, he asked the young Mexican girl. "What's your name, little lady?"

"Camille," she replied.

Mitchell nodded. "Ok, Camille, let's get you home."

The three men and the little lady rode quietly along, following tracks leading them toward the despair left by Pablo and his band of outlaws.

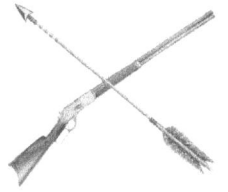

CHAPTER 18
UNFORESEEN HAPPENSTANCE

A RABELLA EYES OPENED, RACING AROUND the room as she lay on the floor. After several moments, she heard the soft voice of her daughter, Laila, calling her name while pushing on her shoulder. Still in a daze, Arabella pushed herself off the floor and felt blood running down her cheek. She eventually sat up and pulled a crying Laila into her arms. Shutting her eyes, she wept and held her daughter close. She looked around the kitchen. When she didn't see Camille, she shouted for her daughter.

Holding Laila away from her, Arabella asked, "Where is your sister?"

Laila cried harder, and Arabella held her close, consoling her before reaching for her dress, which was on the floor beside her.

"Camille!" she shouted, sliding the dress over her head and running through the house. "Camille!" she shouted again, panic flooding her body. Tears streamed down her face.

Laila followed her mother from room to room, crying as Arabella yanked the front door open and ran into the yard. She shouted for Camille before she ran to the barn. She then ran to the other side of the house.

"Camille!" she screamed at the top of her lungs.

Arabella ran back around the house and to the barn, relieved to see the horses still there. Grabbing a saddle, she tossed it onto a horse and looked at Laila as she came across the yard.

"C'mon, Laila, we have to find Pedro!" she said, wiping the tears from her eyes.

Looking past Laila, she saw a few men riding her way. She swept up her daughter and ran for the house. Once inside, she sat Laila at the table, grabbed a rifle that was hidden under a loose board in the floor, and checked its load. "Wait here. I'll be right back!"

Arabella darted out the door, leaving a crying Laila behind her. She ran straight at the approaching men with the rifle pointed directly at them.

The man in the center of the group raised his hands, and a young girl jumped from his saddle and charged Arabella.

Seeing Camille, Arabella dropped her rifle and ran straight for her. Camille jumped into her mother's arms as pure happiness and relief filled Arabella. She gripped her daughter tightly, then quickly rushed back toward the house to get Laila. As she ran up the steps and entered the home, the two girls and their mother embraced as tears streamed down their faces.

Mitchell's horse stood still as he gazed expressionlessly at the small adobe home.

Pete stared at him, a concerned look on his face.

The woman who had run out to get her daughter was bleeding, and the clothes hanging off her gave every inclination that she had been beaten and raped.

Mitchell looked at Frank, and the man shook his head in disbelief. They sat silently before Mitchell drew a deep breath. He looked straight ahead, raised his chin, and gave a small kick to the horse, steering it toward the house. He brought his horse to a stop near the little wooden porch and climbed down.

Tossing the rein to Frank, he knelt and picked up the rifle. He pulled his hat from his head, stepped onto the porch, and approached the door. He lightly tapped, but no one answered. He tapped again.

"Ma'am, can I have a word with you?" he asked, leaning the rifle against the house. He looked back at Pete and Frank and shrugged his shoulders.

He looked back at the door when he heard the sound of a lock sliding over, and the door cracked open. It was the Mexican woman who ran out at him, holding the rifle.

"Hello, ma'am, my name is Mitchell, and that there is Frank and Pete." He pointed to the men, still on their horses. "We're lawmen, and we'd just like to have a word with you if we could."

The door opened a bit further, and Camille peered at Mitchell. He glanced down at Camille with a smile, then back at the woman until she finally spoke.

"My name is Arabella," she replied with a quivering voice. Tears filled her eyes. "Please have a seat, and I will be out shortly."

"That sounds fine, Arabella," said Mitchell. He turned from the door, waving for Pete and Frank to join him on the porch.

They climbed from their mounts, tying them off before walking toward the porch.

The three men sat and talked among themselves about what had transpired between them and Pablo. Now realizing the severity of the man's crimes, Mitchell felt compelled to ride after him.

Thirty minutes passed, and the front door opened. Arabella stepped onto the porch. She went to a chair not far from where Mitchell was seated. She had cleaned up and changed into another outfit.

Looking at the men on her porch, she said, "Sorry for making you wait. I had to clean up the mess inside and see what's missing."

Mitchell's eyes drew close. "Find anything missing?" he asked.

"Just some money and a pistol is all. I am relieved they didn't take the horses."

Mitchell nodded. "Probably didn't feel like dealing with them. I have a feeling they are heading north real quick like."

Arabella bit on her lower lip as her brow creased holding back tears. "My daughter told me what happened and that you saved her from those men. I am eternally grateful." She wiped tears from her cheek before leaning forward to place her hands over her face as she continued to cry.

Mitchell placed his hand on her shoulder, and Arabella jumped at his touch.

"Sorry," said Mitchell, patting her shoulder and moving his hand away.

Her hands still covering much of her face, she looked at Mitchell and shook her head, closing her eyes again.

"Ma'am...where are the men at around here?" asked Mitchell, his brows drawing close.

Arabella wiped her face and nose with her hand, attempting to regain her composure. "Two are in Silver City. and the other is out checking on the sheep," she explained.

Mitchell nodded. "What's the man's name checking on the sheep?"

"Pedro," Arabella replied.

Mitchell looked at Pete and Frank. "You boys ride out and see if you can find Pedro and bring him back here directly."

Pete nodded and stood to his feet, followed by Frank.

"Will do, boss," said Frank.

"We'll find him, ma'am," said Pete, nodding to Arabella as he followed Frank off the porch.

"You boys see Pablo, you either ride like hellfire or start shooting," said Mitchell, looking out at the men as they climbed on their horses.

"Will do," said Pete with a nod. "Yah!"

They rode quickly away from the ranch.

Mitchell looked at Arabella, who held her hands to her cheek. "Ma'am, I assume they did more than just beat you. Is that fair to say?"

Arabella looked away, then slightly nodded.

Mitchell nodded as well. "I am sorry, ma'am. You and your family are safe now."

He reached for his steamer from his vest pocket. He packed his pipe, and the two sat quietly for several minutes. He struck a match and drew several short puffs from the pipe. He stared across the yard at the barn before scanning the horizon for any sight of Frank, Pete, or Pedro.

"Would you like something to drink, Mr. Mitchell?"

Mitchell turned his head to Arabella. "That's mighty kind of you," he said. "Whenever you get a chance is fine. Go on in and check on your daughter. I'll keep guard."

Arabella stood from her chair and approached the door, passing Mitchell. As she went, she placed her hand on his shoulder. "Thank you," she said.

Mitchell raised his hand to pat hers a couple times. "You're welcome. It's going to be ok." He said, placing his pipe back in his mouth.

A slight smile crossed her face as she continued toward the door.

Fifteen minutes passed before the door opened again, and out walked Arabella, Camille, and another young girl.

Mitchell looked at the little lady. "Aww, now, who's this one?" he asked.

Camille smiled and quickly answered for her shy sister. "That's Laila," she said with a wide smile.

"Well, you girls sure have purty names," said a smiling Mitchell.

Arabella sat a glass of tea down beside Mitchell and found her seat a few feet away. Laila quickly climbed on her lap, and Arabella stared in the distance, toward the valley and open plain. Camille stood by her mother's side, keeping a curious eye on the man who had saved her from the outlaws.

Mitchell smiled at Camille and then glanced at her mother. "How you holding up, Arabella?" he asked.

She smiled and bravely nodded. "I'll be ok." She looked at Mitchell momentarily before returning her gaze across the yard.

Mitchell wasn't sure what the young girls had witnessed while their mother was being attacked. He was confident that the men had not hurt the little girls physically, judging by their clothing and demeanor. He watched as the three huddled close together and realized they seemed to be doing better with every passing moment.

Mitchell lifted his glass and took a large drink of tea. "Ahh, that's tasty," he said with a smile. "Thank you kindly." He sat the glass back on the table.

Arabella looked at him and smiled.

Mitchell took off his hat and placed it on the table next to his glass. "We'll catch those men for what they done, Arabella, and bring them to justice," said Mitchell. "We know them pretty well and will have no trouble tracking them down."

"I am surprised you would know such awful men as Quinn, Red, and Eddie," said Arabella.

Mitchell looked at Arabella, his brows drawing together as he knocked the ash from his pipe before putting it back in his pocket. "Quinn and Red?" he asked.

Arabella nodded. "Yes, that's the names I remember, Quinn, Red, and Eddie."

Mitchell now knew that the men had given him fake names, and to top it off, he had heard of an outlaw named Quinn with burns on his face. He looked in the distance, shaking his head, then glanced back at Arabella, wanting to ask her about living in this area. It certainly wasn't the safest place with so many Apache in the surrounding territory.

"How long you lived here, Arabella?" he asked.

Arabella turned toward him. "About five years," she replied.

"Is Pedro your husband?" he asked.

Arabella shook her head. "No. My husband died a few months ago." She pulled Camille closer to her.

Mitchell shook his head. *What in the world has this poor woman been through?*

Arabella looked back at Mitchell, bowing her head. "He was arrested in Santa Fe and killed while trying to escape."

Mitchell's mouth fell open, and a blank stare came across his face. He looked around almost frantically, his eyes darting in every direction.

Arabella noticed his odd behavior and raised her eyebrows.

Mitchell ran his hand down his face and looked back at Arabella. "Domingo?" he asked.

Arabella froze and stared at Mitchell without blinking.

"That's my papá!" said Camille with a big grin.

Mitchell leaned back in his chair, disbelief coursing through him. Arabella locked eyes with him for several moments. She lifted Laila from her lap and sat her on the floor.

"Run inside, girls, so I can talk to Mr. Mitchell," said Arabella, her eyes remaining fixed on the man.

Camille kicked her foot in disappointment. Then she took Laila by the hand and led her into the house, closing the door behind her.

Mitchell exhaled forcefully. "I can't believe it!" His mouth hung open.

"You knew my husband?" asked Arabella eagerly.

Mitchell nodded. "I sure did."

Arabella put her hands together in front of her. "How? Please tell me everything you know," she pleaded.

Mitchell leaned back in his chair again. "My God, Arabella, you were the love of his life," he said. "He rambled nonstop about you and about his ranch near the Gila, but not in a million years would I think this would be the same place."

He shook his head, wrapping his mind around it all. "I found a friend in that man."

Arabella smiled widely. "How did you meet him? Were you in Santa Fe?" Her face changed abruptly, and her smile disappeared. She shook her head, then peered back at Mitchell. "You said you are a lawman. Were you there when he tried to escape?" she asked.

Mitchell exhaled loudly with a low chuckle, still shocked to be sitting in front of Domingo's wife. "No, I was in Taos when he was first captured by some ranchers," he explained.

Arabella wiped at a tear running down her cheek. "Please…," she said, taking a deep breath. "Please start from the beginning and tell me everything."

Mitchell realized he was one of the last people to spend any time with her husband, a man she clearly longed for. He smiled at Arabella before reaching into his vest pocket and pulling out his steamer. He packed the bowl full and struck a match, lighting the sweet tobacco. He shook out the match as he drew several quick puffs, then began. He started from the moment he'd lain eyes on Domingo at the top of a rocky hillside, just above a small cave where the man had slept the night before.

CHAPTER 19
WHO THE HELL IS QUINN?

Frank and Pete rode around the area, looking for any sign of Arabella's ranch hand almost an hour with no sign of the man. They followed tracks in several directions, coming to a dead end every time. The two men brought their horses to a stop and pulled out their field glasses.

After surveying the area, Frank pointed in the distance. "There's a horse over there."

Pete turned in his saddle and put the glasses to his eyes. "Sure is," he replied.

The men looked through their field glasses for several minutes.

"I don't see anyone, just the horse," Pete said.

Frank nodded. "Yeah, same here."

The men put their field glasses away and rode toward the lone horse, checking the area for any signs of Pablo and his gang. Once the men were within thirty yards, they knew it was not Pablo's or his comrades' horse. They searched the area until Pete saw a man about forty yards away, leaning against a tree.

"Over there!" Pete pointed in the distance.

The two men rode toward the tree, stopping a few feet away.

The man was in bad shape and hardly reacted to their presence.

Pete jumped down from his horse and knelt beside the man. "Pedro?" he asked.

The man nodded and grimaced in pain. He had taken several blows to the head, and he held his side.

Pete thought his ribs were most likely broken. He reached for the man and helped him to his feet. "C'mon, now, we have to get you home." He guided Pedro to his horse and lifted him into the saddle. Tossing the rein to Frank, he said, "Start back to the ranch. I'll grab his horse and catch up."

Frank nodded and rode toward the ranch. Pete watched, seeing how Pedro slumped in the saddle, barely able to hold himself up. He walked to Pedro's horse and climbed up, catching the other men within minutes.

In the midst of telling Arabella about his time with Domingo, Mitchell saw three riders approach. They stood together.

"It's them," said Mitchell, seeing Frank and Pete.

He walked down the porch steps, followed by Arabella. The two crossed the yard to get a better look at the approaching riders.

"Pedro!" said Arabella, running toward the men.

Frank and Pete came to a stop, and Pete jumped down from his horse to help Pedro down.

"Let's get him inside," said Pete.

Arabella covered her mouth before reaching out to embrace Pedro. "Oh my God!" she said, seeing the extent of his injuries. "Is he going to be ok?"

Mitchell gave a slight shake of his head. "I hope so." He grabbed the reins of Pete's horse and tied them to a nearby fence, following Pete and Arabella toward the house.

Frank climbed from his horse and tied it off. Then he followed along as well. They walked Pedro up the steps and into the house, taking him to the couch in the living room. After laying him on the couch, Arabella ran to the kitchen and grabbed some damp cloths. She wiped the blood and dirt from Pedro's face.

Camille and Laila stood close to their bedroom door, and the girls began crying.

Mitchell walked to the girls. He got to his knees beside them and drew them close to him. "It's gonna be all right."

The girls relaxed slightly under his words.

Arabella checked the injuries to Pedro's head and abdomen as Pedro moaned in pain, seeming lethargic.

Mitchell stood nearby, worrying the man had a major head injury.

After some time passed, Pedro seemed to be much more relaxed, and his constant moans subsided.

Mitchell motioned for Pete and Frank. They walked through the kitchen and to the porch.

"Boys, we're gonna stay here until the ranch hands return," Mitchell said.

Pete and Frank nodded.

"What do you think? Is he gonna be ok?" asked Pete.

Mitchell shook his head. "I don't know. It looks like he

took quite a shot to the head." He then looked over at the barn and bunkhouse. "Get the horses put up, and place our gear in the bunkhouse," said Mitchell, pointing toward the barn. "I'll let Arabella know we'll wait around until the ranch hands return."

Mitchell nodded to his men then walked back inside. When he reached the living room, he leaned against the wall and crossed his arms. He watched as Arabella hunched over Pedro, holding him. He waited a few moments, then unfolded his arms, and removed his hat.

"How's he doing?" Mitchell asked.

"Same," replied Arabella, rubbing Pedro's head gently.

"We should probably get him to a doctor in the morning if he doesn't seem better by then," he said.

Arabella nodded.

"We'll stay here until your ranch hands return. Then we will set out after those men that did this," said Mitchell.

Arabella wiped the tears off her face. "Thank you." She glanced from Mitchell to Pedro.

Mitchell looked at the girls, who had remained by the doorway, and smiled. "You girls be strong now for your momma." He then moved closer to Arabella. "All we can do is let him rest," he said, placing his hand on her shoulder.

"Thank you for all you done," she said softly.

Mitchell gripped her shoulder ever so slightly. "We'll be outside if you need us."

He removed his hand from her shoulder and walked toward the door. Once outside, he went toward the barn, where Frank and Pete waited.

"Whatcha think, boss?" asked Frank.

Mitchell looked at the ground, then back at Frank. "Well, we're staying here tonight," replied Mitchell.

"What about her ranch hand?" Frank asked.

"I don't know," said a somber Mitchell, shaking his head. "That poor woman can't seem to catch a break." He looked back toward the house, then at Pete. "We'll take shifts keeping watch tonight. That bastard Quinn could come back through here, so let's stay on high alert."

Frank and Pete looked at each other with creased brows.

"Who the hell is Quinn?" asked Frank.

Mitchell chuckled. "Boys, we have a lot to talk about," he said, lifting his gear and walking toward the bunkhouse. "You remember that Mexican feller we had at the jailhouse?"

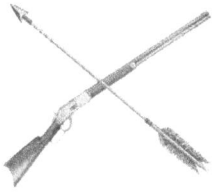

CHAPTER 20

THE FAMILIARLY STRANGE MAN

After one of the longest days of her life, followed by a mostly sleepless night, Arabella was exhausted as the morning sun rose above the valley.

Pedro spent much of the night vomiting, and his eyes remained fully dilated. Arabella grew concerned about permanent brain damage as Pedro struggled to move and talk.

She made breakfast for her guests and the girls, keeping an eye out for Luis and Jose. She was sure they would be returning to the ranch soon. She eagerly awaited their return, as they could take Pedro to Lordsburg to see the doctor. Arabella's anger toward the outlaws who attacked her and Pedro flowed through her body, and she could hardly contain it. Her hands shook as she prepared breakfast. Several times, she stopped preparing the food and wept.

Camille and Laila came out from their room and entered the kitchen. Arabella knelt and embraced them as they entered.

"Mama, is Pedro going to be ok?" asked Camille.

Arabella smiled and kissed her cheek. "I think so, sweetie. He just needs rest," she replied. "Now grab a seat at the table, and I will bring you your plates." Arabella glanced out the window, noticing a wagon approaching in the far distance. She sat the plates on the table. "Eat your food and stay inside." She opened the door and walked onto the porch.

Mitchell, Frank, and Pete were inside the barn, and Arabella called for them. The three men came out of the barn and walked toward Arabella.

"Good morning, Mr. Mitchell. I have breakfast ready for you men when you are ready," she said.

"That's mighty kind, Arabella," replied Mitchell.

Arabella pointed in the distance as Mitchell and his men turned toward that general direction. "Looks like my ranch hands, but I don't know who they would have with them?" said Arabella.

Mitchell took off his hat and stared into the distance.

At the same time, the wagon came to a stop. They appeared to be having a discussion with the man on horseback, and after a few moments, only the wagon continued toward the home. Now just under one hundred yards away, Arabella saw Luis's friendly wave and familiar smile. She waved back, and within minutes, the wagon came to a stop where Arabella, Mitchell, and his men were gathered.

Arabella glanced back in the distance, seeing the lone man climb from his horse and walk the animal toward the ranch. Luis and Jose climbed down from the wagon, going to Arabella's side and embracing her.

Arabella fought back tears, and the brothers seemed to know something was wrong. Puzzled expressions stole across both their faces. They looked at the tall man standing nearby, wearing a tan hat and black vest.

Arabella turned toward Mitchell and his men. "Luis and Jose, I would like to introduce you to Mitchell and his companions, Frank and Pete." Arabella gestured toward each man as she spoke.

"Nice to meet you," said Mitchell, shaking their hands.

"Nice to meet you, señor," replied Luis.

Jose placed his hand to his chin. "You look familiar, amigo," he said.

Mitchell looked at the man. "Hmm, can't say I ever met you, friend," he replied. He then turned to Arabella. "We will get back to the horses and let you talk." He motioned for Frank and Pete to follow him toward the barn.

Luis turned toward Jose. "Pretty sure he was in the saloon just before we cut those Apache free," he said.

Jose nodded, glancing back over at the man. "That's right, I knew he looked familiar."

Arabella looked at Luis and Jose, a tear running down her cheek. "Pedro is badly injured, and we need to get him to the doctor in Lordsburg."

"What happened?" asked Jose.

"We were attacked by outlaws, and they—" Arabella looked at the man walking his horse toward them. Her brows drew together, and she lifted her hand, stopping the conversation. She peered around Luis to get a better look.

Luis stepped aside, and Arabella took a few steps toward the approaching man.

"Arabella, we have to talk to you. Please let us go inside for a few minutes," pleaded Jose.

Arabella kept her gaze fixed on the man only fifty yards

away. She then looked at Luis and Jose. "Who is he?" she asked.

Luis shook his head. "Just someone we met at a saloon in Silver City looking for work. Please let's go inside and talk." He motioned toward the house.

Arabella looked back at the man, her curiosity piqued, and she wondered why Luis kept asking her to go inside.

"Arabella, we need to talk to you before he gets here. Please let's go in," explained Jose.

She nodded, and the three walked toward the house. Arabella turned back several times to look at the strange man. When they entered, Jose and Luis were greeted by Camille and Laila, who were quite happy to see them return.

Arabella pulled the girls back from her ranch hands. "You girls finish your breakfast. We need to talk in private."

Arabella led Jose and Luis into the living room, where Pedro lay on the couch. The ranch hands removed their hats and stood close to him. Pedro opened his eyes and peered at the men.

"How you feeling, amigo?" asked Luis.

Pedro lips moved like he wanted to say something, but they only heard a low moaning noise followed by a deep breath.

Luis looked at Jose, who appeared equally surprised by Pedro's condition.

"We need to get him to the doctor, Arabella," said Jose.

"Yes, I agree," she replied. "I have breakfast ready. After you have a quick bite, you can head out." Arabella sat down by Pedro and rubbed his head. She then looked back at Luis and Jose. "Who is that man?" she asked.

Luis sat in a nearby chair and shook his head as his eyes

circled the room. "His name is Juan, and like we said, we met him at the saloon while having some lunch and a drink."

Arabella continued shifting her gaze between them. "So why did you need me to come in before he arrived? What's going on?" she asked.

Jose looked at Luis before turning his gaze to Arabella. "We wanted to prepare you," said Jose.

Arabella's brow creased. "Prepare me for what?"

Jose sucked his teeth. "Well, we were sitting at the table in the saloon, and he walked in and sat at the bar. Luis and I were both surprised."

Arabella drew her chin toward her chest. "Surprised by what?"

Luis leaned forward in the chair. "Arabella, he looks a lot like Domingo."

Arabella exhaled, relieved that she finally understood, then smiled. "Well, he is not my husband, but I appreciate your concern." She shook her head and returned her focus to Pedro.

Jose looked at Luis again. "There's more, Arabella," he said.

One of her brows rose. "What else?" she asked, turning toward him.

Luis came closer to Arabella. "After we met him in the saloon, we regrouped a couple days later to head here, but when he came riding up, our jaws hit the ground," he said.

Arabella raised her brows. "What was so strange about that?" she asked.

Luis shook his head and put his hand on her shoulder. "He is riding Domingo's horse."

Arabella's eyes darted about the room. Her hands trembled. After coming to terms with what the brothers told her, she asked, "Are you sure?"

"Quite sure," Jose replied.

"And he also has Marcello's rifle," added Luis.

Arabella dropped into a chair and put her hand over her mouth. She sat quietly for several moments. She thought about what Mitchell told her regarding Domingo's arrest, trying to fit the pieces into place. She then looked back at Jose and Luis. "Did you ask him how he got the horse?"

Luis shook his head. "We didn't bring it up to him yet. We wanted to get him here with his guard down."

"If we started questioning him about the horse, he could have ridden off. Having just the wagon, we would never have caught him," said Jose.

Arabella looked around again. "Maybe he is the man who captured Domingo and turned him in?" she asked.

Jose and Luis shook their head.

"We don't rightly know, Arabella, but I think once we go outside, we should ask him," said Jose. "We will have our pistols ready."

"Arabella, can we trust those men out there?" asked Luis.

"Yeah, who are they?" Jose raised his hands.

"Yes, they are good men." Arabella eyes began to tear. "I will tell you about it later, but right now, I'd like to meet this man Juan." Arabella rose to her feet.

Jose stood and moved close to Arabella and Luis.

"Don't mention the horse until I have a chance to talk to Mitchell. He knows all the circumstances of Domingo's arrest," said Arabella. She tilted her head and put her hand to her chin when a thought came to her. "Maybe he already knows him?" she said before stepping away.

They walked through the kitchen and to the porch, Arabella leading the way.

Juan, Mitchell, Frank, and Pete stood in a tight group, having a discussion twenty feet from the porch in the yard. When Arabella, Luis, and Jose emerged from the house, the men stopped talking and turned toward them. Arabella locked eyes with Juan, and they stared at each other for several moments. Jose and Luis walked toward the small group.

The men started talking, but Arabella did not make out a word of it. Her heart pounded, and she found the similarity to Domingo astonishing.

Juan looked down at the ground for a second. Then he glanced back at Arabella with a smile. "Hello, ma'am," he said.

Arabella smiled and walked toward the mysterious man. She reached out her hand, and Juan accepted it.

"Arabella," she said.

Juan smiled a little more. "Juan Moraga," he replied. "Nice to meet you, Arabella."

They let go of each other's hand.

Arabella fought to turn away from Juan when Jose called her name. "Arabella?" he said, tapping her on the shoulder.

She turned toward Jose, who motioned toward the horse in the distance. Walking past the men, Arabella stood alongside the horse, rubbing its neck. She then placed her hand on the rifle and touched the cherry stock. Tears filled her eyes.

Juan glanced at Jose and Luis, his head cocked.

Arabella wiped away tears and looked at the men who had gathered around her. "Please, everyone inside," she said. "I have food ready, and we have much to discuss." She turned toward the porch and found herself looking at Juan.

The men followed Arabella up the steps. As they filed inside, Arabella pulled Mitchell's shirt sleeve, stopping his entrance. Mitchell stood to the side, next to Arabella, until all the other men were inside.

She turned to the lawman and whispered, "Have you met that man before?"

Mitchell scratched his chin. "Juan?"

"Yes," Arabella replied.

Mitchell's eyes narrowed as he thought about it. He shook his head. "I don't think so. To be honest, I thought he looks a lot like Domingo."

Arabella nodded. "Yes, there are some similarities." Arabella leaned closer to Mitchell and whispered, "He wasn't one of the men that captured Domingo in the cave?"

Mitchell shook his head. "No, that, I'm sure of." His eyes squinted. "Why do you ask?"

She pointed toward Juan's mount. "That's Domingo's horse," she answered.

Mitchell looked from the horse to Arabella. "You sure?" He placed his hands to his hips.

She nodded. "Absolutely sure."

Mitchell took off his hat and wiped his brow. "Domingo was captured in possession of a military horse, so for whatever reason, he certainly didn't have his horse."

Arabella's eyes darted side to side. "Do you think he stole it from Domingo?" she asked.

Mitchell placed his hat back on his head. "Well…only one way to find out."

As he turned toward the door, Arabella stopped him. "Yes, but let me do the talking." She opened the door. "Let's get you some food," she said, quickly changing the conversation. "You must be starving."

Mitchell smiled as they walked inside.

Arabella was happily surprised to see Pedro sitting up on the couch. She went to his side, placing her hand on his back. "How are you feeling?"

Pedro stuttered a few times before saying, "Better now."

Arabella smiled and kissed his forehead. "I am so glad you are feeling better."

Mitchell, Luis, and Jose walked into the living room as the other men sat down at the kitchen table.

Arabella glanced at them before turning back to Pedro. "I plan on having Jose and Luis take you to Lordsburg to see the doctor," she said.

Pedro shook his head and, after a couple attempts, finally explained, "No, I think I will be ok I just need some more rest." He noticed Mitchell in the living room and leaned forward to see the men at the table. "Looks like a full house."

"Yes, those are the men that found you and brought you home." Arabella smiled and stood from the couch to help Pedro lay on his side. "I'll get you some food and water."

"Just water is fine," he replied, reaching for her hand.

Arabella held his hand briefly before turning toward the kitchen. Mitchell, Jose, and Luis stepped aside to let her pass. Entering the kitchen, she grabbed several bowls and placed them on the table, along with a pot of beans and a few pieces of bread. She stood over the dough she was rolling earlier, only to find it was dried out. She walked toward the men gathered at the table. "Sorry. That is all the bread I have. I will make more once I have a chance." Jose looked up at her. "This is plenty, Arabella."

"Don't trouble yourself," added Luis.

"Gracias," said Juan, glancing up at Arabella while spooning beans onto his plate.

"Well, help yourselves. I will be right back," she said, returning to the kitchen for Pedro's glass of water.

After bringing that to him, she brought a pitcher of tea and some glasses from the kitchen to the table. Mitchell, Jose, and Luis were helping themselves to the beans and bread. The other men had already filled their plates and began eating.

Camille and Laila walked into the kitchen, but Arabella turned them around. "Go outside or go to your room," she told them. "It's crowded enough in here."

The girls groaned and threw their hands to their sides.

"Go on now. I'll bring your plates to you," their mother said.

As the girls stepped on to the porch, Arabella glanced at the men, some standing and some sitting. "Sorry. I don't have any more chairs," she said, shrugging.

"That's fine, Arabella," said Mitchell, lifting his fork to his mouth with a grin. "Thanks for the food."

Arabella returned his smile. "You're welcome."

She rubbed her chin, thinking for a minute. "Ok, let's start here." She pointed toward Mitchell as the men looked up from their plates. "Mr. Mitchell was with my husband, Domingo, in Taos just a couple days before he was taken to Santa Fe." Arabella turned her eyes from Juan to Mitchell. "He was also there when my husband was arrested."

Juan stopped eating and sat his fork down. "Why was your husband arrested?" he asked.

The room silenced, and Arabella searched Juan's face. After noticing how intently she watched him, Juan turned his eyes to Mitchell, whose studied him just as keenly.

Sensing their apprehension, Juan leaned back in his chair.

He rubbed the back of his neck while biting down on his lower lip.

Arabella turned to Jose. "You and Luis met Juan in Silver City in the saloon. Isn't that right?"

"Si," replied Jose.

"I'm sorry, but I am confused," said Juan, shaking his head and raising his hands from the table.

"So am I," she replied. After a slight hesitation, she glared at Juan. "Why don't you tell me what you were doing in Silver City and where you got that horse?" asked Arabella.

"Lucky?" Juan drew in his chin and creased his brow.

"Yes. Whatever you call him. But that's my husband's horse," she replied.

Juan stared at Arabella, his mouth slightly open. "Really?"

Arabella leaned her back against the counter, her eyes fixed on Juan. "Yes, really," she replied.

Juan shook his head for a moment, his brows lifted. "Well, ain't that something?" He reached for his glass of tea and lifted it to his mouth.

Arabella tilted her head and crossed her arms. "Yeah, it sure is something," she said, her face expressionless.

Moments passed as Juan regarded everyone at the table.

"The lady asked you a question, amigo," said Mitchell.

Juan looked at the lawman, then sat his glass down on the table before turning back to Arabella. "What? Do you think I stole it from him?"

Arabella shrugged. "Why don't you just tell me the story of how you acquired the horse, and I will tell you what I think," she said, clinching her jaw.

Juan drew in a deep breath and exhaled forcibly. "Ok, but

it's a long story, and I told it more times than I care to remember," he said.

Mitchell nodded. "We have all day so take your time and don't leave nothing out."

Juan lifted his hands from the table. "Well, I was robbed of my horse by some outlaws and was left to die," he said.

"Where?" Mitchell asked, his eyes narrowing.

Juan pointed toward the pitcher of tea in front of Frank, and the other man moved it closer to Juan.

"On the Santa Fe Trail about twenty miles east of Santa Fe," he explained.

Mitchell nodded. "Ok, go on."

Juan lifted the pitcher and filled his glass. "I was tied up but managed to get my feet free and fled south on foot. Then after several hours of walking, a man in a wagon gave me a ride to Magdalena. From there, I started back on foot toward Silver City." Juan lifted his glass. "After a couple days of walking, I was dehydrated and completely exhausted. Then I saw a small group of trees up a hill and took a break in the shade." Juan took a drink, then continued. "While I was resting, I heard moaning noises and brush rustling, so I went to investigate. After walking a short distance, I found Lucky tied to a tree. He looked as exhausted as I felt." Juan raised his hands. "I couldn't believe my luck. The horse was well stocked with water, food, and everything I needed," he explained. "After taking some time to get myself and the horse a drink, we went on our way."

"Then you rode to Silver City?" Arabella asked.

Juan chuckled. "Well, not exactly. US cavalry came through and took me…" Juan paused. His eyes lit up like a lucifer match had suddenly flared inside his head. "Wait a sec.

They must have been looking for your husband!" He pointed toward Arabella.

"What did they say to you?" Pete asked.

Juan turned to Pete, sitting in the seat next to him. "They asked me a bunch of questions, then took me clean up to Santa Fe, holding me until they could verify I wasn't the man they were looking for," replied Juan.

Frank reached for a piece of bread. "So then they just let you go?" he asked.

"Sure did. They gave me my horse and rifle. Then I headed for Socorro," Jose replied.

"Gave you my husband's horse and my son's rifle," said Arabella, crossing her arms.

Juan looked at Arabella and gave a small smile. "They are both yours, Arabella. I am glad to return them safely to you."

Jose cleared his throat. "He told us when we met him in Silver City that he'd been doing a lot of traveling, mentioning Santa Fe, Magdalena, Socorro…"

"Yeah, that's true. He did," Luis agreed.

Arabella gave a slow nod, deep in thought.

"You also mentioned Lordsburg. What were you doing there?" asked Luis.

"Well, I was riding with these dumb bastards from Lordsburg when we came across some Indians along the Santa Fe Trail," said Juan, shaking his head. "I wanted to just keep moving, but they were hell bent on robbing them."

Mitchell's eyes squinted. "What happened then?" he asked.

"I told them no, and they pistol-whipped me, tied me up, and took my horse. That's how this whole thing got started," explained Juan.

Mitchell sucked his teeth. "What was their names, those fellers you were riding with?"

"This guy named Red and his friends, Quinn and Eddie," replied Juan.

Arabella, shaken by Juan's response, took a deep quick breath and turned away.

Mitchell met Pete and Frank's eyes, and they all fixed their gazes on Juan.

Juan drew his chin toward his neck. "You know them?" he asked.

"Yeah, we know them all right." Mitchell walked to Arabella, placing his hand on her shoulder. "Let's go outside boys and finish this discussion."

Frank, Pete, and Juan stood and went to the porch, followed by Luis and Jose. Mitchell remained by Arabella until they were alone in the room.

"Let me talk to Juan. I'll also bring Luis and Jose up to speed about what happened," the lawman said.

Arabella wiped her face and nodded, reaching for Mitchell's hand.

"I will find out what he knows," he said.

She gave his hand a gentle squeeze before releasing it. "I don't understand why such good men acquaint themselves with such horrible men like Quinn," she stated.

"They're confidence men, Arabella. They lead you to believe they are something they're not."

"Is it safe to keep Juan around here?" she asked, her eyes fixed on Mitchell's.

Mitchell squinted his eyes. "I believe the man. I'm not saying he's perfect, but he did try and get away from Quinn and his gang." He placed his hat on his head. "Let me talk to him some more, and I'll tell you what he says."

Arabella smiled and turned toward the living room. The screen door shut as Mitchell joined the men on the porch. The room was silent as she sat next to Pedro, who lay sleeping, and rubbed her hand across his head while gazing at the wall. She then closed her eyes, smiling slightly as she thought about Domingo.

A short time later, the door opened. Camille and Laila rushed into the living room, causing Arabella to jump.

"Mama, we're hungry," Camille said.

Arabella smiled at her daughters. "Ok, c'mon." Standing, she walked toward the kitchen, her girls close on her heels.

CHAPTER 21

A BULLET IN THE HEAD

THE NEXT MORNING, MITCHELL, FRANK, and Pete ate a quick breakfast and rode out, searching for Quinn and his gang. They studied the ground and looked for the outlaw's horse tracks as they continued northwest toward Lordsburg.

Mitchell assumed they would most likely head that direction, especially if the outlaws were still after Red Sleeves. He also knew he and his men would have to be extra careful moving through Apache territory after the episode at the river. They would have to move swiftly and quietly. No matter how cold it got at night, no fires would be lit at their camps.

The evening before had been spent talking with Juan, Jose, and Luis about what had happened with the outlaws and Arabella. The men wanted to ride with Mitchell to find Quinn, but they all eventually agreed that three would need to stay back and keep Arabella and the girls safe in case Quinn and his gang returned.

After several hours of riding and searching, Mitchell and his men came upon some tracks they were sure belonged to Quinn, Red, and Eddie. The men spread out, continuing to follow the horse tracks. After a couple more hours of riding, Frank brought his horse to an abrupt stop.

"Boss, over there," he said, pointing in the distance.

Mitchell spotted three riders on the plains ahead. He raised his field glasses to his eyes and studied the men. "Yeah. That's them," he said. He pulled the glasses from his eyes. "Good job Frank." He gestured to Pete. "Come over here a second."

Pete led his horse to Mitchell and Frank, and they discussed their options.

"Listen up, boys. We have two choices here," explained Mitchell. "I figure once they see us, they will run or start shooting." Mitchell pulled his steamer from his pocket and struck a match, watching as several puffs of smoke blew from his mouth. He pulled his pipe from his mouth to continue. "We can just go straight at them and shoot it out, or get in front of them and see if we can ambush 'em." Mitchell took a deep draw from the pipe, and smoke rose above him.

"I say we ambush them," said Pete.

"Yeah, let's do that," agreed Frank.

"All right, let's back track a bit, then loop around, and try to get in front of them," said Mitchell.

Frank and Pete nodded, turning their horses back in the direction they came. After an hour of riding, Mitchell's group placed themselves between the outlaws and Lordsburg.

They located a place—just off the trail to Lordsburg—to take cover and climbed from their horses. After tying them off to a tree, they walked about thirty yards and hid in the high grass and bushes. The men hunkered down amidst the hilly terrain, listening and watching for the outlaws to come into sight.

Not long after, Quinn and his men rode over a hill about two hundred yards away.

"Get ready, men. They're coming," said Mitchell, pulling his Colt Walker pistol from his belt.

At the pace the outlaw trio was traveling, they would be in range within a few minutes.

Mitchell pressed his lips together and then made a slight smack sound, opening them. "Take them alive if we can, but if they don't surrender or make any quick movements, start shooting."

Pete and Frank nodded to Mitchell and continued watching the oncoming outlaws.

Quinn, only sixty yards away, abruptly stopped and looked along the tree line.

"Stay low, boys," said Mitchell quietly.

Quinn focused along the trees, but he seemed intent on an area just south of Mitchell.

"What's he doing? Did he see us?" whispered Frank.

Mitchell squinted and studied Quinn's movements for a few more moments. "I don't know," he said. "Seems to be looking at something down the way." Mitchell motioned down the tree line to his right.

Quinn, Red, and Eddie suddenly turned their mounts and kicked their horses, their movements frantic as they headed the other direction.

Mitchell stood from the brush to get a better look. "What the—"

War cries and thundering hooves sounded before riders

crossed the plain, and Mitchell got a firsthand view of why the outlaws had turned so suddenly.

"Goddamn Indians!" said Mitchell. "C'mon, back to the horses!"

The lawman glanced back as he ran, watching the Indians charge Quinn as gunfire erupted. Within moments, the Indians rode over a hill and disappeared from sight.

Mitchell, Frank, and Pete rushed to their horses. Only twenty feet away, a shot rang out. Frank groaned and fell to the ground. Mitchell and Pete took cover and returned fire.

Four Indians on horseback closed in on them as Frank rolled over the ground, grabbing his side.

"Hold still, Frank," said Mitchell, firing at the Indians as they charged toward him. "We'll get to you."

Pete crawled across the ground. Just as he reached for the horse's reins, another shot rang out, hitting him in the head. He fell to the ground, motionless.

"Pete!" yelled Mitchell, but there was no response. "Goddamnit!" He continued to fire at the swarming Indians.

They yammered and raised their rifles above their heads while circling Mitchell. Frank still lay on the ground, motionless as Mitchell raised his pistol and took aim at the Indian. He pulled the trigger, but the chamber was empty and only clicked. He threw his pistol at the nearest Indian and emerged from the brush to accept his fate.

The Indians rode near him, and dirt and dust filled the air. One Indian knocked Mitchell's hat off his head as their yells continued.

Mitchell looked at his fallen comrades and turned to the Indians, shaking his head. "You fucking savages!" he shouted, and they came to a sudden stop.

Four Indians stared at Mitchell from their horses, and another approached on horseback behind them.

Taking note of the massive Indian riding toward him, Mitchell nodded. "Been looking for you," he said in Spanish.

The Indian rode close to Mitchell and glared unblinkingly at him for several moments.

Mitchell stared back and grinned. "What's wrong, Red Sleeves? Don't feel like talking?" he asked.

Red Sleeves jumped down from his horse to stand face to face with the lawman. The Indian reached out and grabbed the other man by the neck.

Mitchell had never been known for being small, but the Apache chief stood a good few inches over the Taos constable, currently fighting to pull the chief's grip from his neck. Mitchell squirmed and struggled to breathe. Seconds passed like hours, he fell to his knees as Red Sleeves knelt, continuing to choke him.

The chief released his grip, and Mitchell dropped to the ground, pulling large gasps of air into his lungs. After regaining his breath, he rubbed his neck and climbed to his feet, eyes locked on Red Sleeves.

"You know my name. What is yours?" asked Red Sleeves, his voice low.

"Ben Mitchell," he replied, rubbing his neck and shaking off the feeling of the intense choke hold.

"Ok, Ben Mitchell, who sent you here?" asked Red Sleeves as they continued to glare at one another.

Mitchell tilted his head. "The sheriff and the families of those innocent folks you killed in Santa Fe," he said.

"You come with so few men and attack old men and

women at the river. Was that your plan?" asked Red Sleeves with squinted eyes.

"Well, I wouldn't say it was the plan, but there wasn't anything better to do," replied Mitchell as he gave a small grin.

Red Sleeves nodded. "You are brave, but not very smart, Ben Mitchell. I am curious. Was it your mother or your father who handed down this ignorance?" The chief tilted his head to the side, staring at the lawman.

"A little from both I suppose there, Chief." Mitchell scratched his head. He glanced at Pete, lying dead on the ground by the horses.

Red Sleeves turned his gaze in the same direction. "That your friend?" he asked.

Mitchell nodded.

"Your friend was a lousy fighter," Red Sleeves said.

Mitchell looked at the chief as his fists clenched and anger coursed through his body. "That man had something you never will have."

"What's that? A bullet in the head?" asked Red Sleeves. He had the ghost of a smile on his face.

"A little from both I suppose there, Chief." Mitchell scratched his head"Honor, you goddamn savage!" he said through his teeth, his eyes bulging.

The chief's smile widened. "Why were you hiding in the trees from your own men?" he asked.

The lawman spat on the ground, then raised his head to glare at Red Sleeves. "They weren't my men. They were outlaws. They were the ones who attacked the old men and women at the river."

Red Sleeves shook his head. "Does the white man ever speak the truth?" He leaned toward Mitchell. "I heard the old man and woman were taken prisoner, then escaped the white man with the scars."

The chief moved his finger across Mitchell's face. Drawing his fist back, he struck Mitchell in the side of the head. The lawman fell to the ground. When Red Sleeves kicked him in the face, everything went black.

Red Sleeves observed the fallen man's head, paying attention to the scars. Buckskin Hat had mentioned a man with scars on his face bringing great suffering to his people. He continued to stare as Little Feather moved beside him.

"What do you see?" his friend asked.

Red Sleeves motioned to his own face. "Those scars… there is a lot of talk of a man with scars bringing suffering."

Little Feather leaned in to take a closer look. "What do you want to do with him?"

The chief turned to the warriors behind him. "You ride out after the others," he said, pointing to three on horseback.

The warriors turned their horses and raised their rifles above their heads. Giving a war cry, they quickly rode away.

Red Sleeves turned to Little Feather. "Tie his hands," he said. "We'll take him back to the tribe."

Little Feather tied the man's hands with a small piece of rope. He then looked at the other two men who lay motionless on the ground. "What about them?" he asked.

"Leave them," replied Red Sleeves picking up Mitchell's hat and pistol from the ground.

They tied Mitchell in the saddle, and the chief led his warriors to the tribe with the prisoner and three new horses.

CHAPTER 22
GET THE HORSES READY

Two days had passed since Mitchell, Frank, and Pete had ridden out after the outlaws, and Arabella worried about them. After preparing breakfast, she called outside to Juan, Luis, and Jose to eat. The men filed inside and sat around the table. The ranch hands had spent the last couple days working on the roof of the barn, and in the early mornings and nights, hunting wolves that had been attacking the woolies in recent days.

"Good morning, Arabella," said Juan, giving her a smile.

"Good morning, Juan," she replied, setting a plate in front of him.

As the men ate, Arabella leaned back against the counter and placed her hand to her chin, watching them.

"Whatcha thinking, Arabella," Luis asked, lifting his fork toward his mouth.

Arabella shook her head. "It's been two days, and I have a feeling something is wrong," she explained.

Jose nodded. "Well, I am sure they had to ride a ways to catch up to them. Maybe they will return later today or tomorrow."

Arabella nodded. "Yeah, maybe. But I just have a strange feeling." She poured a glass of tea for herself and looked at Juan while he ate.

Juan noticed her gaze and grinned.

Arabella smiled back. She'd only known the man for a few days, but she had come to trust him considerably. Placing her tea on the table, she made another plate of food for Pedro. Walking to the couch, she set it beside him on the side table. His eyes opened and he sat up, allowing Arabella to sit down next to him.

"How you feeling?" she asked, rubbing her hand across his back.

Pedro rubbed his eyes and smiled, stretching his arms above him. "Better," he replied.

Arabella gave him a quick hug and stood from the couch. "Would you like to join us at the table or eat in here?" she asked.

Pedro did another quick stretch. "I will come join you," he said, reaching for his plate. He stood and followed Arabella into the dining room.

Jose, Luis, and Juan greeted Pedro as he sat.

"Good morning, amigos," replied Pedro.

"How are you feeling?" Luis asked.

"Much better," he replied, giving a short nod.

As the men discussed their plans for the day, Arabella returned to the counter, listening to their conversation. For the last two days, she'd struggled with the awful memories of her attackers. After crying more times than she could count, she realized her sadness was turning to anger. She wanted the outlaws to pay for their crimes, but something told her Mitchell would not be the one to bring them to justice. She was convinced only one man could handle Quinn and his brethren.

"I have decided that I will ride out today and find Chief Red Sleeves," she stated.

Every eye at the table turned toward her.

Pedro dropped his fork, and it clattered on top of his plate. "Why…what do you mean?"

Arabella tilted her head and raised her eyebrows. "Because I think something happened to Mitchell, and I think he could help," she replied.

Jose and Luis turned to each other with wide eyes, and Pedro creased his brow.

"That's way too dangerous," Pedro said, his lip curling.

Juan continued eating, seemingly unaffected by the conversation.

"Juan, will you ride with me?" she asked.

Juan lifted his head, his brows raised. "Umm…ok," he replied, shrugging his shoulders and smiling before turning back to his plate.

Pedro's balled his hands into fists, and his face turned red. He glared at Juan.

Sensing the other man's gaze, Juan raised his head again and glared back at him.

Pedro turned to Arabella. "No, I don't think so. I'll go," he said.

Arabella firmed her chin. "You are in no condition, and I am leaving within the hour."

Pedro leaned back and crossed his arms. "Take Luis or Jose then."

Arabella shook her head. "They are staying with the flock; I need you here with the girls."

She reached for her glass of tea and raised her eyebrows at Pedro, who shook his head and uncrossed his arms. "I said no." He pointed at Juan and said through his teeth, "You don't even know this man."

They tied Mitchell in the saddle, and the chief led his warriors to the tribe with the prisoner and three new horses

Pedro locked eyes with Juan, and they scowled at each other.

Arabella slammed her glass down. "I am not asking for your permission, Pedro!" she yelled.

Jose and Luis seemed suddenly very interested in their plates, no longer watching the other occupants in the room.

Pedro looked at the brothers and raised his hands. "Will you guys tell her it's a bad idea? I know you agree with me."

The brothers lifted their heads to Pedro. Luis shrugged, and Jose shook his head.

"It's up to Arabella," Luis replied.

Pedro pushed his plate away and turned to Juan, curling his lip. He stood and stalked to the door, grabbing his hat on the way to the porch. The door slammed behind him.

Arabella narrowed her eyes at the door. She then turned toward Jose and Luis. "Ready my horse and pack it full of mutton and several blankets." She pointed to Juan. "You get my husband's…" She paused and swallowed. "Get Lucky ready, and fill the bags with mutton as well." She drained her glass of tea. "We will head out after I feed the girls," she said, preparing their plates.

Jose and Luis nodded and left the table to answer her request.

Juan scraped the last little bit of food onto his fork. "Will do," he said, smiling. Raising the fork to his mouth, he took the last bite before standing to walk toward the door.

Arabella reached for his arm as he passed, and Juan turned to her.

"Thank you," she said, giving him a small smile.

Juan smiled back. "Of course." He gave her a hug. "It's gonna be ok," he said before releasing her to walk outside.

Arabella's mouth hung open at having experienced the innocent and somewhat pleasant hug. She chuckled as Camille and Laila walked into the dining room, rubbing their eyes.

"Mama, is breakfast ready?" asked Camille.

Arabella knelt in front of her daughters and embraced them. "Good morning, darlings," she said, kissing each of them on the cheek. "Yes, it's ready. Grab a seat, and I will bring it to you."

She picked up Jose and Luis plates to make room for the girls to sit. Glancing out the window, she noticed Pedro and Juan in deep discussion. Their faces were close together, and Jose and Luis attempted to move themselves between the arguing men. She rolled her eyes and sighed heavily.

Opening the window, she yelled, "Get the horses ready now!"

She slammed the window shut and looked at her wide-eyed daughters. "It's ok, girls," Arabella said with a smile. "Just silly boys."

After she placed her daughters' breakfasts on the table,

Arabella rested her hands on their heads. "Now, hurry and eat. Then let's go outside and feed the dog."

Laila giggled. "Mama, Scratchy is in our room."

Arabella tilted her head and made a playfully mean face at her daughter. "Of course, he is," she replied, reaching for Pedro's and Juan's plates and returning to the kitchen.

CHAPTER 23

TWO-HEADED SNAKE

RED SLEEVES WALKED THROUGH HIS camp, met with the greetings of several warriors and children. Still on high alert after running into the bounty hunters only a few days before, the chief knew more men would come for him. Approaching the cook fire, he grabbed a piece of the deer meat propped on a stick. He was in the middle of taking a bite when he noticed Little Feather and Blue Rock riding toward him.

The two warriors had been circling the camp day and night, guarding the area. They halted just feet from Red Sleeves as he chewed on the meat.

"Chief, there are two riders approaching," said Little Feather, pointing the opposite way of the sun.

Red Sleeves nodded and continued chewing. Then he turned and walked to his horse. Jumping onto his mount, he followed Blue Rock and Little Feather from camp. Within minutes, Red Sleeves noticed the aforementioned riders in the distance, and he continued toward them. Drawing closer, he noticed their raised hands just before recognizing a familiar face.

He slowed his horse and addressed his warriors. "Dominga," he said, raising his own hand above his head. The two groups continued toward each other as Red Sleeves noticed the man beside her, seeing a resemblance to Domingo.

Within twenty feet of each other, Arabella raised her hand again and smiled. Red Sleeves raised his hand, and his lips gave a slight curve.

"Chief Red Sleeves, it's good to see you well," said Arabella.

Red Sleeves nodded. "Good to see you, Dominga," he replied. He then looked at the strange man alongside her.

"This is my friend, Juan. He works at the ranch," she explained.

"Nice to meet you, Chief," Juan said.

Red Sleeves nodded to Juan. Then he tilted his head. His brow furrowed as he gawked at the man for a few moments.

"I know what you are thinking," said Arabella, still smiling. "I was also surprised when I met him the first time."

Red Sleeves nodded, then looked back at Dominga.

"I have come here today bringing mutton, blankets, and to warn you of some dangerous men in the area," stated Arabella, motioning toward the large sacks and small pile of blankets before turning back to Red Sleeves. "They attacked my field hand Pedro and took my daughter Camille."

Red Sleeves eyes drew close as an angry scowl crossed his face.

Arabella continued her story. "Then some courageous men rescued my daughter from the outlaws and brought her back to me unharmed," she added.

Relieved, Red Sleeves nodded at Arabella. "Did these outlaws harm you?" he asked, lifting his chin.

Arabella looked away and closed her eyes, giving a slight nod.

"I came across these outlaws you speak of," Red Sleeves stated.

Arabella tilted her head and froze. "You did?"

Red Sleeves nodded. "Yes, some got away. We captured one and killed two," he said.

Arabella shook her head. "Forgive me, my chief, but there were only three?" she asked.

Red Sleeves looked at Little Feather. "There were six?" he asked in Apache.

Little Feather looked at his chief and nodded.

Red Sleeves turned back to Arabella. "Dominga, what did these men look like that attacked you," asked Red Sleeves.

"Three men, one had scars on his face," she replied.

Red Sleeves nodded. "I have the scarred man, tied to a tree." The chief motioning back to his camp.

Arabella eyes grew wide, and her jaw clenched. "Can you take me to him?" she asked.

Red Sleeves thought about it. Then he gave a single nod before looking at Juan. "He will have to wait here," he stated.

"He has mutton for your people in the sacks," she said. Turning back toward Juan, she said, "Here, hand them to me."

Juan reached over his saddle. He unhooked and lifted the rope, swinging two large sacks beside him before extending the two burlap sacks filled with smoked meat to Arabella. She grabbed the heavy sacks, which pulled her slightly off her saddle from the weight, then handed them to Red Sleeves.

The chief looked inside one and regarded Juan with a nod. He then looked at Arabella. "My people thank you," he said.

He tossed the sacks over his horse's rump, leading the group toward the tribe. Arabella waved to Juan, and the man lifted his hand in response. Climbing down from his horse, he tied it off to a nearby palo tree and found a seat under its shade.

Upon entering the camp, Arabella was greeted by many of the tribe. The women and children followed alongside her horse, smiling and welcoming her to their home. Many called her Dominga or Mum Turquoise, and they rubbed their hands along her horse as she rode by. Arabella smiled at the small group following alongside her. One woman emerged by her side and smiled widely, and Arabella recognized the woman as one who had visited the ranch a little over a month ago.

Red Sleeves came to a stop near a cook fire and jumped down from his horse. A warrior lifted the large sacks of mutton from the chief's horse and opened them, and the tribe helped themselves to the mutton inside.

Arabella followed the chief's lead, climbing down from her horse while being surrounded by many of the tribe. She reached over her saddle to pull down four blankets. Much like their first meeting, Arabella extended the blankets toward the woman, who quickly excepted them.

Red Sleeves walked alongside the woman holding the blankets and gestured to her. "White Bird," he said.

Arabella looked back at the woman and smiled. "Nice to see you again, White Bird."

The woman smiled back. "Gracias, Dominga."

Red Sleeves then motioned for Arabella to follow him. Several women and children followed along as well until Red Sleeves instructed them to stay back. The two walked about thirty yards, and a man came into view. He was on his side and tied to a tree.

"Oh no. No," said Arabella, rushing to the man's side and lifting his head.

Mitchell's face was bloody, and one eye was swollen.

Arabella shook her head. "Oh my goodness. Mitchell, are you ok?" she asked.

Mitchell cracked an eye open and looked at her. "Never better," he replied with a grin.

Arabella wiped dirt from his face. "Oh dear, what happened?" she asked, leaning him back against a tree.

"We found Quinn but were attacked by Red Sleeves just as we were about to engage the outlaws," he explained.

Arabella nodded. "I am sorry. Where's Pete and Frank?" she asked.

Mitchell sighed. "Dead."

Arabella moved away from Mitchell and looked back at Red Sleeves, who stood a few feet away with his brows creased. "My chief, this is the man who saved my daughter and then set out after the men who attacked me," explained Arabella.

Red Sleeves glanced at Mitchell before looking back at Arabella. "He is a bounty hunter. He attacked some of my people at the Gila just moons ago, killing one of our women" he replied.

Arabella shook her head and glanced at Mitchell. "Are you sure it was him? This is a good man," she said.

"Maybe good for some, but not the Apache," replied Red Sleeves.

Arabella looked back at Mitchell. "Is that true, Mitchell? Did you attack his people at the river?" she asked.

Mitchell looked at her and shook his head. "Told him it was Quinn, but I don't think he really cares," said Mitchell, readjusting his position against the tree. "To Red Sleeves, any white man is his enemy."

Remembering Juan's story about Quinn along the Santa Fe Trail, Arabella looked back at Red Sleeves. "The men who attacked the Indians along the Santa Fe Trail are the same men who attacked me and took my daughter." She pointed at Mitchell. "He can help us find them," she added.

Red Sleeves stood expressionless and stared at Mitchell. Then he looked at Arabella. "I can see this man is your friend." He looked toward the camp, lined with wickiups, campfires, men, women, and children playing. "But these are my people." He extended his left arm and moved it side to side.

Arabella wiped a tear from her eye. "Chief Red Sleeves, I am your friend, and I am begging you to trust me and release this man," she said.

Red Sleeves looked at her for several moments. "I will talk to the elders about what you have told me." He then looked at Mitchell for a moment, then back at Arabella. "The white man is a two-headed snake. One will promise many things… while the other sinks its fangs into you." Red Sleeves placed his hand on Arabella's shoulder. "Dominga, you know this as much as anybody. Your husband also knew this." Red Sleeves gave a single nod. "That is all I have to say."

Arabella closed her eyes and exhaled, struggling to smile at the wise chief. She walked back to Mitchell and knelt beside him. "Promise him you will never be a threat to the Apache people. Please, Mitchell. Beg for your life. I will do all I can for you," she said, holding his hand in hers.

Mitchell smirked and winced. "I don't think he will listen,"

Arabella rubbed her hand across his head, feeling defeated, then stood. "I will make sure Frank and Pete get a proper burial. Thank you for all you have done for me, Mr. Mitchell." She held back her tears.

Mitchell gave her another small smile. "Thank you, Arabella. It's gonna be all right now." He gazed around him before taking a deep breath and shaking his head. He then turned to Arabella again. "You know, your husband told me you were a great woman. I can easily see what he meant by that," said Mitchell, squinting as the glaring sun hit his face.

"You are such a strong but sweet man," Arabella replied.

Mitchell turned his eyes toward the ground before meeting her eyes again. "In case I don't see you again, can you make sure my wife, Martha, knows what happened to me?" He edged closer to Arabella as dirt and dust fell from his boots and pants. "Let her know she was in my thoughts…until my very last second on this earth," he murmured.

Arabella closed her eyes as a stream of tears rolled down her cheeks. Moments later, footsteps sounded behind her, and Red Sleeves appeared at her side.

The chief placed a gentle hand on her arm. "Come, Dominga, I like to walk with you among the tribe and introduce you to many."

Arabella turned. "I would like that very much, my chief."

They turned and walked toward the tribe. Many were gathered, already waiting for their chief and Dominga, the woman with the turquoise necklace.

CHAPTER 24

THE WOMAN AND THE WARRIORS

A NOTHER CLEAR AND SUNNY AUGUST morning greeted Johnson as he stood from his desk to open the window. As he looked across the yard, he noticed the arrival of several horses and wagons. After watching them a while, Johnson sat at his desk again. He picked up a cigar and lit it, drawing in several puffs until its tip glowed red.

Within moments, there was a knock at the door.

"Come in," said Johnson.

Corporal Rhoades entered, holding the door slightly ajar he saluted his commander. "General Johnson, sir, I have General West requesting to see you," he said.

Before Johnson could reply, the door fully opened and General West swept past Rhoades to stand in front of Johnson's desk. West and Johnson saluted each other simultaneously. Then West sat in the chair opposite Johnson.

Leaning back, Johnson turned his eyes to Corporal

Rhoades. "That's all, Corporal. Close the door on your way out."

Rhoades turned on his heels, shutting the door behind him as he left.

West reached into the box of cigars and pulled one out. He placed it below his nose to smell the tobacco. "Have a match handy?" he asked.

Johnson reached into his pocket and slid the box of matches across the table. West stopped them before they slid off the desk. He opened the box, keeping his gaze fixed on Johnson. After lighting his cigar, he also leaned back, tilting his head back as smoke rolled from his mouth.

"Hope you had easy traveling, General," said Johnson.

"That's a long trek, but we moved along well," West answered. "Congratulations on your recent success here, Johnson."

"Same to you," the other general replied.

"We will be heading out in a couple days, following the Camino Real straight to Mexico City and finally putting an end to this godawful war." West took another puff on the cigar.

Johnson nodded.

"You will be bringing a large portion of your division," West added.

"We're ready, General. Just need to leave a battalion or two to secure the fort and handle the prisoners," replied Johnson.

West glanced around the room, squirming in his seat. "That's good. You have any whiskey around here?" he asked.

Johnson shook his head and raised his palms. "Sorry, General. I'm fresh out."

"That's a shame," replied West. He reached into his pocket and pulled out a small flask. Tipping it to his mouth, he leaned his head back and emptied the can with one large gulp. General West then tightened the cap on the flask and put it back in his pocket. He tilted his head to the side. "What about the Apache?" he asked.

Johnson removed the cigar from his mouth. "What about them?"

West smirked. "Heard they been killing some innocent folks around here. What are you doing about that?" West raised his eyebrows.

Johnson rubbed his cigar in the ashtray, knocking off a large piece of ash and staring at West. "When you say 'innocent folks,' do you mean the Mexican rebels or the outlaws?" quipped Johnson.

West crossed his arms. "Look, Johnson, I know you were friends with the tribes in Alta California, but these Apache are something completely different and need to be dealt with!"

Johnson grinned. "The Apache are allies of ours, General," he replied. "Last time I checked, we are at war with Mexico."

General West's face turned red, and his eyes narrowed as he spoke through his teeth. "Johnson, I have already written to the War Department and stated that we will bring peace to this region. That means striking the Apache resistance."

Johnson leaned back in his chair, running his hand over his head, then rubbed the back of his neck. "I thought we were heading to Mexico City General. There are Apache spread out over hundreds of miles in all directions," he said, waving his arm to his side. "High up in the cliffs and deep in the valleys… terrain that we can't even march, much less get wagons and artillery through." Johnson tapped his fingers on his desk as the men sat in silence. When he realized that sharing the complication of logistics had little effect on West, he reached for the journal on his desk. "This journal is full of reconnaissance reports and information shared to us from our Apache allies, helping us locate and defeat the Mexican army around here."

Johnson extended the journal toward West, who shook his head and raised his hands. "We don't have to kill the entire Apache nation, General. We just need to take out the troublemakers, and you know who that is," he added.

"And who might that be?" asked Johnson, returning the journal to the desk.

West smirked and rolled his eyes. "Oh, that one who killed a group of folks here in Santa Fe a few months ago. The same one attacking the miners, and also the same one bringing the tribes together against the American soldiers and civilians alike."

Johnson raised one eyebrow and tilted his head, grinning. "Sounds like an important man, General. I'd like to meet him someday."

"I'm talking about Red Sleeves, goddamnit!" West hollered, pounding his fist against the desk.

Johnson's smile fell as he peered at the other man. "General West, my orders are to march into Mexico City. If Red Sleeves wants to admit he's done what you accuse him of and surrender, that's fine, but I am not looking for him," explained Johnson, his voice firm. "Now if you don't mind, General, I have matters to attend to." Johnson stood.

West stared at Johnson before also standing. Johnson saluted West, and West saluted back before grabbing his hat from the desk. Johnson remained standing until West left the room. Then he sat and sighed.

What a jackass, he thought.

After taking a few minutes to absorb their conversation,

Johnson reached for a pen and paper to write a letter, the cigar still hanging from his mouth.

Corporal Rhoades eventually walked into the office. "General, sir, is there anything you need, sir?"

Johnson sat the pen down and scratched his chin. "Actually, a bottle of whiskey would be nice."

After spending some time with Chief Red Sleeves and the tribe, Arabella requested to be taken to Pete and Frank's bodies. Red Sleeves complied, asking Little Feather and Blue Rock to fasten a travois to their horses before leading Arabella and Juan to their location. The chief then instructed his warriors to ride with Arabella to her ranch after they retrieved the bodies, ensuring her safe return home.

After saying their goodbyes, Arabella followed the warriors, thinking about Mitchell and hoping Red Sleeves would consider freeing the man. Although she knew that would be an unlikely scenario, she did her best to understand the chief's reasoning. The number of gringos in the area grew almost every day, and Red Sleeves was determined to put an end to it. She feared that if Mitchell were killed, it would draw unwanted attention to the tribe and her own ranch.

As they continued, Juan eventually joined them, and she filled him in on what happened at the Apache camp. She explained that Mitchell was alive, but he may not be for long. Fascinated by the situation, Juan asked many questions about her friendship with Chief Red Sleeves, the notorious Chiricahua Apache whom many in the territory feared.

Arabella smiled. "It was my husband's final gift to me," she said.

Having a sudden thought, she spurred her horse and caught up to Little Feather. The Apache warriors turned to her, and Arabella found it thrilling to ride alongside them. There was a sense of security and belonging, and she could not help but smile. Little Feather gave an awkward grin and turned away quickly.

Arabella's smile grew. She covered her mouth, tickled that such a fearless warrior would be nervous of her. She paid great attention to the Apache warriors as they made a constant survey of the ground and surrounding hills. Whether it was a horse track, a bird flying over, or a tumbleweed blowing across the plains, the warriors spotted it quickly.

She looked at the ground for tracks, hoping to spot something before they did. She noticed something move on the hill in the distance and turned toward the warriors to inform them, but they were already pointing in that direction and discussing it.

Blue Rock looked at Arabella and noticed her interest. "Mule deer," he explained, pointing to the animal.

Arabella nodded and bit down on her lip, frustrated that she hadn't spotted it first. Juan rode behind Arabella, whistling and bobbing his head. Arabella turned back and smiled as he began to sing, but he stopped abruptly.

"Don't let me interrupt you," she said. "I was enjoying it."

Juan smiled and shrugged his shoulders. He cleared his throat and started singing again.

Arabella faced ahead and bobbed her head side to side as Juan sang. Not long after, the warriors rode toward a wooded area. Little Feather turned to Arabella, pointing to the trees and signaling they were close.

Juan stopped singing, and the realization that she was

about to see the dead men began to overtake Arabella. Her anxiety grew with every thud of the horse's hooves.

The sunlight dissipated upon entering the woods, and the warriors looked in several directions. Blue Rock eventually pointed, and they followed behind him. After riding another thirty yards, the warriors came to a stop.

Little Feather jumped from his horse and looked toward the ground before dropping down on one knee, examining the forest floor. Blue Rock climbed from his mount, walked about twenty feet, and stood over the body of Pete. He draped a blanket beside the man, and Juan jumped down from his mount to help. Arabella stayed on her horse and waited. She had no interest in seeing the lifeless men.

Juan knelt beside Blue Rock, helping to roll Pete inside the blanket. They fastened a rope around him, securing the thick cloth.

Arabella glanced at Little Feather, who moved about on the ground and looked at the dirt. He moved into the high brush, disappearing into it as he continued searching. Blue Rock and Juan carried Pete to the travois and secured him to it. A few moments later, Little Feather called out for his party. Blue Rock and Juan quickly moved through the brush.

When Juan called for Arabella, she climbed down from her horse. By the time she reached them, Juan and Little Feather emerged from the brush, carrying Frank.

"He's alive," said Juan.

Arabella's mouth dropped open.

They laid Frank on the ground as he moaned, seeming lethargic.

Arabella asked for a canteen and blanket, and Juan moved to his horse, grabbing his canteen. He tossed it to Blue Rock, who handed it to Arabella. She raised the canteen to Frank's mouth, and as he took several small drinks, Juan carried a blanket to her.

"He's freezing," Arabella said, covering Frank. She tore off one of her shirt sleeves and applied pressure to his bullet wound. "We need to get him to the ranch quickly."

Juan, Blue Rock, and Little Feather lifted Frank, carrying him to the travois. They secured him to it and climbed onto their horses.

The group rode south toward the ranch, and in a little more than a couple hours, Arabella's adobe home came into view.

CHAPTER 25

THE TOOTHLESS COYOTE

As the sun dipped below the rocky cliffs, darkness blanketed the Apache camp.

Red Sleeves walked toward a small fire near his wickiup, where the elders and Buckskin Hat, the medicine man, had already gathered. He placed a small blanket on the ground, sitting next to Buckskin Hat and Gray Sky. Red Elk sat across from him.

"Little Feather?" he asked, looking at the men gathered around the fire.

"He has not returned after leaving with Dominga," said Buckskin Hat.

Red Sleeves nodded and sat quietly, thinking about Little Feather and Blue Rock. He knew the two skilled warriors could handle themselves, and it was unlikely that they would be attacked by the outlaws. The chief looked at Gray Sky. "What do you think of the man Mitchell?" he asked.

Gray Sky raised his eyes toward his chief. "He seems like a fair man, for a hair face."

"Fair man?" said Buckskin Hat. His brow creased in disapproval of Gray Sky's answer.

Gray Sky looked at Buckskin Hat. "I don't believe he was attacking us, but rather, he was protecting us from the burnt man," added Gray Sky.

Red Sleeves also turned to Buckskin Hat. "You had visions of a man with scars to his face bringing great suffering to our people." The chief pointed in the distance at Mitchell, tied to a tree. "The white man has those scars, and the Raven Boy has them." He circled his hand in front of his face. "Maybe the visions were of the Raven Boy and not of this man?"

The medicine man nodded to his chief. "It's true both men have the scars. But if the white man is not an enemy of the Apache, why would he ride with the enemy of the Apache?" Buckskin Hat closed his eyes and tilted his head back, stretching his hands toward the fire. "They are both enemies of our people and both equally dangerous."

Red Sleeves glared at the fire, taking time to digest Buckskin Hat's words.

Red Elk lifted some dirt in his hand and released it. "Buckskin Hat is right. The white man may have protected Gray Sky at the river from the Raven Boy, but he is also the one who brought the Raven Boy here."

Red Sleeves looked at Red Elk and nodded. He sat quietly for a while, thinking of what the elders said. "The Raven Boy attacked Dominga and her children. It was the white man who returned Dominga her daughter." The chief brought his hands down along the sides of his head, simulating the woman's hair. "The Raven Boy attacked Gray Sky at the river, and it was the white man who protected him." He motioned to Gray Sky. "When we attacked the white man along trees, he was waiting in ambush for the Raven Boy."

The medicine man and elders nodded.

"Dominga is convinced there is good in the white man, that he would be no threat to our people if set free." Red Sleeves looked at them. "When I captured the white man, even facing certain death, he did not cower and tell me false words. His words were of anger, but there was truth in them. A man afraid of the spirits will tell many lies to live another day." Red Sleeves reached for a log and tossed it into the fire. Then he looked into the bright stars amidst a dark sky. "I will offer the white man a way to life and a way to death." He regarded Mitchell in the far distance. "It will be up to him which path he chooses."

Red Elk, Gray Sky, and Buckskin Hat all nodded, then they sat quietly for several minutes. From the dark shadows around the fire emerged Little Feather. He sat down beside them.

"How was your journey?" Red Sleeves asked.

"Traveled well, my chief," Little Feather replied, crossing his legs in front of him. "When we returned to the woods, one of the white men was gone from where we left him."

"Gone?" asked Red Sleeves, lowering his brow.

"I followed a trail of blood into the bushes and found him alive," said Little Feather.

"Is he with Dominga?" Red Sleeves asked, knowing Dominga would not have wanted Little Feather to kill the man.

Little Feather nodded. "He is. I do not know if he will survive."

Red Sleeves regarded all the other men gathered around

the fire. "If the white man chooses life or death, he will also speak for the white man of the bushes."

Buckskin Hat nodded in agreement.

"What about the Raven Boy?" asked Red Elk.

"Little Feather, Blue Rock, and I will set out at first sun to put an end to the Raven Boy and all who ride with him," said Red Sleeves.

"We should send a hundred warriors," Gray Sky replied.

Red Sleeves turned to Gray Sky. "The Ghost Child became the Raven Boy. The Raven Boy became great medicine throughout the Apache." The chief swiped his hand across the flames. "Now, the Raven Boy became Quinn the Coyote." Red Sleeves looked around the fire as he read the expressions of his friends. "The tale of the Ghost Child has been in our hearts for too long, Sending one hundred warriors would give too much respect to Quinn, the toothless Coyote who attacks old men, women, and children," explained Red Sleeves. He placed a hand on Little Feather's shoulder. "The Apache warriors are the greatest fighters of the plains and valleys. We will bring swift death to Quinn, the Coyote bitch." Red Sleeves looked at Buckskin Hat. "All the stories will end tomorrow, and it should be understood by our people that he was just a toothless coyote and deserves to die and be forgotten like one."

Buckskin nodded to his chief.

Red Sleeves reached for his pipe, lifting a small stick from the fire that burned on one end. Placing the small flame into the bowl of the pipe, he drew several puffs before passing it to Buckskin Hat. "Let us smoke and find peace in our hearts," said the chief. He raised his hand above his head, bringing it down slowly in front of his chest to make a fist.

The next morning, Red Sleeves woke before sunrise and kissed his wife on the forehead while she slept. He crept to the other side of the wickiup and knelt by his children, watching them sleep. The chief's smiled and placed his hand on his son's head before leaving the wickiup.

"Father."

Red Sleeves stopped and looked behind him to see his son, who shared his name, sitting up. "Watch after your mother and sister while I am away," he said.

Mangas the younger nodded. "I will, Father," he replied.

Red Sleeves grinned with pride. "Sleep now, son. I will see you in a few days."

The chief pulled the animal skin flap to the side and left the wickiup. Crossing the camp, he approached the cook fire to grab some meat, where Little Feather and Blue Rock already sat. Blue Rock held out his hand when Red Sleeves reached them, holding a large piece of mutton for his chief. Red Sleeves nodded, taking the meat from the warrior's hand. He took a large bite while glaring across the camp.

The sunlight was just reaching the sky above the plains in the distance, creating a tiny orange glow. Smoke layered across the ground of the windless morning.

Red Sleeves turned toward Little Feather and grinned. "Good day to die."

Little Feather smiled back at his chief, the fires reflected from his teeth. "When we return, I will be looking at you and you will be looking at me, Chief Red Sleeves."

Red Sleeves smiled wider, exposing the dark gap of his missing front teeth. He put the last bite of meat in his mouth before placing his hands on each of his warrior's shoulders. "This is a great day, my friends," said Red Sleeves, chewing on the piece of meat. "Get our horses ready. Bring me Whom'tu and the white man's horse."

The warriors walked away to do as their chief instructed.

Grabbing a water pouch hanging a few feet away, Red Sleeves raised the pouch and took a large drink before grabbing another piece of meat. He then walked briskly across the camp, heading for the tree where the prisoner had spent the last few days.

The man lay on his side, sleeping, and Red Sleeves stared down at him for a brief moment before kicking the man's foot. Mitchell lifted his head, and the two stared at each other without a word. Red Sleeves knelt beside the man and handed him the water pouch. Resting on his elbow, Mitchell chugged it down. A moment later, Red Sleeves handed him the piece of meat.

"Gracias." Mitchell took a bite, then sat up to lean his back against the tree.

Red Sleeves sat beside Mitchell and looked at the sun rising above the plains and bringing its glow further across the sky. "I remember in the woods…when you raised your pistol at the warriors, but there were no bullets," said Red Sleeves, grinning. "Then you slung your pistol at them." He grinned wider.

Mitchell nodded, chewing on the meat as he listened to the Apache chief.

"If there was a bullet in the pistol, maybe a warrior would be dead. But you most certainly would be," explained Red Sleeves.

Mitchell nodded, raised his brows and shrugged. "Dumb luck, I reckon."

Red Sleeves looked from the sky to Mitchell. "I have thought about that many times. I believe there was a reason the chamber was empty," he said.

Mitchell tilted his head, and the corner of his mouth quirked up. "Because I already fired six rounds?"

"No," said Red Sleeves gazing back up the sky, then turning back toward Mitchell. "I believe we both needed to be alive for what we are to do today."

Mitchell swallowed down the meat and reached for the water pouch. "Oh yeah? What are we doing today?" He took another large drink of water and stared at the sky.

"We are going to kill Quinn the Coyote," said Red Sleeves, glaring at Mitchell.

Mitchell sat the water pouch beside him. "I suppose if I say no…that would be bad for me?" He tilted his head as he watched Red Sleeves.

The chief nodded. "It would be bad for many," he replied.

"Well, I accepted my fate days ago, and I can't see myself riding with another group of outlaws and murderers," explained Mitchell, drawing in a deep breath.

Red Sleeves grinned. "It's not just for your life, Mitchell. One of your men is still alive."

Mitchell leaned forward. His eyes darted back and forth.

Red Sleeves noticed Mitchell's surprise. "The man that was hit in the side," he said.

"Where is he?" Mitchell asked.

Red Sleeves looked at the eastern sky, taking note of the sun's position. Then he turned back to Mitchell. "He's safe for now." The chief stood and stared down at Mitchell, who had reached for the water pouch again to take another drink. The sound of horses nearing could be heard as he glared at the lawman. "So, what's it going to be, Ben Mitchell?" He clenched his jaw and leaned his head back, waiting for a response.

Mitchell lifted the ropes that secured him to the tree. "Cut 'em, and let's go coyote hunting."

Red Sleeves grinned and pulled his knife from his hip, cutting the ropes.

Mitchell stood and placed his hands on his hips to stretch his back. Then he turned, unbuttoning his pants and pissing on the tree that had secured him for days. "I'll be needing my hat, Chief," he said.

Little Feather walked toward Red Sleeves, leading Whom'tu and Mitchell's horse.

Red Sleeves reached for his horse's reins and turned to Blue Rock. "Get the white man's hat."

The warrior turned his mount and rode toward the cook fire.

Red Sleeves tossed Mitchell his horse's rein, then turned to Whom'tu, placing his forehead against the horse's muzzle. The chief said a few short prayers, followed by, "Carry me safely, old friend." He rubbed the horse's neck and pulled himself onto his mount.

Whom'tu blew large amounts air though his snout, followed by a whinny. The horse raised its hooves and brought them down forcefully, pounding the ground with loud thuds that echoed throughout the camp.

Mitchell mounted his own horse, glancing at Red Sleeves while putting his hand to his hip. "Pistol?" he asked.

Red Sleeves shook his head. "Not yet, Ben Mitchell," he replied with piercing eyes and a low, monotone voice.

Moments later, Blue Rock returned and tossed Mitchell his hat.

Mitchell placed it on his head and nodded to the warrior.

Red Sleeves turned his horse and headed northwest, leading his war party out of the camp. A few Apache men and women emerged from the wickiups and watched their warriors and the white man ride into the distance until they disappeared behind the cliffs.

CHAPTER 26

AN UNWELCOME VISIT

Arabella sat on the porch with the girls, Scratchy at her feet. Inside the barn, Juan fed the horses and chickens. Jose and Luis worked on fences, planning to head out and check on the woolies within the hour.

The door to the house opened, and Pedro stepped outside. He nodded toward Arabella then put his hat on his head and walked off the porch.

"How you feeling today?" asked Arabella.

Pedro continued walking like he didn't hear her.

Arabella tilted her head as the girls moved closer to her.

"What's wrong with Pedro, Mama?" Camille asked.

"He's still healing, sweetie. He will come around soon," she explained.

Pedro walked past Juan, who had just stepped out of the barn after sprinkling cracked corn across the ground for the chickens.

Arabella shook her head, knowing darn well what was eating at him.

Juan sat the bag of feed on the ground and walked to the porch. "How you doing, ladies?"

Arabella smiled. "Just fine. Would you like something to drink?"

Juan took his hat off and walked up the steps. "Gracias. I'll get it, though," he replied, opening the door. "I'll run a glass out to the bunkhouse for Frank, see how he's doing." He disappeared into the house.

Arabella fixed her gaze back across the yard and caught a glimpse of Pedro's stare. She clenched her jaw, tired of Pedro's antics. She made up her mind to address it later when she had a moment alone with him.

Scratchy jumped from his spot beside Arabella's feet and ran into the yard, barking.

Arabella studied the direction he barked. Dust rose in the sky as a large amount of horses approached. Standing, Arabella glanced at the brothers.

They had already heard the commotion, staring into the distance as blue uniforms emerged from the dust.

Arabella forced herself to stay calm as she reached inside the door and grabbed a rifle. She noticed Juan, pouring himself a glass of tea. "Horses approaching. Grab your pistol and come outside." Moving back to the porch, she turned to her daughters. "Go inside, girls."

The soldiers were rapidly approaching as she stepped off the porch and walked across the yard toward them. She thought fifty US cavalrymen closed in, and she clutched her rifle to her side as the horses came to an abrupt stop. Dust blew across the yard, and the many horses snorted while Arabella used her sleeve to cover her mouth.

One of the men leading the group removed his hat, knocking the dust from it and returning it to his head. "Hello, ma'am, my name is General Johnson," he said in Spanish.

Arabella glared at the man, stone faced. "Arabella," she said flatly as Jose and Luis moved to each side of her.

The man nodded at the brothers and turned back to Arabella. "Is this your ranch, ma'am?" he asked.

Arabella gave a stiff nod. "It's our ranch."

Quick footsteps sounded behind Arabella and the brothers, and Juan appeared beside her. Pedro stood by the barn door, observing from a distance.

The general glanced back at his men, then turned back to Arabella and her ranch hands. "I suppose you are aware we are at war with Mexico," he stated.

Arabella nodded. "Well, too aware."

Johnson looked around the yard. "We're going to need to take some supplies, ma'am, and it's in our authority to do so."

Arabella stood stoically and glared at the general. "You and your authority are unwelcome here."

Johnson removed his hat. "I'm sorry, ma'am, might be unwelcome, but necessary, to bring freedom to this land." He waved a few horses forward, followed by a wagon. "We will only take what we need. I'll pay you for the trouble."

As the horse and wagon rode around Johnson and toward the barn, Arabella and Juan stepped back, allowing it to pass. Arabella's breath hitched, and she turned toward the house. The similarity of this situation took her back to the last time American soldiers rode onto her ranch.

She wiped away a tear and moved to the porch, Juan following close behind.

"You ok, Arabella?" he asked.

"I'm fine," she said, taking a breath and forcing her voice to come out sternly. "Just help them get what they need and get them out of here." She walked into the house, shutting the door behind her.

General Johnson watched the Mexican woman walk into her home, and the field hand who had been standing by the barn door crossed the yard toward the house. He thought about the woman's reaction to their presence as the soldiers loaded up hay, feed, eggs, water, and mutton.

Watching the wagon being loaded, Johnson made a mental note of the items being placed inside. One soldier exited the barn with saws and tools, another with blankets.

Johnson stopped the soldiers. "Food and water only, men," he said loudly to ensure everyone heard.

The field hands were in the barn, and they even helped carry out a few items.

As one man approached, Johnson called for him. "What's your name, señor?" he asked.

"Luis."

Johnson nodded and pulled a cigar from his pocket. "Have you seen any Mexican soldiers come through here lately?"

Luis shook his head. "Not for many months."

Johnson nodded and lit his cigar. "The woman…she seemed quite upset by our presence. Any idea why?" he asked.

"She has many reasons," replied Luis.

Johnson removed the cigar from his mouth. "Well, go on," he encouraged.

Luis looked at the house, then back at Johnson. "American soldiers killed her son," he replied.

Johnson nodded and bit his lower lip, deep in thought. He looked at his wagon. "That's enough, men. Let's move out!" The general pulled a pouch from his pocket, pouring some coins into his hand. He counted out ten and handed them to Luis. "Give these to the lady," the general requested as he returned the pouch to his pocket.

"Gracias," Luis replied as the general turned his horse and spurred it forward.

He rode past his men, placing the cigar into his mouth, while the soldiers filed in two lines behind him.

Arabella shut her bedroom door and sat on her bed, tears streaming down her cheeks. Thoughts of Marcello and Domingo flooded her mind. The presence of the American troops jolted her to the core. She wiped her face when she heard a tap on the door.

"One second," she said, attempting to regain her composure.

When she felt ready, she opened the door to find Pedro on the other side, hat in his hand.

"I'll come back later," he said, noticing her tearful eyes.

"No, it's fine. Come in," she replied, returning to her bed and sitting down.

Pedro stood by the door watching her. "You ok?" he asked.

"Yes, just hard to be out there with the soldiers."

Pedro nodded. "Yeah, I imagine so," he said quietly.

"A lot happening these days." Arabella turned her head to stare aimlessly across the room.

A long silence passed between them, and Pedro stared at the floor, dragging his foot back and forth across it. Arabella could sense Pedro had something to say.

"What is it, Pedro?" she asked.

Pedro gave a timid smile. "You know, when I came here with you, it was under the agreement we would be friends and wait for Domingo's return," Pedro explained.

"Yes, Pedro, and we are friends."

Pedro smiled and looked at the floor. "Yes, we are. But now I think it's time to be more than friends." He raised his head to stare into her eyes.

Arabella closed her eyes and shook her head. "I am not ready for that, Pedro. You know that."

Pedro's gaze remained unblinking "Do I?" he asked.

Arabella's eyes narrowed. "What do you mean?"

Pedro looked behind him, hearing the girls in their room. After waiting to make sure the girls were not coming, he turned back to Arabella, who stared at him with eyebrows raised.

"Oh, forget it," he said, placing his hat on his head.

Arabella stood and moved closer to him. "No, tell me what you mean by that?"

Pedro put his hands on his hips and looked down, then raised his head, and met her eyes. "I see the way you look at him, Arabella." He motioned toward the barn.

"Look at who? Juan?" She tilted her head and furrowed her brow.

Pedro gave a short nod. "Yeah, Juan," he grumbled.

Arabella clenched her jaw. "I do enjoy his company, but that's all." She drew in a breath and closed her eyes. Opening them again, she placed her hand on Pedro's shoulder. "Just as I do yours, Pedro," she added.

Pedro smirked. "Yeah…ok, Arabella." He turned, but Arabella pulled back on his shoulder, stopping him. "You have been there for me and the girls through some of my darkest days, and for that, I am grateful," she said, her eyes tearing up, "But I never once asked for anything else, and I never will."

"Well…you're welcome," he said, walking away.

Arabella sighed. She walked backward and sat once again on the bed. She covered her mouth as her loud sobbing carried through the house, gaining the attention of her daughters. They ran into their mother's room and wrapped their arms around her. She embraced her children.

"What's wrong, Mama?" Camille asked.

"I miss your papá and your brother," she explained, and all three wept together.

Not too long after, they lay in bed, holding each other. They talked about the good days, like hearing Domingo banging his hammer on the roof for hours at a time.

"Papá always was on the roof!" said Camille.

Arabella laughed, and they giggled together. She kissed her daughter's foreheads. "C'mon, let's go find Scratchy and go for a walk."

"Ok!" said the girls simultaneously.

They jumped from the bed and reached for Arabella's arms, nearly pulling her off. Their laughter resonated through the house, as did the slam of the front door. Arabella and the girls stopped laughing and looked at each other with wide eyes.

"What was that, Mama?" asked Laila.

Arabella scratched her cheek playfully. "Maybe Scratchy chasing after the soldiers?" she joked, but she knew darn well it was Pedro.

CHAPTER 27

A SHEEP AMONG WOLVES

R ED SLEEVES LED THE WAY through open plains and rocky terrain as he, Mitchell, and the warriors zigzagged throughout the territory, searching for signs of Quinn and his men. After several hours, Red Sleeves spotted a campfire and steered Whom'tu toward it. Upon reaching it, he jumped down and placed his hand into the ash, feeling for heat.

He shook his head. "Nothing," he said, standing to search for tracks. He spotted three sets of hoof prints, and he was sure the Coyote and his pack had been there. Climbing on his horse, he turned to Mitchell. "Where do you think they are heading?"

Mitchell removed his hat and wiped his brow. "I would say Silver City. Quinn could never stay away from a saloon too long."

Red Sleeves nodded and gave a kick to his mount. They raced across the terrain for another hour before reaching a small creek, and they stopped to let the horses drink. The chief searched up and down the creek, finding more tracks in the muddy ground.

After resting for a few minutes, they climbed onto their mounts and followed the tracks. After riding another hour, the tracks had much more definition, indicating the Coyote was much closer.

Five miles from Silver City, Red Sleeves brought his horse to a stop and allowed Mitchell to lead the way. He wanted to put a good hundred yards between Mitchell and himself, believing if the Coyote saw Mitchell riding alone, he would approach the lone man rather than run. Red Sleeves tied Mitchell's hands to the saddle horn in case he tried to escape.

"Whatcha thinking, Red Sleeves?" asked Mitchell as the chief tied his hands.

"Sending you ahead. See if you can draw them out," he explained.

Mitchell looked in the distance, then back at Red Sleeves. "You might as well shoot me now," he said, shaking his head. "If they see me, they are gonna come straight at me a shootin'."

"We will be close behind, watching for them." Red Sleeves then smirked. "Besides, Mitchell…that's exactly what we want them to do."

Mitchell shook his head again. "At least untie my hands so I can race back toward you if they come?" he said.

Red Sleeves grinned and hit the horse's rump, sending it in motion. "Keep riding straight toward Silver City," Red Sleeves said, watching Mitchell disappear down the hillside before emerging onto the open plain.

The chief climbed back up on his mount and glanced at Little Feather, who had an expression of concern etched across his face. "The white man won't try to escape. We still have his friend," said a calm Red Sleeves.

Blue Rock reached into a pouch near the horse's neck and pulled out a few pieces of meat. He handed one to Red Sleeves and Little Feather. They all ate in silence, watching Mitchell ride farther into the distance.

Several minutes later, Red Sleeves raised the field glasses he had taken from Mitchell, scanning the tree line and hills ahead. He pointed to the trees along the plain. "We will ride along the trees, keep cover."

He turned his horse and journeyed down the hill, and Blue Rock and Little Feather rode close behind him. Mitchell was just over a hundred yards away when Red Sleeves reached the tree line. He lifted the field glasses, keeping a close watch out for Coyote. After riding a safe distance behind Mitchell for around half an hour, Red Sleeves saw the man suddenly stop. Red Sleeves raised his hand, halting his warriors while placing the field glasses to his eyes, but he could not see down the hill in front of Mitchell. Red Sleeves removed the field glasses and gave several kicks to Whom'tu, increasing the horse's speed to a trot while riding along the trees. Red Sleeves kept a sharp eye on Mitchell, although he had no sign of why the other man stopped.

Blue Rock came up alongside Red Sleeves. "He must see something," said Blue Rock.

Red Sleeves nodded, steering his horse deeper into the trees, only seventy yards from Mitchell and his mount.

The early afternoon sun beat down on the Taos constable as he rode across the open plain. The sweat from his brim rolled down his forehead. He squinted, trying to keep it from running into his eyes.

His heart pounded, sounding like the horse's hooves beating against hard ground as he further distanced himself from the Apache warriors. He raised his shoulder as high as he could to wipe the sweat from his face. Meanwhile, he continued twisting and pulling the rope that secured his hands to the saddle horn, trying to break them free.

Observing the wide-open land around him, Mitchell felt like a lone sheep among wolves in the open plain without his pistol. Mitchell knew that's exactly what he was.

As the landscape rolled slightly down hill in front of him, three riders moved in the direction he headed. Unable to see the men through droplets of sweat hanging from his eyebrows, he brought his horse to a stop. He closed his eyelids tightly and blinked repeatedly, but the sweat pooling there and its burning sensation, made it difficult to keep his eyes open.

Just down the hill, the three horses were less than fifty yards away. They came to an abrupt stop, and the riders turned toward him.

After examining the riders, Mitchell caught a glimpse of a familiar face. It was none other than the outlaw, Quinn, alongside his comrades, Red and Eddie.

A few miles outside Silver City, Quinn rode along the ridge after a hard night of drinking and playing poker. He reached for his canteen, pouring water over his face to shake off the long night, and took a large drink. He was screwing the lid back on when one of his men called out to him.

"Over there," exclaimed Red.

Quinn looked in the direction he pointed, and his lip curled in a smiled. "Well, well, is that our old cowboy friend Mitchell riding alone out yonder?"

Eddie pulled out his field glasses, and after staring at the rider on the hill, he smiled as well. "Sure as hell is!" he said with a chuckle.

Red shook his head. "That man is one dumb son of a bitch."

Quinn raised his field glasses to his eyes and scanned around the lawman. "Yeah, but where's his compadres, Frank and Pete?"

The men looked for several moments.

"Looks like he's alone," said Eddie.

"It sure does," Quinn said quietly. He put his field glasses into his pouch. "Well, let's go say hello boys." He pulled out his pistol and checked the cylinder before snapping it back in place with the flip of his wrist. He started toward Mitchell, keeping his horse at a walk.

Mitchell's horse stilled as the man glared down the hill at them. He showed no sign of reaching for a pistol or fleeing.

Quinn's brow creased, and his eyes narrowed. Something was very odd in the man's behavior, he thought. The outlaw watched closely until a strange feeling overcame him, and he brought his own mount to a stop. Red and Quinn also stopped and turned.

"What is it, boss?" asked Eddie.

Quinn stared up the hill at Mitchell, only forty yards away. "I don't know. Where is his men? They might be setting us up for an ambush."

Red and Eddie looked around, looking for other riders.

"I don't know. He is awful wide open for that," said Red.

Eddie nodded. "Yeah, what kind of dullard would put himself in harm's way?"

Quinn tilted his head, staring at Mitchell and watching his movements closely. After a few moments, he raised his hand above his head and waved to Mitchell. Quinn waited for a response, but there was none. He raised his hand again, and there was still no response.

Quinn chuckled, then he laughed loudly.

"What is it?" asked Red.

Quinn gave another deep laugh. "This poor dumb bastard," he said, pointing at Mitchell. He angled his head toward the lawman while looking at Red and Eddie. "Go up there and shoot that fucker for me."

Red looked from the hill to Eddie before returning his gaze to Quinn. "What if it's an ambush?" he asked.

Quinn reached into his pocket and pulled out a cigar. "Well, just shoot him when you get close enough, then turn around, and ride back down here," he explained. "I'll stay back and cover our escape route just in case."

"Ok, boss," said Eddie, spurring his horse forward.

Red hesitated and looked back up the hill at Mitchell.

Quinn chuckled and kicked Red's horse. "Git up there, you goddamn chicken."

Red's startled horse lunged forward, and Red spurred his mount lightly. He caught up with Eddie, who rode slowly and cautiously toward Mitchell.

Once alongside Eddie, Red glanced left to right, looking for any movement.

"Can't see a damn thing over this hill," said Eddie, shaking his head. "No telling what's behind him."

Red stood in the horse's stirrups, attempting to see over the hill as he continued to look side to side. He sat back in the saddle and pulled his pistol. "If Frank and Pete are up there, I'm gonna blow their fuckin' heads off!" he said through his teeth.

Twenty-five yards from Mitchell, Eddie drew his pistol as well. The men rode a few yards closer and stopped.

Mitchell stared at the men, showing no sign of reaching for his pistol.

Red glanced around again, seeing no signs of other riders, before his eyes found Mitchell again. "Whatcha doing there, Mitchell?" he asked.

Mitchell leaned his head to the side and spat. "Heading to Silver City Red. What about you, boys?" he asked.

"Just leaving Silver City," Red replied.

Mitchell nodded. "How's the whores?" he asked.

Red grinned a little. "Sore," he replied.

Mitchell smiled. "Well, you boys gonna let me ride through?"

Red raised his brows and shrugged. "I don't see why not?"

"Where's Pete and Frank?" asked Eddie.

Mitchell angled his head behind him. "'Bout ten miles back that way. Frank's horse stepped in a dog hole, so I went on ahead to fetch another one in Silver City."

"Ride down here to us," Red instructed, creasing his brow.

"I'm fine where I am, Red," replied Mitchell.

Red held his pistol up, as did Eddie, and took aim at Mitchell. "Ride down here now, or die where you are!"

Mitchell nodded. "All right, boys, no need to get upset.

We're all friends here," said Mitchell, spurring his horse forward.

Eddie and Red kept their pistols drawn as their old riding buddy came to a stop about ten feet away.

"Hello, Eddie," said Mitchell. "Man, you look rough, boys. Bad night?"

Red noticed the constable's saddle and gun belt. "Where's your pistol?" he asked.

Mitchell shrugged. "Lost it a ways back."

Red shook his head. "How dumb you think we are you fuckin'—"

Eddie's eyes darted around when Red abruptly stopped speaking. "What is it, Red?"

Red pointed at Mitchell's saddle. "His fucking hands are tied to that saddle horn." He turned to Quinn and hollered, "No pistol! His hands are tied!"

"What?" yelled Quinn, riding closer.

Red turned back to Mitchell. "What's your story now, you bastard?" He moved his horse toward Mitchell and held his pistol close to the man's head. Pulling the hammer back, he asked, "Who did this to you?"

From a distance, Quinn yelled. "What's going on!"

Red looked at Eddie. "Tell Quinn what we got here."

Eddie placed his pistol in the holster and turned his horse. "His hands are tied to the saddle!" Eddie hollered.

A few seconds later, Quinn yelled back. "Shoot 'im, and get the fuck out of—"

Quinn's words were cut short by the sound of hooves against the ground behind Mitchell on the other side of the hill. Red looked in the direction of the sound, and Mitchell spurred his horse, turning to go back up the hill.

"Bastard!" yelled Red. He fired three shots, striking Mitchell's horse each time.

The animal reared up, and Mitchell slid off the saddle. With his hands still secured to the horn, the lawman bounced about the horse as it bucked and neighed. Then it tumbled to the ground, taking Mitchell along with it.

Red noticed Eddie's fear-filled eyes. "Yah!" he shouted. He smacked the reins and spurred the horse while turning toward Quinn, who watched in the distance.

Eddie followed Red's lead, spurring his horse and glancing back toward the top of the hill.

The men rode less than twenty feet before they heard the sounds of hooves and war cries directly behind them. An Indian jumped from his horse, yanking Red off his mount. The men tumbled across the ground, and the Apache delivered several quick blows to his head.

From the ground, Red looked at Eddie through blurry eyes. The other man had toppled from his mount, and two other Indians punched him. Red saw Quinn in the distance, hightailing it out of there.

Fuckin' chickenshit, he thought.

He felt another blow to his side followed by one to the head, and all went dark and quiet.

After beating the man unconscious, Red Sleeves stood and glanced in the distance toward the fleeing Coyote. Running full speed at Whom'tu, the chief jumped up over the horse's rump and landed on its back. He grabbed the rein and kicked, and Whom'tu moved at full speed. The animal's hooves pounded the arid ground, sending dirt and dust in all directions.

The Coyote was almost a hundred yards ahead of Red Sleeves, but within minutes, Whom'tu had cut that distance in half. The Coyote turned his head several times as Red Sleeves continued gaining ground. The man steered his horse into the trees and disappeared from the chief's view. Red Sleeves soared into the woods without slowing. Riding through heavy brush, he maneuvered his mount around the trees and caught a glimpse of the Coyote, less than thirty yards ahead of him.

The Coyote looked back, and his horse collided with a tree, throwing the man from his mount.

Red Sleeves slowed his mount as the Coyote disappeared into the brush. Stopping Whom'tu, the chief jumped off the horse, grabbed his rifle, and took cover by a nearby tree.

The Coyote's horse was on its side, moaning and snorting, unable to get to its feet. Red Sleeves peered around the pine tree as he tried to spot the man. He raised his rifle, taking aim at the Coyote's suffering horse, and fired a round into the animal. It stopped moaning and lay motionless.

Bang! Another shot rang out from the brush, sending bark flying from the tree.

"Jackass!" shouted the Coyote. "You shot my horse!"

Red Sleeves sat quietly as he looked for the man's position.

"What's a matter, Red Sleeves?" grunted the man. "You too afraid to fight?"

Red Sleeves looked around the tree again. As he watched smoke from the Coyote's gun rise from the brush, he knew where the other man was located. "Afraid of a toothless coyote who attacks old men and women?" Red Sleeves replied.

Quinn fired several more shots at the tree, sending more bark flying as Red Sleeves took cover. "Don't worry, Red

Sleeves. I have plenty of bullets and two pistols, so we will be here a while."

Red Sleeves got to his knees, hiding under the tall brush while looking for the Coyote through it.

"You nasty bastards murdered my family over twenty years ago. Did you know that?" asked the Coyote.

Red Sleeves ducked behind the tree. "I wasn't there, or I would have killed you too," replied Red Sleeves.

"You wouldn't have killed shit! I got my revenge, though, didn't I, Chief?" said the Coyote with a chuckle. "How'd you like your squaw hanging from that tree?" he asked, still snickering. "She was pretty on the outside, but her insides were awful."

Red Sleeves clenched his fist.

After a few moments of silence, the Coyote said, "Where did you go, Red Dick?" His words were followed by another chuckle before a grunt, signaling the pain of laughing.

"You should save your strength, Coyote Boy. You'll need it," replied Red Sleeves.

The Coyote then fired two more rounds into the tree. "My name is Quinn, or the Raven, dumbass. Don't know where this Coyote shit is coming from," he added.

Red Sleeves raised his rifle. "You remind me more of a coyote bitch, especially after running like you did back there, deserting your own men." The chief fired into the brush toward the area he thought Quinn hid. He then heard brush rustling.

"Damn it to hell," moaned Quinn.

Red Sleeves picked up a large rock and threw it to his right about fifteen feet. When Quinn rose to fire at the source of the sound, Red Sleeves swiftly moved around the other side of the tree and ran straight toward Quinn.

The startled outlaw raised his pistol just as Red Sleeves threw his rifle at him. The chief yelled a war cry and leaped toward the man. Quinn managed to get one shot off. It caught Red Sleeves left hand, sending his pinky finger backward to hang loosely from his hand.

Grabbing the man's pistol, Red Sleeves tossed it away. He grabbed Quinn's shirt and delivered blow after blow to the man's face. The blood from Quinn's nose combined with the blood pouring from the chief's hand covered the outlaw's face as Red Sleeves continued delivering punches, feeling no pain from his finger.

Quinn stopped fighting back and lay still, moaning.

Red Sleeves stood and grabbed his loosely hanging pinky. Pulling it off his hand, he tossed it in the brush. He grabbed his knife, knelt to cut Quinn's shirt, and wrapped his hand with it.

"Coyote bitch," Red Sleeves mumbled to himself, spitting on the man.

The chief grabbed Quinn's arm and pulled him to a nearby tree. He tied him to it, using rope fastened to the saddle of the outlaw's dead horse.

A short time later, Red Sleeves heard noises behind him and turned. A quick glance through the trees showed his warriors, Mitchell, and what was left of the Coyote's pack with their hands tied behind them. Before walking toward the men, he stopped beside his horse and rubbed his neck.

"You did well, my friend," said the chief, placing his hands to the horse's cheeks and his forehead against its muzzle.

Little Feather and Blue Rock led the captured men on their horses to a stop ten feet from Red Sleeves. Noticing the blood on Red Sleeves arms, the two Indians yelped, raising their rifles simultaneously and celebrating the great victory.

Red Sleeves walked between them, placing his arms out on each side to drag his hands along their mounts. He moved toward Mitchell, who had walked since his horse had been shot. The chief grabbed a canteen from one of the outlaw's horses and tossed it to him.

Mitchell opened it, taking several large gulps. "Gracias," he said, lowering it from his mouth.

The chief's eyes fixed on the man for several moments before he nodded. "It's hard to find a white man who speaks the truth," he said. "It's sometimes hard to know your true friends and true enemies when so many hide behind their own lies, afraid to be honest, and too weak to be their true self."

The chief turned, pulling one of the outlaws from his horse and hurling him to the ground. The man moaned as his face pressed against the dirt. Red Sleeves led the man's horse to Mitchell.

"I said you had two roads, Mitchell, and you chose well." Red Sleeves handed the horse's reins to Mitchell.

The white man nodded. "I believe we all have two roads, Red Sleeves," said Mitchell, wiping his brow before placing his hat on his head. "And as fun as this has been, I sure hope our roads never cross again." Mitchell grinned, climbing onto his new horse.

Red Sleeves returned his grin before walking to one of his warrior's horses and grabbing a pistol. He then walked back to Mitchell, handing him his Colt Walker.

Mitchell smiled at having the pistol in his grasp again, and he put it in the holster.

"You will find your friend at Dominga's ranch," said Red Sleeves. He turned toward his warriors.

"What about those men?" asked Mitchell. "Let me bring

them to justice. They will hang for what they have done. I will see to it personally."

Red Sleeves paused. "A quick death by a white man's rope could be considered justice to some, but it is not true justice. Since there can be no true justice for lives the Coyote has taken, the only true justice left is for those who are living." The chief then looked at the sky as a raven flew overhead. "It can only be true justice for the living if the justice is delivered slow and painfully."

Mitchell looked at the chief before nodding.

As the constable turned his horse, Red Sleeves called to him. "Ben Mitchell, if you see that squinty-eyed sheriff in Santa Fe, tell him I'm coming for him, and I will gut him like the pig he is." He then turned back toward his warriors.

Mitchell smirked. "I'll tell him, Chief," he said, giving the horse a light kick.

Once Red Sleeves reached his warriors, he turned back just in time to see Mitchell disappear into the woods and out of sight.

Tied to a tree, Quinn's eyes were wide open as Red Sleeves moved closer to him. Once he was close enough, Quinn spat at the chief.

Red Sleeves instructed his warriors to bring the other men closer. Blue Rock dragged the one already on the ground, and Little Feather yanked the other from the saddle, dragging him closer.

The two men had their hands tied behind their backs, on their knees.

"Gather up some sticks and branches and place them

around the tree," instructed Red Sleeves, going through the saddlebags on the horses until he located a tinderbox. Gathering handfuls of dry grass along the ground, the chief approached Quinn.

"Whatcha doing?" stuttered Quinn.

Little Feather and Blue Rock returned, placing the sticks around the base of the tree where Quinn was tied.

"No…no…wait," said Quinn as he tried to kick away the warriors and the sticks.

Red Sleeves motioned to Quinn's feet, and Little Feather pulled them behind the tree, bringing the man to his knees. Little Feather secured the man's feet together with leather straps, then he tied another one around his neck, drawing Quinn's head firmly against the bark.

Quinn struggled and shouted at the warriors before begging for his life. The other two men in front of Quinn stared, their eyes wide open as horror filled their faces.

Blue Rock returned with more sticks and branches, and the stack reached midway across the outlaw's chest.

Red Sleeves stood before Quinn and gazed at him. "This should have been your fate many years ago." He packed the dry grass into the sticks.

Quinn struggled to get free before he finally gave up. "Fuck you, Red Sleeves," said Quinn. "I killed many of your people, and my death will never bring them back."

"My people are with the spirts and still live," said Red Sleeves, kneeling by the pile of branches and dry grass surrounding the man. "Once you are dead, you will be gone forever and never live again." He pulled the flint and striker from the tinderbox.

Quinn struggled again, and the strap wore through his

skin, causing blood to run down his neck. Tears streamed from the man's eyes, and he stopped resisting to look at Red Sleeves.

The Apache chief struck the flint several times, and the dry grass began to burn. He stepped back, watching as the outlaw attempted to twist away from the rising flame.

"There will be no mercy for you, Red Sleeves! You and your entire tribe will die for your crimes!" he shouted.

"You first," replied the chief, pointing to the straps. "If you hold still, they may burn and set you free."

Fire climbed around the man, and Quinn shouted as flames licked his skin. His pants and ragged shirt burned, the flame inching closer to his face. Burning sticks and branches snapped between the outlaw's yelps and groans. Moments later, flames rose above the man's head. The outlaw gave a final scream before his chin fell to his chest and he stilled.

Smoke rose through the trees and into the blue sky. Red Sleeves turned his head up, watching it disappear into the distance. There was no sign of the raven. He turned to the two men, tied and on their knees.

Red-faced and eyes watering, they begged for their lives.

Red Sleeves nodded to Little Feather and Blue Rock, and the two warriors moved behind the men and pulled their knives. "Today, we avenge my people and the Mexican woman," he said. He looked to the sky again, and a smile appeared on his face. "This is a good day for the Apache and a good day for the mothers and fathers, brothers and sisters of the lives you stole." The chief knelt in front of the men, glancing into each of their eyes, and smirked. "I will hang your scalps on a lodge pole in our camp so we can celebrate this day for many moons."

Little Feather and Blue Rock grabbed the men's hair simultaneously, pulling it back while running their blades across the men's foreheads. A cry rang from them as blood poured down their faces. After pulling the scalps from their heads, the warriors raised them into the sky and danced around, yelping to celebrate the victory.

A few moments later, Blue Rock and Little Feather returned to the men and cut their throats. Blood poured down their necks and through their shirts before spilling onto the ground.

Red Sleeves rose to his feet, tightening the makeshift bandage on his hand. He looked back at the Coyote. Flames continued to burn, leaving a charcoaled corpse—mouth and eyes wide open—visible behind the flames.

The chief mounted Whom'tu, and Little Feather and Blue Rock followed his lead. Having cleared the land of the Coyote and his pack, the Apache warriors and their chief steered their mounts through the woods and onto the open plain. Riding in silence, they finally experienced the contentment of true justice.

After an hour of riding, Red Sleeves stopped his horse and climbed down. He stood on the edge of a high rocky cliff, gazing in the far distance as dust rose into the sky. He placed Mitchell's field glasses to his eyes, watching as several hundred horses and many wagons moved southeast into the Apache territory.

Studying the men closer, he knew they were American soldiers. As he continued watching, Little Feather and Blue Rock climbed down from their mounts and stood beside him.

"American soldiers," said Red Sleeves, removing the field glasses from his eyes and handing them to Blue Rock.

The three men watched until they were sure the soldiers were not heading toward their tribe. Red Sleeves clenched his jaw. He stood motionless, watching the Americans ride into the distance before vanishing from the trails.

Red Sleeves turned to his warriors. "Let's follow the sun," he said, walking back to his horse.

Little Feather and Blue Rock followed their chief to the horses.

"We will ride to the burial grounds, then to the chief of the Western Apache," said Red Sleeves, pulling himself onto his mount. "We will make camp at Dominga's and tell her the Coyote is no more."

Little Feather and Blue Rock climbed their horses, and the three rode down the steep rocky cliff to smoother ground, bringing their horses to a gallop. Before the sun's last bit of rays left the plains, they were within a mile of the woman's ranch.

CHAPTER 28

THERE WILL BE NO PEACE

After tucking the girls into bed, Arabella walked into the kitchen to get a drink of water. As she lifted her cup, Scratchy barked from the porch. Setting the cup down, she walked to the window and looked out. The sun was just setting, and although the sky became darker by the minute, she could make out three riders approaching the house.

A lantern came out of the bunkhouse, signaling the men had been alerted. She opened the door and stepped onto the porch as Luis crossed the yard, Jose and Juan close behind. Arabella focused on the approaching riders until she could recognize them, smiling at the sight of Red Sleeves, Little Feather, and Blue Rock.

The chief raised his hand in front of him. He brought his horse to a stop and climbed down. "Hello, Dominga," said the chief as Blue Rock and Little Feather raised their hands.

"Hello, Chief," she replied, looking at the warriors. "Hello, Blue Rock and Little Feather,"

The chief walked closer to her, and Juan drew nearer, stopping several feet from the chief.

Red Sleeves nodded to the man. "We are heading west, like to make camp here tonight," he said.

"Of course," she replied before looking at Juan. "Can you help with the horses?"

Juan tipped his hat to Arabella, then stepped closer to the warriors.

Red Sleeves looked toward Little Feather and Blue Rock, then motioned toward the barn.

Little Feather jumped down from his horse, handing the reins to the outlaw's horse to Juan before leading his own mount toward the barn. Blue Rock climbed down from his mount and reached for the rein of Whom'tu, then led the two horses, following close behind Little Feather.

Once they disappeared inside the barn, Arabella invited the chief on the porch for water and mutton, and he quickly accepted.

Arabella smiled at the chief. "Be right back," she said, opening the door to go inside.

As Red Sleeves sat on the porch, Jose and Luis crossed the yard and stood on the steps.

"What brings you out this way, Red Sleeves?" he asked.

Red Sleeves glanced at the man. "Santa Rita's our sacred ground," he replied.

Luis nodded. "Be careful. There are a lot of American soldiers out this way," he stated.

Red Sleeves glared at Luis.

The ranch hand continued. "Had fifty of them come through here earlier today."

"We saw the American soldiers on the way here," said Red Sleeves.

Luis scratched his cheek. "Which way were you coming from?"

"Silver City," Red Sleeves replied.

Jose shook his head. "Must be more than one group of them, because the ones that came through here headed southwest down the Camino Real," he explained.

Luis nodded in agreement.

The chief sat quietly as he thought about what the men had told him, and he realized there must be thousands of American troops moving through the territory. "Where do you think they are heading?" he asked.

Jose scratched the back of his neck. "Mexico City would be my guess. That's where the Mexican soldiers are." He then looked around the yard and raised his hands. "Sure ain't none around here," he added.

Red sleeves stayed tight lipped.

The front door opened, and Arabella came out, carrying two cups of water and a plate of mutton and bread. She sat the plate and a cup on a table by the chief.

"Here you go, Chief," she said before sitting and taking a drink from her own cup.

"The chief said he ran into troops coming from Silver City," said Luis.

Arabella lowered the cup from her mouth and held it in her lap. "We had troops come by here earlier," she said, glancing at the chief.

"Yeah, we told him," said Jose.

Red Sleeves took a bite of mutton and looked around at the group. "Mitchell. Did he tell you we found the men that attacked you?" he asked.

Brows raised, Arabella glanced at Luis and Jose before turning back to Red Sleeves. "We haven't seen Mitchell. Why would he be here? Did you free him?" she asked.

Red Sleeves nodded, and Arabella smiled widely, her white teeth reflecting off the light of the lantern.

Red Sleeves narrowed his eyes. "Mitchell should have been here by now," explained the chief.

"Maybe he ran into the soldiers and was held up?" she replied.

Red Sleeves sat thinking for a few moments and looked at Arabella. "Mitchell, Blue Rock, Little Feather, and I set out after Quinn the Coyote this morning." Red Sleeves looked at her and gave a slight grin. "The Coyote and his pack are dead."

A smile returned to her face. "You are so brave, Chief Red Sleeves. Thank you for going after those men and freeing Mitchell." Her eyes teared up just before noticing the bandage on his hand. "How's your hand?" she asked, standing to approach Red Sleeves. "Let me have a look."

She reached out for his hand, and Red Sleeves extended his arm. Arabella gently unwrapped the makeshift bandage. She gasped when she saw the pinky completely gone.

"Did Quinn do this?" she asked.

Red Sleeves nodded. "He got off one lucky shot."

"Please come inside so I can clean the wound," Arabella said.

Red Sleeves grabbed another piece of mutton then stood from his chair. The two walked into the house, and Red Sleeves had to duck when he entered. Arabella led him to the kitchen and grabbed an oil lamp. She placed it on the counter and cleaned the wound. Red Sleeves watched as she applied a little yarrow plant to the wound.

"This needs to be stitched," she explained, reaching into a cabinet to grab a needle and some thread.

Red Sleeves sat still while she worked on his hand. "Where is the man from the bushes Little Feather and Blue Rock brought here?" asked the chief.

"Frank? He is in the bunkhouse," replied Arabella, tilting her head to the side and raising her brows. "I guess he would be none too happy to see you here."

Red Sleeves grinned. "White men…never happy to see me," he replied.

Arabella smiled. Then Red Sleeves clenched his jaw when she ran the needle through the loose-hanging skin, drawing it closed. Arabella stitched the wound and asked many questions about Red Sleeve's run in with Quinn.

Red Sleeves kept the story brief, saying simply that the man was a coward and died the way he deserved.

A few minutes later, Arabella finished stitching and placed yarrow plant on the wound, wrapping it with a clean rag and tying it tightly. "There, that should heal fine," she said.

Red Sleeves flexed his injured fist.

"Careful. You don't want to rip the stitches," said Arabella, placing the needle and thread back into the cabinet.

They returned to the porch with Luis and Jose, where Pedro had joined them. Red Sleeves returned to his seat and grabbed another piece of mutton. Leaning against a post, Pedro didn't say a word.

Arabella gazed at him. "Aren't you going to say hello to our guest?" she said, squinting her eyes while placing the oil lamp on a nearby table.

Pedro looked at Red Sleeves. "Hello, Chief."

Red Sleeves nodded as he chewed on the mutton.

An oil lantern in the distance caught Red Sleeves's eye as Little Feather, Juan, and Blue Rock left the barn and crossed the yard to join them.

Arabella waved at Blue Rock and Little Feather as she stood. "Sit here. I'll go get you some food and water," she said, opening the door to the house.

"Thank you, Dominga," said Little Feather.

She disappeared inside, Pedro on her heels.

Luis stretched his arms above his head. "Well, I am going to turn in," he said, looking at Red Sleeves. "There's plenty blankets in the barn. Help yourself to them."

Red Sleeves nodded as Luis walked away.

"I'm gonna turn in too. Good night," said Jose.

"Good night," replied Juan.

Moments later, the front door opened, and Pedro walked out. He glanced at Juan through squinted eyes before continuing on, shaking his head. He stalked across the yard toward the bunkhouse, fading into the distance.

Arabella emerged from the house with another plate of mutton and two cups of water. She set the food on the table and handed a cup to Little Feather and Blue Rock. The men lifted the cup for a drink, then reached for the mutton.

Juan looked at Arabella. "You doing all right?" he asked, his brow creasing.

"Fine," she replied, giving a slight smile.

Juan nodded. "I'm sleeping in the barn, but there's plenty room for all of us," he said, looking at Red Sleeves and the warriors. "Good night." He walked off the porch and toward the barn.

"Good night, Juan," replied Arabella.

She sat next to Red Sleeves, watching Juan disappear into the darkness.

Red Sleeves looked at Juan before turning back to Arabella. "Your friend Pedro does not like that man," he said.

Arabella bit down on her lip and shook her head, gazing toward the barn. "No, he sure doesn't," she replied. "He told me he is leaving in the morning, and I didn't argue with him. I just looked at him and said…just go."

"A man with love for a woman who doesn't want him is a lonely man, then blames that loneliness on the woman," stated Red Sleeves.

Arabella sat quietly for a few moments. Then she nodded. "I have known Pedro for more years than I can remember, and I truly care for him as a friend," she said, looking at Red Sleeves. "Domingo, never cared for him, and I always felt that was just him protecting me, but now, I don't know. Maybe there was more to it?"

Red Sleeves held up his hand to Little Feather, and the warrior tossed him another piece of mutton.

"There is plenty more inside," said Arabella, standing.

Red Sleeves raised his hand, motioning for her to sit. "We had plenty, Dominga," he said with a nod.

Arabella sat back down as Red Sleeves gazed across the yard. He lifted his cup for a drink. "Tomorrow, we will be gone before the sun rises."

"Where are you heading?" asked Arabella.

"To the chief of the Western Apache," replied Red Sleeves.

"The white soldiers move about our land, destroying all things in their path. We have to stop them."

Arabella shook her head. "There are so many soldiers now," she replied. "Isn't there any way of peace?"

Red Sleeves shook his head. "Until we have our lands, there will be no peace. Not for me. Not for the Apache."

Arabella and Red Sleeves sat quietly for several moments, and Red Sleeves set his eyes on the starry night.

"The lights in the sky can guide you to where you want to go, but never tell you which way you should go," said Red Sleeves, turning his head toward Arabella. "It has been good for me and my people to know you. It has been good to have you as friend when there are so few left."

Arabella smiled. "I will always be a friend of yours and the Apache," she replied. "Thank you for going after the outlaws. They were some really bad men, and I am forever grateful for your bravery."

Red Sleeves nodded, then rose to his feet. "You have done well, Dominga," he said, staring into the darkness toward the barn. "You are strong in heart and mind." He turned toward her. "Whatever path the sun god and great mother may lead you, the path among the Apache will always be there." He motioned to Little Feather and Blue Rock, and the warriors rose from their seat and walked toward their chief.

Arabella smiled at the man. "This was a great day, my chief," she said. Then she looked at the warriors. "I look forward to us meeting again."

The warriors each raised a hand and smiled. The chief grinned. Then he squeezed his fists in front of his chest before turning and walking across the yard toward the barn.

As Arabella watched the light of the oil lantern fade in the distance, she noticed Scratchy peeking his head out from under one of the chairs on the porch.

She smiled and shook her head. "C'mon, you can sleep inside, you big chicken."

She moved to the door and held it open, and Scratchy ran inside. Arabella then picked up the plates and cups, carrying them inside before shutting the door behind her.

Early the next morning, Arabella poured a cup of coffee and stepped onto the porch. She looked at the fences and saw many horses gone, signaling the departure of Red Sleeves, Little Feather, and Blue Rock. She looked farther in the distance and noticed a single rider heading west. After a few moments of focusing, she could distinguish Pedro heading back to Tucson, as he'd said he would the night before.

The sound of an opening door caught her attention as Juan stumbled out, smacking his hat against his leg, apparently still exhausted even after a night of sleep.

"What happened to you?" she asked smiling.

Juan jerked his head toward Arabella, as if he hadn't noticed her standing there. "Good morning, Arabella," he said with a smile and wave. "My goodness, that was a long night. Those Apache stay up way too late and get up way too early," he said walking from the barn toward the house.

Arabella chuckled. "Come inside. I have coffee ready." She turned and walked back into the house.

Scratchy sat by the door, anxiously waiting for it to be opened.

Arabella patted him on the head. "Good morning, Scratchy," she said, then held the door as he raced inside.

Shortly after Juan came inside, Luis and Jose entered. They sat at the table, talking for a few minutes about the woolies and the day's work ahead.

"Where did Pedro head off to?" asked Jose.

Arabella tilted her head and raised her eyebrows. "Back to Tucson," she said.

Luis nodded. "I expected he would. He's been acting strange since taking that hit on the head." He reached for the coffee and filled his cup.

Juan looked at Arabella, and his eyes squinted. "I don't think he much cared for me." Juan bit his lip and then shrugged his shoulders.

Arabella returned to the kitchen, grabbing a bowl of beans and plates. "I don't think he cared much for anyone lately," she said, placing them on the table.

The girls came into the kitchen, and Arabella embraced them.

"Who didn't care, Mama?" asked Camille.

"Nothing, honey, we were just talking," said Arabella, preparing a plate for them.

Scratchy followed Arabella around the kitchen, waiting for a morsel of food to hit the floor. Arabella grabbed a small chunk of bread, luring Scratchy toward the door, and tossed it outside. The multicolored mutt took off after it, and she quickly closed the door behind the animal.

After everyone had a plate, they gathered around the

table. Laila sat on Arabella's lap as they ate in silence for several minutes.

Arabella looked over at Luis and Jose. "How's Frank feeling this morning?" she asked.

Jose scraped some beans onto his fork. "I believe fine. He was still sleeping when we left the bunkhouse," he replied.

Arabella focused on Camille. "When you are finished, I want you to run a plate of food and coffee out to him," she said.

Camille nodded. "Yes, Mama."

A few moments later, Scratchy barked, and Arabella moved Laila from her lap.

"What now?" she asked, walking to the window and glancing outside.

She noticed a man riding their way and instantly recognized the man's large hat. "It's Mitchell!" she said before stepping onto the porch.

Mitchell raised his hand above his head. "Hello, Arabella!" he said in his low rumbling voice.

Arabella waved back, then looked over at the bunkhouse as the door swung open.

Frank emerged, fidgeting with his boots as he walked across the yard toward Mitchell. Upon seeing his friend, Mitchell smiled widely and climbed down, and the two men shook hands.

Mitchell placed his free hand on Frank's shoulder. "How you doing, ole boy?" he asked.

"Better," replied Frank. "But I am damn glad to see you well!"

"Same here," replied Mitchell, and the two men laughed.

Arabella walked toward Mitchell and embraced him. "I

have been so worried about you," she said as Mitchell's hat fell to the ground.

Arabella reached down and grabbed his hat, placing it on her head. "Come inside, you two. I have fresh coffee and breakfast ready," she explained, pulling off the hat and tossing it to Mitchell.

"That sounds rightly fantastic," said Mitchell, stepping toward the porch.

Once inside, they all cheerfully conversed around the table for almost an hour. Mitchell told them some of the story of Quinn and his gang being caught outside Silver City, but he left most of the details out since the girls were still at the table. He explained to them that he was so exhausted after being tied to a tree for days and then riding in search of Quinn, he'd decided to stay in Silver City for a night.

"I never slept so long in all my years," he said with a smile.

Arabella told him Red Sleeves had come by and had left sometime early that morning.

Frank shook his head. "I would have killed him while he slept had I known that," he said.

Arabella turned to the man. "There will be no talk like that at the table, Frank."

Frank looked around the room as his fork hovered a few inches from his mouth. "Sorry, Arabella, I didn't mean no disrespect."

Luis and Jose stood from the table.

"We're going to head out to the flock. Back in a while," Jose said.

As they reached for their hats and headed for the door, Luis asked, "You gonna be around for a bit, Mitchell?"

Mitchell looked over at Frank, then to Luis. "No, we'll be heading out fairly soon, get back up to Santa Fe," he replied.

Luis reached out a hand, and Mitchell quickly accepted it.

"Safe travels then," said Luis.

"Much appreciated," replied Mitchell.

Jose shook Mitchell's hand, then nodded toward Frank. "Take care now," he said before following Luis outside.

Arabella glanced from Mitchell to Frank. "I will pack you boys up some food for your journey home."

Mitchell smiled at her. "We'd appreciate that, Arabella," he replied.

"I'll saddle your horse up and fill the canteens," Juan said, standing from the table.

"Thanks, Juan, that's rightly kind of you," Frank replied, as Juan walked out and toward the barn.

Arabella lifted several plates from the table. "Run along, girls. I want to visit with Mitchell before he leaves," she said.

The girls ran outside to catch up with Juan, excited to see the horses. Mitchell and Frank continued eating, and Arabella sat next to them after clearing the table.

"What happened to you after I left?" she asked, shaking her head. "I begged Red Sleeves to set you free, but a large part of me feared he wouldn't."

Mitchell took another drink of coffee and placed the cup back on the table. "Well, I must admit I was surprised he let me go to," he replied. "After he told me Frank was alive, I figured I would do whatever he said just to get out of there."

"What happened to Quinn? How did he die?" she asked.

Mitchell cocked his head sideways and sucked his teeth. "Well, I wasn't there when he killed them, but I rode back by there the next morning." He shook his head. "It wasn't pretty, Arabella." He reached into his pocket for his pipe.

Frank looked at Arabella. "These Apache friends of yours are dangerous, Arabella," he stated.

She glanced at Frank, then turned to Mitchell, not deterred by Frank's opinion. Mitchell packed his pipe, striking a match and raising it to the bowl before drawing in several puffs. "He's right, Arabella. They are some very dangerous people to be in such close quarters with."

Arabella tilted her head. "Well, it seems to me there are many dangerous men, and not all are Apache."

Mitchell nodded. "That's for sure," he said, placing the pipe back in his mouth.

"The Apache just want to keep their land and way of life," she said, pulling up her hair and wrapping it up in a bun. "I think we all want that, don't we, Mitchell?"

Mitchell nodded. "Yeah, I suppose we do," he replied.

Arabella bit on her lip, wanting to ask something, but then she changed her mind.

"Something on your mind?" said Mitchell, noticing her expression.

Arabella took a deep breath. "You're not going to come back down here again looking to arrest Red Sleeves, are you?" she asked.

Mitchell grinned, then shook his head. "No, not me. But plenty others will," he replied.

Arabella regarded both men. "Surely, you could talk to the governors and the sheriff. Tell them Red Sleeves let you go. That has to count for something?" she pleaded.

Frank jumped in. "He didn't let me or Pete go."

Mitchell lifted his hand from the table at his friend before addressing Arabella. "No one is going to listen, Arabella. It's way past that now."

Arabella sat back in her chair staring at the floor.

Mitchell reached toward her, briefly placing his hand on her shoulder. "I just want you to be safe. Chief Red Sleeves can take care of himself." He stood and put on his hat before refocusing on Arabella. "Before we head out, I'd like to go spend some time where Pete is buried if you don't mind?" he asked.

Arabella looked up and slightly smiled. "Of course. He is buried next to my son." She slipped her shoes on, and the three walked to the porch.

Juan had Frank and Mitchell's horses tied at the hitch post.

The trio strolled to the resting spot of Pete and Marcello, close to a small grouping of pine trees. Juan followed along, reaching for Arabella's hand as they walked. She accepted.

CHAPTER 29
GENERAL INTERMISSION

GENERAL JOHNSON'S DIVISION MOVED SOUTHEAST along the Camino Real, two days from Mexico City. General West and his division had left Santa Fe and followed along the Rio Grande River. West's division was at least a day's ride ahead of Johnson. The separation was planned to ensure they did not bottleneck the troops and slow their advance.

Johnson rode toward the front, along the road. Some men scouted miles ahead of them, making sure there were no Mexican soldiers or rebels lying in wait. They passed many Mexican civilians in the towns, who stared vacantly at the American soldiers.

The dusty road and heat was taking its toll on the troops as they marched. Johnson did his best to give the men an adequate number of breaks, but he also knew the importance of reaching Mexico City as soon as possible. General Scott waited for reinforcements in the small town of Pachuca, located just north of Mexico City. After an unsuccessful two attempts to take the city, General Scott had been ordered by the War Department to wait for the arrival of West and Johnson before commencing another attack.

The plan was to hit the city from the north and the west simultaneously, spreading the Mexican defenses along two fronts. With the fall of the Mexican capital and the capture of the Mexican president, Antonio Santa Anna, the war would finally be over.

Johnson relished the idea of returning to the Oregon Territory after the war. He would first journey home to Virginia and see his wife and children for a couple months before his redeployment to the west coast. He hardly cared where his next deployment was, as long as it was a cooler climate than where he currently marched.

Johnson had just lit a cigar, and he was speaking to recently promoted Sergeant Major Warden—who rode alongside him—when they noticed a horse hastily approaching. The general pulled his field glasses and recognized one of General West's men. Placing the glasses back in their pouch, he placed the cigar back into his mouth.

"One of West's soldiers," he stated as the sergeant major focused on the rider in the distance.

Within a few minutes, the soldier was less than thirty feet from Johnson. The rider brought his horse to a stop then turned, waiting for Johnson to ride closer.

As they approached, the soldier rode alongside the general and saluted him. "General, sir, I have a letter here from General West," he said, extending the envelope to Johnson.

The general placed his cigar in his mouth to break the seal, then opened it.

The letter informed Johnson that in a surprise move, the Mexican forces had launched a counterattack against General Scott in Pachuca. It read that Johnson must move quickly and attack Mexico City from the west immediately upon arrival. General West further explained that his division would move northeast to reinforce Scott's defensives before heading south to lay siege on the capital.

Johnson handed the letter to his sergeant and removed his cigar from his mouth. "Corporal Rhoades," he said.

"Yes, sir," the corporal replied.

"Ride back to the supply wagons. We will be moving swiftly and well into the night before the next break. It's a forced march, Corporal."

Rhoades saluted his general, spurred his horse, and headed toward the rear of the line.

"I will inform the men and their commanders," said Warden, saluting the general before turning his horse.

Johnson placed the letter in his pocket and looked toward the messenger, "Thank you, Corporal. Godspeed."

"Godspeed, sir" the corporal said, saluting before making a quick pace down the road.

His horse's hooves kicked up a line of dust, sending it high into the air, as the general watched him disappear in the distance.

Mexico City came into view the next afternoon, and Johnson reached for his field glasses. He wasted no time ordering the artillery to line along a high ridge, which stood five hundred yards from the western side of the city.

His exhausted soldiers moved to obey his orders. On his

command, one company after another formed shoulder-to-shoulder lines for the upcoming attack. Dragoons reconned the area to look for any Mexican soldiers, and within an hour, they returned after having seen no signs of the enemy. Johnson figured they were all within the city walls or possibly north, fighting Scott and West.

A few hours of daylight remained when Johnson gave the command to fire. Artillery fire thundered through the hills and canyons, and smoke rose into the sky. The cannonballs flew high into the distance and disappeared. Loud crashing and explosions followed seconds later as Johnson ordered the men to reload.

Johnson looked through his field glasses, seeing no sign of troops. Turning to his artillery commander, he shouted, "Fire!"

Boom! Another round of cannonballs pierced the clouds to land directly on the capital. Raising his field glasses, Johnson saw around fifteen riders moving the opposite way of his army.

"Should we pursue them, sir?" asked the dragoon commander.

Johnson shook his head. "They're running, let them go."

The general ordered the artillery to fire once again. Cannons rang out, filling the hillside with smoke and collapsing several small buildings in the middle of town.

"On the double, men," he shouted, ordering his men to march.

Two brigades moved toward the town. His line of men reached almost a quarter mile deep and eighty feet wide. The narrow column of men approached the causeway, leading to the walls of the city. They found no counterattack from the enemy, no returning fire of cannons, and Johnson was convinced the battle would be inside the walls with the enemy using the buildings as cover.

He ordered his dragoons to keep watch for enemy cavalry, knowing their tightly formed brigades left the soldiers susceptible to a cavalry attack. After thirty minutes, the first group of soldiers filed inside the walls of the city using ladders and pickaxes to infiltrate the Mexican capital.

Johnson spurred his horse down the hillside and up a ridge to get a better view, hearing the crackle of gunfire from the city. At first, there were just a few shots, but it was followed by an all-out eruption.

Smoke from rifles rose above the town, making it difficult to see. Johnson surveyed the area and watched for the enemy. Over a hill in the north, he spotted the Mexican cavalry flooding back toward the city. Johnson ordered the dragoons to meet the enemy in the open plain before they could reach the Mexican capital.

The size of Mexican cavalry versus that of his own were closely matched, around two thousand each. The hooves of his dragoons thundered against the ground as a cloud of dust covered the hillside. Within minutes, the two armies collided, throwing men and horses in all directions. Almost half of the Mexican force retreated in the other direction, leaving the other half greatly outnumbered.

The battle of the cavalries continued for less than twenty minutes, until the last of the Mexican soldiers and their mounts retreated or died on the field. Johnson's dragoons pursued the Mexican cavalry for a short distance before riding to the city walls. They scaled the walls and poured into the city as fire from rifles continued cracking.

Johnson and several of his commanders rode closer to

town, just a hundred yards from the city. Both of his brigades and his dragoons were within the city walls. Rifle shots filled the air, although not as many as before.

Sergeant Major Warden rode from the town to General Johnson, breathing heavily. "Sir, we have pushed them back and secured the west side of town."

"Good job, Sergeant Major," he replied, motioning for his officers to follow him.

They rode just outside the walls of the city. Several hundred men were grouped there, securing that portion of town from the enemy and attending to the wounded.

Johnson turned to Corporal Rhoades. "Bring up the supply wagons and medics," he ordered.

"Yes, sir," said Rhoades, saluting before riding hastily away.

The rifle fire became more sporadic, and Colonel Merrick of the Eight Infantry Regiment approached and saluted his superiors. "Sir, they are on the rooftops, sniping us."

"Find some ladders and get your men on the rooftops," the general ordered. "Control the ground and the roofs, Colonel."

Merrick saluted and returned to the ensuing battle.

"Sergeant Major, lead a company toward the palace and find Santa Anna. He's hiding here somewhere," Johnson commanded.

Warden saluted the general and spurred his mount toward town.

After half an hour, the American forces controlled three-quarters of the city. Johnson entered the city walls, the victory imminent. Johnson looked into the sky and realizing there was a good hour of light left, he ordered his men to push forward.

The approaching sound of hooves caught the general's attention. Turning, he noticed General Scott's men.

"From General West, sir," said the captain.

Opening the letter, Johnson narrowed his eyes as he read. He had been ordered to immediately stop his attack.

Johnson looked at the captain and shook his head, knowing exactly why the order was called. He ordered his commanders to halt their attack but hold their positions.

Officers rode to their field commanders, and the message was conveyed through the ranks. Within twenty minutes, the gunfire had completely stopped.

Johnson climbed from his horse and paced, stalking to and fro as he thought about the frustrating order.

Supply wagons and medics flooded the town as they helped the injured men who were scattered about. The wounded and dead were swiftly carried away, and they set up the field hospital in a white adobe church.

Johnson gave himself a moment to cool down before walking about his men, congratulating them on a job well done. He spotted Sergeant Warden and approached him.

The sergeant major saluted the general. "Sir, just as we reached the palace, we were told to halt the attack."

"No signs of Santa Anna?" Johnson asked.

"No, sir," replied Warden. "My guess is he's still in the palace."

Johnson looked at the small hole in the other man's uniform where blood ran down his forearm. "Get that arm looked at, Sergeant Major," he said, pointing toward the man's sleeve.

Warden stood at attention and saluted the general. "Yes, sir."

Johnson saluted back. Then Warden walked toward the church.

Corporal Rhoades advanced toward Johnson and saluted him. "Sir, we have your headquarters prepared."

Johnson followed Corporal Rhoades as he led the general to a small adobe home. The soldiers who stood guard saluted the general when he walked past. Inside, he found a desk, a bed, and his belongings. His maps, a pen, and a box of cigars had been placed on the desk.

The general looked about the room before turning to Rhoades. "Thank you, Corporal."

Moving to his desk, Johnson opened the box of cigars and lifted one from the box. He placed it in his mouth and lit it with a match from his pocket.

"I'll get you some water sir," said Rhoades, heading for the door.

Before Rhoades exited, Johnson called to him. "Have the commanders question the prisoners about Santa Anna's whereabouts."

"Yes, sir," replied Rhoades.

Johnson sat at the desk after Rhoades left, reviewing his map of Mexico City. He thought about the order he'd received to halt the attack and gave a low growl.

After a couple hours had passed, Johnson met with his officers, who pinpointed their men's positions on the map. The general requested a full battle report from each of them as soon as possible. After he relieved them, Johnson removed his boots and jacket and sat on the bed.

Saying a quick prayer, he lay in the bed, unable to sleep. Even within the heart of the Mexican capital and only hours from the war's end, he found no tranquility. He knew his deployment after the fall of the Mexican Republic would not be Oregon or Virginia. It would certainly be in New Mexico against America's newest enemy, the Apache nation. Little did he know, the biggest battle that awaited him would be lost without a single gunshot.

CHAPTER 30

SOL DE COLORADAS

On an early September morning, Arabella and Juan sat on the porch, drinking coffee and watching the sun rise in the distance. The sun cast a reddish-orange light as the glowing colors spilled across the sky.

Enjoying the beautiful morning sunrise, Arabella shared with Juan the stories of her youth, when she first met Domingo, and how Pedro had once been her boyfriend. Juan shared with her his stories of growing up in La Barca, and they both soon realized they'd grown up not far from each other. It wasn't long until they were laughing and really enjoying each other's company as they talked about their younger years.

Riding under a magnificent morning sun, Red Sleeves entered straight into the camp of the Western Apache and was quickly greeted by many of the tribe.

Red Sleeves was about to meet the new chief of the Western Apache for the first time. He was a young man with the reputation of being a fierce fighter. Once the news of the new arrival had reached the young chief, he quickly left his wickiup and walked across the camp toward the now-legendary chief, Red Sleeves.

The two chiefs stood face to face, placing their hands on each other's shoulders.

"Red Sleeves," said the man.

Red Sleeves grinned. "Cochise."

Another beautiful morning sky greeted General Johnson as he fastened the last button on his shirt, reached for his newly shined shoes, and put on his coat and hat. Within minutes, General Scott walked into his headquarters, followed by General West.

The three men stood in a circle as Scott questioned Johnson about his attack on Mexico City the day before. Not long after, the conversation became heated, and General West had to break the two men apart.

General Scott stormed out, threatening to have Johnson court-martialed and relieved of his command.

Johnson walked to his desk and shook his head. He looked up, noticing the glare General West aimed at him. Johnson removed his hat and tossed it on the desk as he faced West, pointing toward the door.

Pedro rode down the crowded streets of Tucson, stopping in front of his house. On the porch next door sat Vicente, gazing at the morning sky and hardly noticing as his old friend climbed down from his horse.

Seeing Pedro, Vicente stood and raced down the porch steps to greet the man. The two embraced each other and walked toward the house as Pedro told Vicente why he'd left the ranch. Maria stepped outside and joined the unexpected reunion.

Sheriff Ricks sat at his desk in the jailhouse, eating his breakfast and reading the paper. The front door of the jailhouse slammed open, knocking against the wall and overturning a nearby coatrack. The sheriff dropped his fork to the floor. His eggs spilled onto his lap as he reached for his pistol.

The bright morning sun poured into the jailhouse. It lit up the room as Ricks saw the silhouette of the man at the door. Upon noticing a familiar hat followed by a familiar voice, the sheriff threw one of his boots toward the man and hollered at him.

Mitchell grinned and sauntered toward Ricks. He tossed his hat on the desk and found a seat.

After Ricks calmed down, he asked about Red Sleeves.

Mitchell smiled and told him Red Sleeves was on his way.

Ricks smiled, bellowing, "You got him!"

Mitchell raised his eyebrows, then leaned back in his chair, and scratched his cheek, staring at the desk.

The sheriff leaned toward the man. "Mitchell? Did you get him?" he asked.

Mitchell sucked on his teeth. "Well, Sheriff, not exactly."

Sheriff Ricks leaned back in his chair, his jaw clenched and eyes fixed on Mitchell. "Then what do you mean? He's on his way?"

Mitchell shook his head and smiled.

The sheriff's fearful expression further tickled Mitchell as he put his feet up on the desk. Tilting his head back, Mitchell's deep rumbling laugh echoed throughout the jailhouse.

CONTINUARÁ

If you have enjoyed reading this novel, please return to your favorite online retailer and leave a review. The author appreciates any and all feedback from readers.

ABOUT THE AUTHOR

Born in 1973, Bozwick Abel resides in Pinckney, Michigan near the chain of lakes. He spends a fair share of time boating, fishing, and eating ribs with the wolf pups. Abel is a firm believer that passion is the marrow of the soul and can take you anywhere you want to be.

Visit the author's website: https://bozwickabel.com/
Connect with the author on Facebook:
https://www.facebook.com/bozwick.abel

ACKNOWLEDGEMENTS

Inspired by a song several years ago put the wheels in motion for Pariahs of War, and without the continuous support of my friends and family, this book would not be possible. Having a great support team around you is key in any endeavor, and I am thankful for all those who contributed to making Pariahs of War a reality.

I'd like to personally thank Debra L Hartmann and her team at The Pro Book Editor and IAPS.rocks. I cannot say enough about their expertise and knowledge of not only editing and proofreading but the entire self-publishing process.

I'd also like to thank all those who read this book and the unspoken heroes of days of old.

SAMPLE FROM *DOMINGO*

(PARIAHS OF WAR VOLUME ONE)

"Ready up, men! They're coming again!" yelled Sanchez, watching the Indians through his field glasses. He watched the lead warrior spin his horse around three times and let out another war cry. "Red Sleeves."

"Who, sir?" asked the major.

"Red Sleeves," replied Sanchez, looking across to the Apaches heading back up the hill. "He stopped General Pico and his men a couple years back. He's a murderer, thief, pillager… He's done it all." Turning to his men and pulling out his sword, he shouted, "All right, men! They're coming! This is it!"

Milton Keynes UK
Ingram Content Group UK Ltd.
UKHW040135170224
437973UK00001B/32